Totally Bound Publishing books by Sara Ohlin

Graciella
Handling the Rancher
Seducing the Dragonfly
Flirting with Forever

Rescue Me
Salvaging Love
Igniting Love
Promising Love
Embracing Love

Rescue Me

EMBRACING LOVE

SARA OHLIN

Embracing Love
ISBN # 978-1-80250-990-8
©Copyright Sara Ohlin 2022
Cover Art by Erin Dameron-Hill ©Copyright October 2022
Interior text design by Claire Siemaszkiewicz
Totally Bound Publishing

EMBRACING LOVE

Dedication

This one's for survivors.
And to new beginnings, which we all deserve.

Chapter One

Connor Duggan pulled out the chair on Sasha's right and sat beside her. His toned and tan forearm brushed against hers and Sasha's calm night was ruined. This one evening a month was one she'd come to anticipate with joy, where she'd grown comfortable with these newish people in her life, and in two seconds, her comfort whooshed right out of the window.

Crap! It wasn't only her peace that disappeared. His presence, all his larger-than-life muscles, invaded her space and took all the breath from her body. She grabbed onto the table to calm the dizziness.

And the way he smelled. *Oh my Lord, his smell is intoxicating.* That singular delicious woodsy scent called to her. Her pulse jackhammered beneath her skin and a flush heated her cheeks. She was vaguely aware of the hum around her, the others sitting and diving into dinner, laughter and chatting, but it was all a warped background, with the sound coming slow and the movements fuzzy.

The monthly dinner with her friends had gone from enjoyable and almost lovely to a chaotic scraggly mess in her head and hormones.

Sasha forced her body still. For some reason, her body had a mind of its own around Connor Duggan lately. It wanted to sway into him, link her fingers with his, ask him where he got the slew of rainbow-colored friendship bracelets, both silly and sexy on a man his size, listen to his deep voice and maybe crawl into his lap.

What the heck? *Stay,* she ordered her body, like she would her dog. Images of her face shoved into his strong shoulder inches from hers, breathing in his essence, seared across her mind. And when had she ever drooled over someone's essence before?

We could do this, we could just lean in and take a tiny sniff, one tiny breath of him. Pretty please, her body begged. *Yes,* her fingers agreed. *We could finally stroke that strong jaw of his and see how his stubble feels against our fingertips or find out if his skin is soft or rough. Or,* her skin chimed in, *he could touch us, stroke us with those work-roughened fingers of his. I bet he'd make us hum. Wouldn't that feel delightful. We've never hummed before.*

Sasha's fork clattered on her plate, and she shoved her chair back. "I have to go." Fumbling with her napkin and trying not to make eye contact with anyone, she rounded the table. Without tripping down the steps to Jackson and Ellie's sunken living room, she managed to leash her dog, who'd been snuggled up in a pile with Ellie's dogs and Connor's dog, Kitten.

Kitten, arguably one of the cutest, rowdiest dogs on the planet. *Do you think his owner is rowdy too?* her body asked with a hopeful, wistful tone. Sasha shook her head. What the heck was going on in her head and…uh, other body parts? She made her way toward the front hall.

"Sasha," Ellie said in her sweet, calm voice. "You okay?" Ellie squeezed Sasha's hand, and Sasha didn't pull away. That alone was heaps of improvement from where she'd started with these people, these friends. A year ago, when she'd feared any kind of touch at all.

I'm not okay, not okay at all. "I'm sorry, I have to go." *I've gone from fearing men and touch to wanting to be stroked by your handsome friend and I can't tell you or anyone else. I don't even understand it myself.* She was going to faint. No, no, she could hold it together.

Secrets. She was collecting them, she knew, but there was no way in hell she could admit *this* truth to Ellie, standing right there in the entryway, that sitting next to Connor Duggan had her so tangled up she'd lost her balance completely, that she ached to *explore* him. Nope. There would be absolutely no explaining. She wouldn't be able to find the words.

The thing is, she knew Ellie wouldn't make her spell out anything. No one sitting at the dinner table, not Jackson, Ruby, Lachlan, Katie or Leo, Natalie or Gage, none of their children, and certainly not Connor, would demand an explanation. They all knew her past. They allowed her room and time to feel comfortable with them. And right or wrong, tonight she would take advantage of that kindness because she needed to get out of this house. Immediately.

"I'll take you home," Ellie said.

Sasha deflated, grateful to Ellie and annoyed with herself. Twenty-seven years old and she still didn't know how to drive, so her friends were often forced to give her rides. If she were already in downtown, she'd walk, but Ellie and Jackson lived up in the hills, miles from downtown.

"We can take you, Sasha darling," Ruby said.

"I'm so sorry to make any of you. I've ruined your dinner. I—"

Ruby grabbed her purse and Lachlan's hand and led the way outside, shouting out their goodbyes behind them. "It's nothing to be sorry about. We were going to leave in a few minutes anyway. Lachlan has his volunteering tonight."

Ellie gave her hand one more gentle squeeze, then let her go. Sasha gave a jerky nod toward the rest of the table and took her unsettled nerves outside and away from the tight confines of the house where Connor's heat and presence seemed to have permeated everything.

She didn't speak on the ride home. Well, not out loud at least. Inside, her hormones and body parts had a gossip-fest. *Why are we running away from him? I know. I thought we should have climbed on his lap. Or stroked that new beard he's growing in. I'm dying to feel those whiskers. I think I like him better clean-shaven.* For crying out loud, she was absolutely losing her mind.

She was glad when the car stopped and she could hurry out. Lachlan and Ruby waved. Ruby blew air kisses and drove off, leaving Sasha by the front door to the apartment above The French Connection Bakery where everyone thought she lived. Instead of heading upstairs, she unlocked the bakery doors, relocking them quickly behind her and disengaging the alarm.

"I ruined our night, bud," she said to her dog. Boy, had she. Bolting out of dinner with her friends like a skittish colt. *Better than stay and act like a hussy,* she told herself. Ha, a hussy. That was hilarious. Funny ha ha, as Natalie's teenagers often said, in tones dripping with sarcasm.

Braveheart padded over to his dog bed in the back of the kitchen and plopped down. He stretched out his legs and was asleep within minutes. Her good boy, so patient with her. No sense going home this early. After her debacle at dinner, she had too much energy to get out. Making bread would help. She shoved her unruly emotions and all her loony body part personalities out of her way and got to work.

There was a beauty in making bread. To begin with simple bland ingredients and turn them into a pleasure for all the senses. Even creating it engaged her fully, the sound of the mixer churning flour and water together, the slap of the dough on the bread board, kneading it with her hands, leaning her body into the work. She transformed it into a smooth ball ready to be proofed, humid scents of yeast and flour warming the air. Then, to taste it, fresh out of the oven when it was still warm and oozing steam, the perfect crisp of the crust mixed with soft insides. The entire process was a soothing meditation for Sasha. Tonight, she eased her way through loaf after loaf, settling her nerves in the routine.

The downside of baking was that she could lose track of time. Now it was past ten at night. Worse, it was raining, and she and Braveheart still had to walk the ten blocks home.

She grabbed a few recycled bags and loaded up bread and butter, a hunk of cheese, the leftover pasta salad she'd made at lunch and strawberries. Not nearly as delicious as Jackson's grilled chicken and lemon pasta she'd left behind in the dust of her embarrassment, but not too shabby either. After all, she had made the artisan bread herself and the strawberries were fresh from the pots on the bakery's back patio.

"Okay, pumpkin." Sasha peered out through the doors. "I know you hate the rain, but it seems to be our destiny tonight." Gloomy, too, without the hint of stars or moonlight. The darkness attempted to twist her newly meditative state into knots.

Walking in the rain with her large cross-body bag, her arms full of groceries and a tired but loyal dog next to her, Sasha tried to hurry. Her jacket had a hood which rested against her shoulders. Considerate though it was of the brand to attach one, Sasha never used a hood. It blocked too much of her peripheral vision. An umbrella would have hindered any quick escape she would ever potentially have to make. So even in the rain with all of society's weather-proof advances, Sasha would be soaked by the time they made it home. *It's fine. It's fine.* It kept her alert.

She managed to squeeze herself between some people on the sidewalk and race through the puddle-filled crosswalk just before the light changed. The steady downpour forced her to adapt, honed a sharper edge to her anxiety. She gripped the leash. Her dog walked beside her, soaking too. *I'm sorry, love,* she silently whispered, hoping he understood. *I'll get you warmed up as soon as we —*

Her head snapped up and she glanced around. Instinct had her picking up their pace. *Is someone watching me? No. Stay calm. Don't forget to breathe.* Gripping the leash tighter, she dashed across the last street. She was off her game tonight. Normally she crossed two blocks back to avoid this large main intersection. *You're exhausted. It's nothing.* No ominous presence lurked nearby even if one always lurked in the hidden depths of her mind. *Then why do I feel something odd?* Her instinct had her looking around again.

Mostly the crowded downtown helped calm her anxiety and fears a bit. Easier to hide in a large group. But the rain, plus her irritated nerves, made the night difficult to tell if...something was wrong. And Sasha knew that all it took was one tiny thing out of the ordinary to destroy one's world. It was imperative that Sasha spy these villains immediately.

Because she hadn't that one time that had changed her life from quiet luxury to a violent nightmare.

Sasha shook off the ghosts of the past. With her words of encouragement playing in her head, she entered the automatic turning door of Hotel Marisol, making sure Braveheart was tucked close to her side as the doors swung round. Her mutt did not enjoy the swinging circular entrance.

Hotel owners Marisol Ruiz and her husband, Guillermo, stood behind the glossy black and gold concierge desk. She nodded at them, and they smiled back at her as she passed. Some days they spoke, but other times they asked no questions. They knew who she was. Before she'd stayed one night in their hotel, she'd researched them and approached them with her desire for privacy.

Once the elevator doors closed, Sasha allowed herself to let go of a tiny sigh. *Almost home. Almost there.* As soon as the elevator dinged on her floor, she gathered her sharp focus around her again, checked both directions in the hallway and headed left to her suite. Building strength, resilience and smarts were her goals and she was determined to do this on her own. As soon as she entered her room, closed and engaged both locks, she sank down to her butt and allowed her ragged breaths out. Braveheart pressed up against her side, whimpering his own relief or concern. She wrapped her arm tightly around him. "I know. It's okay. We're going to be okay. I've got you. We're safe."

When she was certain she could stand again without fainting, she rose, cranked up the thermostat and used the fluffy towels to dry off her dog. Once he seemed more settled, as in claiming half the bed and snoring away, Sasha peeled off her soggy clothes and climbed into the hot shower, erasing the chill and the fear of the night.

Will I ever be normal? Will I ever not be on guard? The steam knocked her walls down and let her grieve without anyone noticing. Her warm tears mixed with the water. Sasha let it all out, amazed every time that she had more tears, more regrets to drain from her body.

After an exhausting shower, she checked the locks again. Too tired to eat, she put her groceries neatly away in the kitchen, microwaved herself a cup of tea, set her alarm—repeating the steps she did every night—and climbed into bed.

She was a survivor. She'd survived her abusive marriage.

Yet I still feel trapped and afraid.

Five years of hell married to Anthony Lucciano, a liar and a cheat at best, a powerful slithery monster at worst. A magician with his personalities, changing from the smooth handsome charmer into a sadistic abusive scum the next. Five years he'd beaten her down, physically and mentally, until she was unrecognizable to herself.

Last year he'd almost killed her. There were moments she wished he had. He was the one who was dead, and yet...and yet getting over it all, dealing with it, leaving the worst behind was its own kind of torture.

It seemed like it had taken forever, almost ten months now of physical therapy to get her arm strength back. She'd been seeing a psychologist to help her mental state. Yet for some reason tonight, she'd felt thrust all the way back to the beginning of her healing journey, or maybe twisted onto a different path. It was all so confusing.

"You understand, don't you, my boy?" She ran her hands through her dog's fur. He stretched his back paws out at her touch. A few months ago, Braveheart had lost his marbles at some loud boom and shot out of her grasp, charging through the neighborhood as if an inferno had been nipping at his heels. Ellie, a gifted veterinarian and animal whisperer, and Sasha's first real friend had said, *"Even for animals, trauma can reappear at surprising times."*

Why? Sasha wanted to yell. *Why can't I be done with it all, the shame, the fear, the grief, the leftover scars?*

Sasha didn't know how to understand this fear of a ghost, let alone acknowledge it, or ask anyone about it. Relying on people left her vulnerable, and that was the scariest of all. Unfortunately, she hadn't anticipated that being alone could also allow such a heavy loneliness to creep around her. It sucked. It was a feeling she was familiar with, and it hollowed her out and made her wonder if it was her curse, to always feel the pit of emptiness. It wasn't until she was nearly asleep, a pillow clutched to her chest, that she remembered that nudge of awareness on her way home and wondered, *Am I crazy or was someone following me tonight?*

Chapter Two

It was early, the sun stretching long rays onto the backyard, brushing the last hints of night away. Connor Duggan and his blonde Labrador both lay sprawled out on the back deck, breathing hard.

Must have coffee. He dragged his aching body up and, rubbing the pain in his lower back, limp-walked in through the back door. *God, I hate running.* If it weren't for the fact that it shocked his unsettled emotions into gear and helped calm his rambunctious one-year-old dog, Kitten, he'd settle for never, ever, *ever* running again. But after the restless night he'd had worrying over Sasha Kincaid, he'd needed the exercise.

What a massively embarrassing mistake Connor had made at Jackson's house last night. *Why did you sit right next to her and scare her away, you idiot?* Because she'd been smiling and laughing and he'd gotten so lost in watching her that he'd lost his cool. He'd been pulled in by her lure, placing himself in her aura as if he belonged there. Dinner had been ruined after she'd bolted. They'd all mostly been finished eating anyway, but the mood had changed. He'd gone back to the office to grab a few contracts to review. Then, right after locking his door to leave, he'd been jostled by a woman on the street, a woman racing through the rain and downtown crowds—Sasha.

He'd paused, then crossed the street and headed in the same direction. It wasn't any of his business what she'd been doing out so late by herself in the rain with grocery bags in her hand. He was surrounded by confident, strong women who could take care of themselves. He'd heard earfuls from his nieces about how women needed men for almost nothing, but that didn't mean he'd tossed his manners out the window, or his concern. Christ, Sasha hadn't even bothered to put her rain hood up, and she'd been rushing, her body held tightly together. Like she'd been afraid of something, or someone, until she'd disappeared into Hotel Marisol.

Frustrated at himself for ruining her dinner, he'd rammed his muscles through ten miles instead of his normal six this morning. Now his body screamed its displeasure at the punishment.

"Criminy," he cursed as he bent over and stretched his thighs. "Doing manual labor doesn't kill my body as much as this hated exercise. I feel ninety-three instead of thirty-three. Oh, sure I'll have a cup of day-old drip coffee from my ancient Mr. Coffee." Kitten barked in answer, although Connor wasn't quite sure what she was saying.

The nice thing about having a conversation with his dog was that he could interpret her barks however he wanted.

"Gross. Why am I torturing myself with this swill?" He tossed the brown crap down the sink and rinsed out the coffee pot.

The bummer in a man-dog conversation was that it reminded him that he was alone. He missed the fluffy flavored creamers his nieces used to stock the fridge with. The way his niece Brie would brew the perfect strong expresso, with hints of chocolate and smoke she used to say. The frothy milk his oldest niece, Rosie, would pile on top of his caramel-flavored coffee. The youngest pipsqueak, Cece, used to sneak the flavored creamer into her own chocolate milk and lie about it whenever any of them discovered the empty carton in the fridge. The little firecracker hadn't had one guilty feeling about the lies, as long as she'd gotten her sweet fix. He was kind of proud of the kid.

The pipes under his sink whined at him even after he'd turned off the water. He needed to fix the plumbing. *Or I can put it off for one more week.*

He took in the state of his old craftsman home and gave a laugh. How ironic that he was renowned for his ability to take any run-down, or nearly destroyed building and renovate her until she shined like diamonds, yet his own house was stuck in a bad eighties re-muddle. The peeling linoleum floors in the kitchen and rust-colored scallop design faux backsplash must have been picked out as a joke. The rest of the house needed new paint, updated flooring, original woodwork stripped and brought back to its original glory…and, well, Connor didn't have the heart for any of it.

Originally, he'd intended to renovate this home eight years ago. Young and in love, he'd envisioned his future in this house, married to Nina, a handful of kids, happiness and laughter for an eternity. He'd only fixed up the outside before their world had imploded. His brother-in-law and best friend John died from cancer. Nina had left him. His sister Katie and his nieces moved in, and full house renovations had been tossed out the window.

All those before dreams of his were layers of dust he wanted to sweep away. Old house. Old memories. He craved…something different? New house, new adventures? New city? Uncertainty shifted in his gut. *I want to make Sasha Kincaid smile.*

He rarely let himself dwell on that thought, because there might never be anything more between them aside from friendship. He thought they'd had at least that lately. Their dogs often played together in the park and she'd begun coming to more of their friends-and-family get-togethers. He'd always been so careful of her personal territory and feelings. But last night he'd gone and squashed any headway he'd made, barging into her space as if he were the uncontrollable dog.

His stomach chose that minute to drum out its hunger. He opened his refrigerator. Plenty of fruits and vegetables, some chicken breasts for dinner. No double hazelnut or butter pecan creamer, no pudding or leftover cookie dough. In fact, he decided, slamming the door shut and watching the handle sway because it was also broken, breakfast was as good a place as any to start with change.

And a great excuse to grab something yummy to eat and drink from his favorite bakery in Corvallis before he went to his first job site of the day. No one needed to know, as much as he was addicted to the sugary coffee drinks and the sticky-sweet morning buns at The French Connection, that his motives for visiting had nothing to do with food, or almost nothing, because those morning buns were no joke. If he was lucky, he'd be able to apologize to Sasha for making her so uncomfortable last night that she'd fled.

* * * *

Sasha stood at the long wooden baking bench behind the expresso counter, mixing something delicious in a large bowl, concentrating, lost in her task. Almost ninety degrees outside already, probably warmer in here, and she was wearing a long-sleeved blouse and apron over some goofy baggy pants and weird clog shoes. A blue baseball hat covered her head. The entire outfit was too big on her, like she preferred to hide. She was taller than most women he encountered, and even in her baggy, indistinguishable clothes, he'd recognize her. His heart thudded. It did every time he saw her. *Uh-oh.*

"Hi, Janie." Connor spoke to the barista. "I'll have a double grande chocolate caramel latte and a morning bun, please."

"Sure thing, Mr. Duggan."

Connor met Sasha's gaze as she turned to look at him. Seeing her drew his smile out automatically. Fuck, his heart was trying to beat out of his chest. He forgot his intentions to be cool and instead, acting like a thirteen-year-old dork, he gave a goofy wave. What was he doing? It must be the lack of food in his belly and being surrounded by so much sugar.

She set her bowl and hand mixer down, wiped her hands on her apron and stared at him through the lenses of her cute silver-framed glasses. Nope, he couldn't blame the baked goods. *It's all her.* Then, in the blink of an eye, she turned and walked away.

"Mr. Duggan? Mr. Duggan?"

"Huh?" He dragged his eyes back to Janie.

"That's eight dollars."

"Right." He forced his smile back into place, paid and tipped her, then stepped to the side to wait for his order.

You have a crush. You have a crush, his inner adolescent teased. *Ha ha ha ha ha ha!*

"Shut up," he mumbled to his idiot child self. He crossed his arms and scowled at the woman standing next to him who was giving him the raised eyebrow. "Sorry...I'm telling myself to shut up."

She hugged her coffee to her body and moved away.

Shit. He rubbed his eyes. *What the hell is wrong with me?* He did, he had a crush on a woman who had lost all trust in men. A woman who he'd thought he might be becoming friends with, but who lately couldn't stand to be in the same room with him.

When they called his name, he grabbed his order and stalked out of the crowded bakery into the stifling heat. Connor walked to his job site at the other end of the long park. He ignored anyone who waved to him, didn't smile at the kids already cooling off in the spray water park, forgot to hand out treats to the familiar dogs he knew from the neighborhood, treats he routinely carried in his pockets, and shoved his way through the doorway of the old Art Deco mansion, an iconic building some idiot had turned into tiny, uninspired apartments in the eighties. His crew was busy demoing the entire place before they could restore her glory.

His chocolate caramel latte tasted bitter on his tongue, and he chucked it into the large garbage bin. Cranky, unsettled, pissed at himself, he'd nearly lost his appetite. But his still-warm bun, layers of croissant dough laced with sugar and cinnamon and hint of orange, was a thing of genius and it'd be a shame to waste. He stuffed the pastry into his mouth and devoured it.

Sweet butter and orange sugar calmed his pissy mood, a bit. He closed his eyes and savored. God, how did she do it, how did she make something so warm and delicious and sublime? He imagined her rolling the dough, layering it with butter, putting all her love into it. How those graceful, strong fingers of hers would work the ingredients together. Magic, pure magic. He wanted to study her hands, map them with his own, trace over her bones to the soft skin on the underside of her wrist. *It's got to be soft, but how soft?*

"Everything okay?"

Connor choked on his breakfast. Jackson Kincaid, his best friend, business partner and brother to the woman Connor had a taboo crush on, stood staring at him from the staircase, confusion settled into his features.

"Pardon?" Connor said. He spit out the words, smacked his chest and tried to calm the choking, now seriously regretting the lack of coffee

"I don't think I've ever seen you stomp into a job site, angry. And..." Jackson gestured to the garbage can. "You tossed your sugared drink away without sucking every last drop of it. We usually have to listen to you moan over how delicious it is. You attacked that pastry as if it had insulted your mother. Are you sick or something? Feverish?" Jackson walked over and rested the back of his hand on Connor's forehead.

Connor tried to laugh. What came out sounded more like a chicken being strangled. Jackson raised his eyebrow.

"Fine, I'm fine. Tired, that's all. Rough night." He wasn't angry, was he? Confused, frustrated, sad. Jesus when was the last time he'd been sad? Or admitted to it? His niece Brie was constantly urging him to get more in touch with all of his emotions, not just the happy ones. His little sage. If she only knew how well-versed he was with them all, deep painful grief, envy, desire. It was easier to shove them down. Most of the time.

Connor tried to ignore his friend and opened his clipboard to see what stage of demo his crew was on. Maybe they had lathe and plaster to rip out or old plumbing to destroy. The dirtier and harder the job the better. He needed to take his mind off his ridiculous crush, or whatever the hell it was. What he needed to do was burn it to the ground, because Sasha Kincaid was off limits for more than one reason. And one of those was standing here trying to get his attention.

"Right," Jackson drawled. "Another hot date keep you up all night?"

Connor closed his eyes and took a deep breath. His reputation as a one-night stand hot shot, although so far from the truth lately it wasn't even funny, had been his own fault. When Nina had left him, he'd decided he'd enjoy sex if he found a partner with the same agenda, but that would be it. No more relationships for him, no more dates and getting to know each other, no more sharing dreams and...*hoping*.

Over the last few years, he'd grown weary of not hoping. And standing right here, feeling beaten down by his past and lost about what his future could be, he wished his best friend knew the truth, that he wasn't the playboy he pretended, that he was plain lonely and that, well, that he, Connor Duggan, had felt his heart start beating again when Sasha Kincaid had walked into their lives last summer.

He couldn't admit everything to Jackson, but maybe a part of it wouldn't hurt. "I...ah, haven't really had a date in months." Over a year, if he was being honest. *Has it been that long?*

"You?"

Connor faced his friend. They'd never lied to each other, and Connor knew, if Jackson could see his expression, he'd believe Connor was speaking the truth.

"Shit, you're serious."

Connor gave a lift of his chin.

"Maybe you are sick?" Jackson joked and punched his biceps.

"Hey," Connor said and rubbed his arm. "No teasing me when I'm feeling tender about my absolute sandpit of a love life." He even sounded grumpy to himself. *What a shmuck.*

Jackson barked out a laugh. "You're serious?"

"Well, yeah…" *Am I?* He thought about the way Jackson always had Ellie on his mind, how he took her lunch every day at her clinic, how her face lit up every time she saw Jackson coming. How Ruby and Lachlan held hands, Lachlan gazing at her with pure adoration when they did, as if Ruby had gifted him with the most precious thing ever. How his sister, Katie, and her new man, Leo, gravitated toward each other and seemed to have a silent communication between them, that always had them glowing. How Leo enjoyed caring for her and cooking for her. That even though it was Katie's gift to feed others with her amazing food, Leo knew her so well that he understood how much she appreciated being fed herself. Fed with love.

I am one hundred percent turning into a sap, and I'm…huh. Connor breathed out clearly for the first time all day. *Huh? I'm one hundred percent okay with that.*

"You do know the difference between a love life and a sex life, right? One actually requires an emotional investment."

Wow. He felt those words like a serious punch to the sternum, no joking around with that hit. Did his best friend really see him as such a shallow asshole? "Yes," Connor said, "I'd almost forgotten what a know-it-all bastard you could be, so thanks for enlightening me."

"Duggan, I was joking—"

"Yep, got it. No worries. Gotta bust out some walls. I won't be able to make lunch today. Say hi to Ellie for me." No way was he meeting Jackson and Ellie for lunch at The French Connection. His gut could only handle so many hits in one day. He put on his safety glasses, grabbed a sledgehammer and walked away.

Chapter Three

One of Sasha's secret safe places was the tiny fenced-in garden area by the back door of the bakery, a spot mostly enveloped in shade from the lilac bushes and overgrown lemon tree. Last week she'd added a cushiony chaise-longue and some chairs, but today Sasha chose to sit on the ground and lean her face into the cool bricks of the building. It might be hot as Hades outside, but she was mostly flushed from her near encounter with Connor. It was an allergy or something, lately. He came within ten feet of her, and she could sense him. Her skin tingled. As soon as she saw him, a blush heated her face and her chest, and the only cure would be to rub her body all over his powerful muscles.

She knocked her head against the wall. *It's not like I'll ever get close enough to touch him. I'm a wimp! I can't even talk to the man.* "Ugh!"

Connor Duggan had crept into her awareness slowly over the seasons. Last summer when she'd reunited with her brother, after being adopted and losing him over twenty years ago, she'd been introduced and welcomed by all Jackson and Ellie's friends. She'd met Connor, but he'd never pushed into her space unless their dogs tangled. That made her smile.

The first time Braveheart and Connor's dog, Kitten, had met, it had been insta friendship and love all rolled into one. Literally as they'd rolled around each other and nipped and played, as if they'd known each other their entire lives and celebrated being together every time they were reunited. Sasha didn't have any person in the world she felt that way with and it made her chest ache.

"Your pal was here," she said. Braveheart, napping on the wicker loveseat cushion in the shade, flopped his tail in acknowledgment. "Not the big K, but her owner."

Her dog sat up and thumped his tail. "You fancy him because he gives you scrubs and treats." Ahh for things to be that simple, to crave a person's presence because they scratched at that perfect spot behind the ears. Sasha rested her head against the rough brick wall, sweat beading on her forehead as the heat beat down on her.

"There is something about him," she whispered. *So many somethings*. A heady warmth that drew her attention. He was completely at ease with the way he and his powerful muscled body swaggered through the world around him. Always joking, making people laugh. As if his goal in life was to put others at ease through humor. Then why was she such a lame fool around him the last few weeks?

She smacked her cheeks with her hands. When he'd shown up at the bakery a few minutes ago, with that boyish grin on his face aimed her way, instead of listening to her brain and walking toward him, she'd followed her whacked-out emotions again which had screamed, "*It's too much to handle – we have to hide!*"

"Oh my goodness! That's twice in less than twenty-four hours I've run away from the man. And this time, what's worse is that he looked right at me and waved." And she'd run away. Because she might fall flat on her face in embarrassment? Or perhaps it was more than that.

Her husband had been her only real relationship, and it had turned from idyllic to terrifying soon after her marriage. From there it had nearly killed her. Although, she knew now what she'd thought of as idyllic in the beginning had been an act on Anthony's part. Unfortunately, that made it all the more difficult to trust her own judgment now.

Her past was always hovering like a busy hive full of bees, waiting to sting if she ever let herself get close to someone again in such an intimate way. *Is that what I want, to be with someone again?*

All this trying to figure out how to be in the world again was exhausting. Sasha knocked her head against the bricks, not reassured at all. She was so tired of feeling and acting stupidly around him, any of them. Sasha slipped back inside to see if Connor was still there. Hopefully she could salvage the morning and say hi. But when she surveyed the café, he was already gone.

I think I messed up. Sasha sighed and turned to work. She let the magic of the place calm her. Voices intertwined with the constant hum of the espresso machine. The bakery was still hopping. It was never too quiet here and she cherished the noise, how it made her feel wrapped up in a big hug, safe, connected without having to be too engaged. Scents of warm lemon and sugar came from the oven as one of her bakers removed the lemon meringue mini tarts. Bread cooled on the racks and a humid breeze stole through the entire place.

Normally these thoughts surged through her with happiness, a knowing that she'd come through such darkness to this paradise. Demons might still come alone at nighttime, but this, all around her, was goodness. And it was all hers.

Sasha uncovered the large sheet pan of laminated dough to fold in more layers of butter. Nearly ready, then she could form it into pinwheels and croissants and…Connor Duggan's favorite, morning buns. *I noticed what his favorite is.* She'd noticed more than that, like how the man drooled every time he ate from here, his face warm and open and delighted. A blush stole up her neck every time she thought of him. *Mm-hm, we should jump him, kiss him, see how he kisses.*

"Hush," Sasha whisper-ordered the hussies in her mind. *Work will center me.* Setting one of the doughs on her baking table, she began rolling it out into a large rectangle. Next, she smashed the slightly softened butter into a smaller rectangle and placed it in the middle of the dough. Working quickly, her hands having memorized the actions, she folded the dough up over the butter and set all the layers together, pressing down, using the strength she'd gained from the daily repetition, putting her entire body into the motion. Then she wrapped it up and returned it to the refrigerator until it was time to bake. She followed the same routine with each batch, getting lost in the hypnotic motion of the rolling pin, the movement, the exercise.

Working her body, allowing her mind to ease, her emotions to settle, turned morning to afternoon. The bakery was quieter now. Only one person sat at a table reading the newspaper. No one ordered coffee. The huge freezers and refrigerators hummed a quieter symphony in the background.

Her employee Bo walked past and set a mug of tea on the counter for her. A routine he did nearly every afternoon, a tiny kind gesture she treasured. He was the only man who worked there. Tall and lean, his skin covered in gang tattoos, he had a slight limp and rarely spoke. But it didn't bother her. She understood a person not wishing to speak ever again.

Her brother, Jackson, had brought Bo by one morning last fall, and Sasha's dog had gone crazy over the man, slobbering kisses all over him. If Sasha hadn't been able to tell by the kindness in Bo's eyes, her dog's reaction toward him would have solidified that he wasn't a man she had to fear. When he'd asked for an application, she hadn't hesitated. If Jackson trusted Bo, Sasha could as well. The Heelys had hired him the next week. And when Sasha had bought the business, she'd promoted him from dishwasher to baker, teaching him as they went.

One by one, she'd accumulated a few men in her life she could trust. Her brother, her friend Katie's husband, Leo, the owner of Lachlan's pub, Lachlan MacGregory. She slightly feared Natalie's husband, Gage, not because she thought he'd hurt her, but because he nearly exploded whenever Sasha's past came up.

"Hey, Sasha," Ellie called from the counter and interrupted Sasha's pondering. Jackson stood behind Ellie with his hands around her. On Ellie's chest, tucked into his baby carrier, was Alex. A smile filled Sasha's face. There was one male in her life she was absolutely head over heels in love with, her three-month-old nephew, Alexander Samuel Kincaid. The love of her life.

Sasha waved, tossed her apron in the laundry and washed her hands before she went to sit with them in the café. She'd forgotten about their weekly date. Every Friday they tried to meet her for a late lunch.

"Want to hold him?" Ellie was already untangling her sleepy baby from the carrier when Sasha approached.

"Yes, please." Sasha let Ellie hand the warm bundle over and carefully snuggled him close. She closed her eyes and placed tiny kisses on his head, breathing in his sweet baby scent. "He's so peaceful."

"Ha!" Ellie snorted. "He's milk drunk and most likely won't stay that way for long. Thought you could enjoy him for a few minutes before his personality flips. I might even be able to snarf down one of those grilled veggie and cheese sandwiches you guys make before my little monster wakes up hungry again. I swear, he eats like a starving man." Even though she was exhausted and complaining, Ellie's words and expression beamed.

When Jackson returned with their food and drinks, Sasha kept Alex in her arms and gave Ellie and Jackson a chance to eat. It was no hardship to cuddle this precious love. Right here, right now she felt grateful for getting a second chance in life, if for no other reason than to be an aunt.

She was also thankful her face was buried in the soft, downy hair on Alex's head when Ellie said, "Why did Connor cancel on lunch, honey?"

"Don't really know," Jackson answered. "He was in a weird mood at work when I saw him this morning. Then he disappeared into demo mode."

"Weird how?" Ellie asked.

"Grumpy."

"Connor Duggan grumpy?" Ellie said. "That is weird."

Sasha kept her head down.

"I've never, *ever* seen that man anything other than happy and focused." Confusion laced Ellie's words.

"Me neither," Jackson said. "It was…it kind of reminded me of when you and I first got together."

Sasha peeked. Jackson's gaze was all for Ellie.

"When…" Ellie's face bloomed into a small smile and her cheeks got rosy while she regarded Jackson. "Oh, you mean you think he's grumpy over a woman. Someone's got him tangled up in love?"

Jackson wagged his eyebrows at Ellie, indulging her romantic ideas. Sasha adored the way they were with each other. How Ellie softened all the rough edges of Jackson. How he was not shy in showering her with affection. But she didn't understand what they were talking about. How could Connor being in love make him cranky? And who was the woman he was, in Ellie's words, tangled up over?

"I don't know if I'd go that far yet. Not sure he's really that type," Jackson said. "He's more the appreciate-their-body-and-leave type."

Ellie smacked his arm. "You know that's not true. You haven't been paying attention, honey. That man is so full of love and happiness—he's simply waiting to shower it on someone."

And Sasha wasn't hiding her face anymore. She was fully invested in following the conversation.

Jackson chuckled. "To be fair, I don't really pay that much attention to my friend's love needs," he teased Ellie.

"Well." Ellie softened her voice, serious now. "Maybe you should. He's your best friend and he's lonely. Anyone can see that."

Connor Duggan lonely?

"Anyone?" Jackson asked. "He's the chilliest, happiest guy I know."

Exactly.

"That's what we see on the outside. You and I both know people often act one way in the world because..." Ellie glanced at Sasha. "Well, because sometimes it's too difficult to expose our true selves, our true feelings and desires."

Sasha felt the tension change at their table. All the sudden she was witnessing a private moment. The way Jackson and Ellie looked at each other, the force beating between them, nearly took her breath away. *That, that's what I wish for, to know a person so intimately that even the darkest parts can be shared and cherished.*

Sasha started to get up. "I'll go grab us some cookies."

"No," Ellie said. "Let Jackson do it." Jackson stood, leaned down to kiss his wife, brushed a tear off her cheek and left them.

"Are you...are you okay?" Sasha whispered. Something had happened. Sasha wasn't certain what it was, only that it was intense between her brother and his wife.

"Yeah," Ellie said and let out a small huff. "Wonderful." She wiped her eyes with her napkin, a bright smile lingering on her face. Her tears were a result of happiness. *What a strange concept.*

Ellie took a sip of her tea, fixed Sasha with her sparkling blue eyes and said, "So Connor Duggan, grumpy and tangled up over a woman."

"Hmm," Sasha said and buried her face back in the baby, hiding again. Why was Ellie all the sudden interested in talking about Connor with her? He was like a feather brushing against Sasha's skin. More than that apparently — her face flamed at the thoughts she'd had at dinner last night. There was no way she could meet Ellie's gaze now. No way.

She closed her eyes and tried *not* to think about Connor Duggan being tangled up in love over some other woman.

Chapter Four

Well, I can't run away from him now. Braveheart lunged across the grass to get to Kitten, and Sasha lost control of the leash. The expanse of park began across the side street from the bakery and stretched for several blocks down to the river. Peaceful in the mornings, busy during Farmer's Market days and Music in the Park evenings, and flowing with all kinds of people on a warm summer day, it was essentially her yard since she didn't have one. *Yet.*

Nope, she couldn't run from Connor Duggan here. Unless she wanted to leave her dog behind. Today, when she spied him tossing the frisbee to his excited Lab, she felt both the small sigh of joy and the churning of her belly nerves. It had been a week since she'd seen him last, since she'd snubbed him that morning in the bakery. It had been lingering at the front of her mind, bugging her, challenging her.

At a quick glance, Connor was intimidating in stature. Enormous, tall, powerful tight muscles, making everyone else around him seem smaller, less significant. She'd learned enough about him these past months to know he was also a huge goofball, a teddy bear. Standing right in the middle of the green grass, with his dog and his larger-than-life grin, the sun anointing his smile, he gave Braveheart a rubdown, then laughed as Kitten tackled Braveheart in a spiral of dog hug. Connor was also carrying Sasha's nephew, Alex, tucked tight against his chest in a cozy gray baby carrier.

She could handle this, talking with a handsome man, in the daylight with dogs and her nephew. With one hand holding the carrier protectively to his chest, Connor leaned down to grab the frisbee, tossing that engaging smile of his around like he had infinite to share. When he looked her way, she swore his smile got brighter. Maybe he was happy to see her and she hadn't ruined their fragile friendship.

"Hi," he said. And if she wasn't acutely attuned to people's expressions and vibes, she might have missed the hesitancy in his greeting. Was it because she'd bolted the last few times he'd gotten near her?

"Hi." She smiled and tried to act warm and casual because her nerves had whooshed right back in. "You have...you're..." She paused and fiddled with her hands because he had a bit of spit-up smudged across his cheek and her fingers ached to brush it away for him. "You're babysitting?" Instead of touching Connor, she ran her fingers over Alex's warm head.

"Yeah." His voice got soft, and he gazed down at his godson. "He's having a cranky day. I offered to give Jackson and Ellie a break so they could have a quiet second or a nap, you know."

"He doesn't seem cranky." She was so close she could see the flecks of gold in Connor's brownish hazel eyes. They sparkled when he smiled at her. She'd never noticed that before. *I wonder if his eyes change color with his mood?* " He likes you."

"Mm." Sasha could feel the rumble of Connor's response all the way to her toes. He was studying her, aiming that crooked smile right at her, in full force. "Watch this." He took a step away and attempted to sit down on the bench. As soon as he began to bend, Alex started crying. When Connor stood back up, the baby quieted. Connor made the same move two more times with the same results. Sasha watched with astonished eyes. "Every time I try, *anyone* tries, to sit down, or be still, he starts crying."

"Oh no," she said and covered her mouth to stifle her laugh.

"Go ahead, laugh. It is funny. Poor thing," Connor cooed to the baby. "You finished with work?" he asked her.

The man was so easy in his body, coordinated, comfortable, talented, big. *He is big, isn't he. One big slice of deliciousness. Hush,* she told herself. She got lost in watching him.

"Yes, I'm finished at the bakery and I thought I might…" *I hoped you'd be here. This is your chance. Say it.* "I was looking for you."

"Me?" His face softened completely, no more wariness. He carefully held Alex to him with one of his strong, protective arms while he tossed the frisbee and watched the dogs race after it. When he faced her again, his smile was still there and it felt like it was all hers, as if no one else on the planet even existed.

Ahh, she really could melt into a puddle right here. His gaze was that powerful. Lines curved around his mouth, the slight flush that crawled up his cheeks, the way his beautiful eyes saw everything. *We should really spend hours concentrating on his eyes, see if they do change color. Yes! While he's naked.* She nearly took a step back from the force of his gaze and what he would see in her, when he spoke.

"Sasha?"

"Oh, I…here." Sasha held out the small bakery bag. "I tried a new recipe this morning. I thought you might want…to…to taste it." *Good job, almost no stuttering.* His eyes lit to the bag so fast she laughed. And just as quickly his eyes were back on her face, on her mouth to be exact.

"That's a great sound," he said, his voice rougher. He hadn't stepped closer, hadn't invaded her area. He was so careful about that. Then why with that one sentence did it feel like he was touching her, as though he'd wrapped his arms around her and tugged her close, in a spectacular way, aligning his body fully with hers, setting every single skin cell of hers on fire?

She needed to sit down, before her legs gave out. She *really* wanted to be aligned with his body. She did neither, barely. He couldn't sit, not with Alex behaving like a mini devil, and Sasha didn't want to be rude. And smooshing her body up against his would…uhm…*it might feel really amazing.* Connor took the bag and she let out a breath, unsure if it was for relief or disappointment. The world seemed to simmer around her whenever she was in his presence, like a too-humid afternoon, and even the air felt wavy.

Connor grabbed the pastry out of the bag, took an enormous sniff, and this time when he looked at her, his eyes were darker, piercing, like she'd offered him her body as the warm tasty treat. *I mean could it get any hotter out?* Sasha tugged at the front of her T-shirt, sweat dripping down her back, from the sun, from nerves, she didn't know.

"I…uhm…added caramel and nuts and dark brown sugar, so it kind of gets all sticky and gooey." Her words felt thick coming out. Someone had stuffed her mouth with cotton and she didn't know how to move her lips or her tongue.

"Sticky and gooey," he said reverently. "My favorite." Without taking his eyes off her, Connor devoured the caramel pecan pinwheel in three enormous bites. Savoring each taste, she imagined, as it burst on his tongue. When he finished that last swallow, she was unprepared for it, for the show to be over. But it wasn't. He licked his lips, peered into the empty bag as if he might dare to find all the secrets of the universe. Then, *then* he took a step closer.

She should have stepped back, but she couldn't, frozen in place by his sparking brown eyes, by the force of him. She was tall, but not Connor-Duggan tall, so she was forced to either stare at the baby attached to his chest or look up. She knew what the safer choice would be. But somehow her body didn't care right this minute as a warm breeze swirled around them, as if they were the only two people in the park, no neighbors, no babies, no dogs, no responsibilities, *no pasts*.

"Damn." His voice was hot and hushed, pure disbelief in his words. "That was the best thing I've ever tasted. In. My. Life."

He still had spit-up on his cheek, and now he had a dusting of brown sugar at the edge of his lip, where his tongue hadn't reached. He didn't speak, didn't say anything else after his last words whispered around her, but still his body spoke to hers. She reached up without a thought and brushed the sugar off his mouth. "Sugar," she whispered.

Neither one of them moved, and when she started to pull her hand away, he caught it in his large, warm one. Sasha sucked in her breath and watched as he carefully ran his thumb over her fingers, studied them with his intense focus.

"There's something special here, in these fingers, that can create something purely outstanding." He met her gaze again. "Something that tastes so good it makes a man swear."

Sasha huffed out a laugh, not feeling one bit humorous. "Damn is hardly a swear."

"Trust me." He rocked her world again with those hooded eyes. "It takes something pretty serious to get a damn out of me."

"Oh."

Connor smiled then, broad and gorgeous, like he'd discovered something amazing or secretive or she couldn't tell, but it caused her own smile to bloom, and she didn't care if she was an idiot, nerves fluttering, standing in the park mooning over a man while he held her hand, inspected it. A man who stared deeply into the lines on her skin and told her fortune. An amazing one, at that. When his phone blared out a pop song, he dropped her hand and fumbled with the device. "Babysitting time is up."

"Oh." She sighed. It was all she could get out. He'd stunned her speechless.

"I need to get this pumpkin back to Ellie so she can feed him."

"Right." Sasha stepped away and called Braveheart to her side. She had to swallow back her disappointment at the broken moment. *Can it really be called a moment?* Yes, she was going with yes. It was to her, a lovely one, even though it was also full of tension, but not in a negative way. She'd have to unpack all her emotions about that later and see if she could understand everything simmering between them. It could be a whole lot of nothing. Right? Hmm. *Sugar, that didn't feel like nothing.* Were her inner hussies onto something?

"I hope you enjoyed it then." She fumbled with her words, trying for polite. She could do polite — after years of practice she'd bet she could out-polite anyone.

"Oh, I did," he assured her. "Couldn't you tell?"

Again, she didn't know how to answer. *Yes, I can tell you enjoyed the pastry.* But was that what they were really talking about?

"Would you have dinner with me?" he asked. There was his confidence again, straightforward, bold. "Ahh...or..." He shook his head.

Oh, maybe he hadn't meant to blurt that out. "I should have..." he started. "Could have eased into that better. I meant to. But I guess I'm trying to be in touch with my feelings and my feelings really want to have dinner with you. I can't promise not to trip over my words, but I can promise good food and even some laughter." His eyes traveled to her mouth. "Sure would enjoy hearing you laugh again." He said it so quietly she wasn't sure it had been meant for her ears.

Sasha breathed easier, even while her nerves danced again. "I...uhm..." Braveheart pressed up against her leg, sensing the flutters under her skin.

"It's okay if you can't. I mean, it'll bum me out, but I don't want you to be uncomfortable. I...we could eat at my house, outside on the deck, with the dogs. Chaperones, you know." He cupped his hands over

Alex's ears. "All right, tiny mate, pretend you can't hear your cool role model making a complete bungle of this invitation. I'm meant to teach you how to be charming in life."

His awkwardness softened her nerves into a slower song, where she could focus better. "On the deck with the dogs sounds nice," she said. Silence. And like a needle slicing across a record, her heart tried to jump out of her chest at the idea that she'd said yes to dinner with a man.

"Great. Awesome." His face beamed with excitement, and she was instantly glad she'd said yes, despite the nerves. "Awesome. I mean…yeah," he said, and his face settled into a soft grin. "Come on, Kitten, we've got some errands to run and something delicious to make for a pretty lady for dinner. Seven work?" He'd already started walking backward, still grinning at her like a fool, a super sexy, hunky fool, when he added, "Should I pick you up?"

No! Her thoughts clouded for a minute. "That's okay, we'll walk. Seven's good."

"Perfect. Come around to the backyard. That way the dogs can maul each other and not us. You know the way, then."

The dogs would be better in the yard. She knew that from family dinners at his house, but she also suspected he made the offer to keep her comfortable. The least she could do was thank him. "We'll bring something sweet."

His smile grew again. And she'd thought it couldn't get any bigger. The man had an endless energy for joy. And Sasha hadn't had enough in her life. She wanted to be swept up in those smiles of his, carried away on the cloud and leave all her fears behind her on land. She watched until he was out of sight before she turned back toward the bakery.

But then she stopped, as Ellie's words came back into her mind. *Connor Duggan tangled up over a woman. Oh shoot, is he?* Just because Ellie thought so didn't make it true. But he was the kind of man people were drawn to. She'd bet he'd had lots of women tangled up over him.

Maybe she could…uh…ask him. Maybe he could be the kind of guy friend she asked those kinds of questions, about being tangled up over someone and how to go about getting untangled, or tangled in a much, *much* better way. Oh, Lord, she was confusing herself now. It was dinner, that was it, not a date, not therapy. Dinner with a friend, all by themselves. And the dogs of course. She could do this. It was time she did the kinds of things she craved no matter what anyone else thought.

Chapter Five

Well, now you've gone and done it, idiot. He'd gotten
the lady to agree to eat with him. Most wouldn't call
that being an idiot. But this was Sasha, and this was so
much more than dinner. He set the grocery bags on the
counter and ran his hands through his hair. *Pull it
together. Straight ahead, forward thinking and all that. Put
the groceries away, make the marinade, get showered. Not
complicated.*

Olive oil, lemon, garlic and rosemary, easy. He
tossed the lamb chops in the baggie with the marinade
and set it in the fridge, chopped some vegetables for the
salad and threw two potatoes in the microwave to pre-
cook.

The house was clean. Simply because it still
belonged in the eighties and required a makeover
didn't mean he was a slob. Besides, he'd been doing
major cleaning to put the house on the market. He
scrubbed down the counters anyway, put the dirty
dishes in the dishwasher that sometimes worked and

sometimes didn't and picked up the newspapers he had strewn across the coffee table. A quick vacuum and he felt better.

Kitten sprawled across her bed and watched him, tongue hanging out. "Yeah, I know why *you're* so exhausted." *Lazy bum.* "How can one dog shed so much?" he asked her. "Must take all your energy to produce enough fur we could turn into another complete dog, then scatter it over the entire house."

Sasha had been to his house before with groups of people. Too bad he felt like a ball rolling down the hill with no way to stop. He needed a run. *Too late, pal, too late for that. She'll be here in an hour.*

Sasha Kincaid was coming to dinner. He hoped. Hoped she didn't decide this was one of those times to turn and run as far away as she could from him. He still didn't understand why she'd done that lately. Not that it was any of his business. And she had found him in the park, deliberately.

"I've been looking for you." One simple phrase in her pretty voice had sped up the thumping in his chest. A bright day full of sunshine in the park, lazy and uncomplicated, had turned on a dime when she'd appeared. Not in a bad way, just that suddenly, like always, all his focus zeroed in on her and nothing else seemed to exist. He'd had to deliberately keep his hand on Alex's tiny back to remind himself the baby was there. Sweet, quiet snoring little bugger that he was.

But Sasha. *Talk about sweet. And sexy.* They'd shared something special. He'd felt it, hoped she had too. He'd watched her eyes dilate, felt the brush of her thumb against his lip, almost as if she hadn't had a choice in the matter.

He let that thought, and her seductive eyes taking him in from behind those frames of hers, frames that did nothing to hide her beauty, keep him company in the shower. A quick shower, the quickest, because he was a man, and thoughts of his hands on Sasha Kincaid, while water heated his naked body had him hot and hard instantaneously. And he wasn't going there to that fantasy, not yet. Not until he was certain she might want him too. It seemed sacrilege or like cursing himself in the same breath. So, a short chilly shower it was.

Now, what to wear? He wasn't a man who'd ever thought too much about impressing women with clothes, not that he was a complete nincompoop when it came to fashion. He *had* lived with a house full of women for seven years, and whether they wanted to help him altruistically, or not be completely embarrassed by his fashion choices, he now had a closet full of clothes he knew were approved of by his very own garment squad. Even if Cece had tossed in the occasional unicorn T-shirt. He'd been surprised someone made a T-shirt bearing a sparkly unicorn in his size.

Casual, tonight was casual—he'd said it himself. Back deck, grill, dogs as chaperones. "For cookies' sake, man, you're losing your cool. All right, gray T-shirt, jeans, flip-flops. And a bit of cologne, just in case." He opened his bottle of Calvin Klein, stepped closer to the bathroom vanity, and that was where the evening began to go downhill. He fumbled the cologne and lost hold, the bottle flying into his chest…and liquid pouring all over him.

Damn, that was spectacular. Cologne dribbled down his face and drenched his shirt. Some had even landed in his hair. Broken pieces of the bottle were in a puddle on the floor.

The noise of dogs outside in the backyard reached Connor as he stepped out of his second shower of the evening five minutes later. He stuck his head out of the window and watched Sasha for a minute. She stood in the grass, wearing a sundress the color of pale spring buds on trees. Jesus, she was pretty. He hadn't seen her in a dress before. She'd paired it with white canvas tennis shoes. Her hands were in her pockets, and she held herself in a tiny nervous huddle.

"Hi," he yelled, and cringed as she startled. He hadn't meant to scare her. "Sorry, be right out, uh, cologne mishap." He toweled off quickly and threw on a different shirt. Short-sleeved black button-down went with khaki shorts, right? He really did need a keeper, as his niece Rosie was fond of reminding him. His hair was still wet when he made it out through the back sliding doors.

"Hi," he said again like the dolt he was. "I'm glad you're here." Was that the right thing to say? Was it too much? It was how he felt, but should he have told her? He put his hand on his chest to try to calm the sprinting inside. Nope, it didn't work. All it did was remind him that he was on a first date with a woman he'd been dreaming about for months, or perhaps a lifetime.

When she'd walked into his life last year, his entire world had flipped over from steady to brilliant. He'd been changed internally, all his bones breaking and readjusting, his heart answering, *Oh yes, there you are.* The months since had been both amazing and torturous. Somehow, he was aware he could never face going back to that boring place he'd been before Sasha.

It left him in an uncomfortable spot, not knowing how she felt. "You look really nice."

"So do you. I mean thank you." She let out a huff. "Wow, I really suck at this whole communicating thing."

"I think you're doing fine." He ached to walk right into her arms and dance with her in the grass under the evening sky, still too light out for stars. He'd imagine the stars. He had a ridiculously specific imagination.

"You, uhm, do look nice too."

He sighed. "Outfit two, after the ah…massive spill. I was trying to impress you, WWRD."

"Pardon?"

"What would Rosie do? My niece. When in fashion doubt, she always said I should picture what she would suggest for the occasion."

"Are you in fashion doubt often?" She studied him, her mouth almost curved in a smile. Her eyes certainly were. In fact, he was pretty sure her eyes were laughing at him.

"Uh…no, nope, sometimes?" Why was he acting like that thirteen-year-old boy at his first school dance with the prettiest girl in the school paying him attention? "I did think the occasion suggested cologne, but I did not anticipate the bottle jumping out of my hands and exploding all over the bathroom."

"Oh no," she said, her face scrunched up. She put her hand over her mouth to cover the giggles.

"Yes." He exaggerated his debacle. "The bad news is, despite taking another shower, Calvin Klein will mostly likely be joining us for dinner tonight."

A laugh exploded out of her. She couldn't help it, and it felt wonderful. "That bad, huh?"

"It went *everywhere*." He threw open his arms and shuddered.

She laughed harder, picturing him fumbling with a bottle of cologne as it sailed out of his hands, spraying all over the place before it shattered on the tile floor. Laughter subdued her nerves. She imagined most men wouldn't have admitted it had happened to them, let alone be self-deprecating about it. But Connor wasn't most men.

He was as easygoing as everyone thought, but he was also simply funny and — she'd noticed over the months she'd gotten to know him — egoless. He enjoyed making people laugh. And he never seemed to mind being laughed at. *A healthy self-confidence.* She hadn't ever realized how sexy that could be for a man. Large, strong, successful, handsome, and yet he loved being funny too. The combination was irresistible to her.

"Well," she said and handed over her small backpack cooler. "Good thing I brought enough dessert for a threesome."

Connor gaped at her. She opened her mouth in a large *O*. Silence poured out.

"Did you just say what I think you said?" His voice cracked.

"I…" She slammed her hand over her mouth, mortified. Absolutely mortified. Where had that *come* from?

They stared at each other for a split second then, like he couldn't help it, a choked laugh burst out of him. Her eyes got bigger, and a giggle started in her too. He lost his cool and bent over with the force of the big bold laughs bursting out of him.

"I'm sorry…" He tried to speak in between. "I can't help it."

She laughed with him, hard. Eventually he slowed down, took a deep breath and blew it out. They both calmed, with a few more giggles and tears before they could carry on a conversation. Inside, Sasha felt buoyant, dizzy with the feeling of pure joy tingling through her body.

He sobered and pierced her with that intense focus of his, and for a minute she nearly lost the joy, wondering if she'd done it wrong, until he spoke. "You have such a great laugh." Another one of his million smiles danced across his face, this one a bit surprised and dreamy.

"I'm…it's a bit out of practice." *More like being resurrected from the dead.* Sasha hadn't laughed in a long, long time, ages.

His face softened. "Guess we'll have to work on that."

Oh. She put the back of her hand on her cheek, feeling the heat flame. Was that a challenge he was going to put his whole body and mind to? If so, sign her up right this instant. Could laughter be sexy? Sasha had never contemplated that thought before. This wasn't going how she'd imagined, but was completely lovely all the same.

"Well." He grinned. "That's one way to start the evening. How about a glass of wine or a beer?"

"Not right now, thank you. I don't like to drink when I'm nervous."

"I have some lemonade. It's a bit on the sweet side."

She followed him into the kitchen. "That doesn't surprise me," she teased. Whoa, where had that come from? Teasing wasn't something she did.

"Can't help it." He grinned. "And now I'm dying to know what you brought for dessert," he said, a chuckle escaping from his lovely mouth again.

"Stuff to make chocolate brownie sundaes."

"Seriously?" His mouth dropped open, and his eyes grew huge. He flipped open her cooler and poked around. A man on a dessert mission. *Wonder what it would feel like if he put that mission into kissing us?* Hmm, her body hummed with the electricity sparking around the room. His excitement over dessert was hot. *All of him is.* Mm-hm.

She could agree, standing there in nice summer short-sleeve black button-down, shorts and bare feet, proudly displaying those silly friendship bracelets he wore all the time, eyes wide as he pulled out the brownies she'd wrapped in plastic. He put the parcel to his nose and breathed in.

"These are going to be downright delicious, I can tell. And..." His eyes got bigger. "Tell me you made homemade salted caramel sauce." It was a whisper of reverence and hope and wishes do come true all in one plea.

"I did." And she got to see his face change from delight to desire when he looked from the caramel sauce to her. She felt the pull of his gaze as if he had a hold on her dress and was tugging her toward him, physically.

Unfortunately, or fortunately, depending on how much of a fool she'd almost made of herself, he heaved out a sigh and took a step away from the cooler with his hands up as though he couldn't bear to see the goods anymore without being able to touch them, eat them. *Oh, we'd like for him to eat the goods — he can lick them and taste them to his heart's content.* She was flushed, she knew it. *Ice cream and brownies, not sex!* She wanted to shout to her libido, which now was having full-on erotic fantasies anytime Connor got near her sweets. Jeesh! Even her thoughts were ridiculous.

But she'd gotten a little confused there herself. Because…well, she enjoyed the images of him touching her, tasting her. She certainly daydreamed of exploring his body. She thought it might be…that sex with Connor Duggan might be…not only passionate, but fun. And wasn't that a novel and glorious image.

"As much as I want to head straight to dessert, I invited you to dinner and I even have something delicious to serve you."

Whoa, had she gotten carried away. Flushed and confused, she took her own step back. Because suddenly she *wanted* so much and from experience it wasn't good to admit that. Except she was trying to live a new life, one where she made her own decisions and didn't let anyone, alive or dead, dictate how she was supposed to behave. And she somehow thought Connor would be the kind of person who would want to know her choices, her desires. But could she simply put them out there in the open for his perusal? And what of the woman Ellie hinted he was into?

"I'll see *you* pals later." He reverently palmed the brownies and caramel sauce and set them down on the kitchen counter, then put the ice cream in the freezer. "Lemonade will have to tide us over."

He smiled and poured her the largest glass of lemonade she'd ever seen. She had to giggle. This whole evening so far had been ridiculous.

"Are you tangled up over a woman?" She blurted it out.

Connor startled and tipped the giant size glass of lemonade over. Too quickly for action — they both watched as the liquid fanned across the counter and poured all over her shoes and the kitchen floor. If the earlier silence outside when she'd mentioned the threesome had seemed to stretch on into eternity, now it was a tsunami roaring toward land. Or perhaps it had already crashed.

After years of holding herself tightly together and perfectly quiet while trying to anticipate Anthony's moods, it was refreshing to say what she felt without any filters. Apparently refreshing also came with a huge dose of embarrassing, by Connor's expression. Was he confused? Disappointed? It was hard for her to tell. He almost seemed hurt, but why would he be hurt by her question?

The glimpse of emotion that briefly flashed across his face was replaced by apologies. "I am so sorry." He recovered quickly. Hmm that wasn't quite the response she was anticipating. "I can't believe I'm living my best idiot self tonight. Why tonight?" he said mostly to himself. He came around the island and studied the mess. "I…uh…here."

He lifted her onto the stool so fast she almost didn't feel his hands on her waist.

"Sasha, I'm so sorry. I didn't mean to touch you without asking." Now he definitely looked hurt, pained.

She shook her head. "I didn't mind." It was all she could get out because it was the truth and it surprised her. Then he was bending down, down, and taking her shoes off, his warm hand on her ankle, so confident but gentle, secure.

"I'm not usually this much of a klutz." She almost couldn't focus on his words.

Kitten tore through the open back door, tongue hanging out, a bloodhound on the scent of sugar. The mutt slid to a stop by the puddle of lemonade and started lapping, defying the laws of most dogs who hated anything lemon.

"Kitten, no!" Connor tried to pull her back. "I can't believe I did that. This date is not going at all how I planned, uh, hoped. I'm going to toss these in the washer, if you're comfortable with that, then I'm going to clean up this mess and..."

"No, it's okay. I..." She grabbed her shoes and hopped down. Now the blood wasn't rushing to her cheeks, because it had already flooded them. "It's still sunny — we'll put them on the deck and they'll dry and it'll be fine. It's fine. Or I can run home." The mess was her fault. She'd made a fool of herself with one stupid question and she didn't know how to recover the evening, the lighthearted dinner between two almost-friends.

"Sasha," he called and followed her outside. "Hey." Connor put a hand on her arm, a gentle touch, not a grip, a nudge. "Please don't go. I'm not tangled...I mean...I'm not with anyone."

"Oh."

He put his hands on his hips and gave her a long steady look. "Why would you think I'd ask you on a date if I was seeing someone else?"

Oh. Oh! It had been hurt she'd seen wash across his face, however briefly. She'd bruised his feelings. She guessed she had a lot longer to go before she understood so many social cues. First of all, she hadn't known it was a date, and she wasn't about to admit *that* to him. Besides he could probably see the stupidity written all over her so there was no reason to shout it out loud.

Hmm, could Ellie be wrong about him being into someone? But he did date lots of women from what she'd heard. And this was a...a date? The thoughts in her mind rolled over like an out-of-control bicycle. Could she be one of those other women he dated? He could teach her what she lacked. "But you enjoy sex, right?"

Chapter Six

Connor worked hard to choke down his embarrassed laughter. He covered his mouth and coughed through the absurdity of this conversation. No way in hell was he going to come off as if he were making fun of her. But damn, she was cute and funny and confusing. Where had this line of conversation come from? Her honesty and bluntness were refreshing. But something about this screamed of awkward and uncertain.

First of all, how in the world had she not known this was a date? And secondly, what in the heck *did* she think this was tonight? He'd been attracted to her for months. His attraction had only grown stronger. She might never have feelings for him, but he'd tossed the Hail Mary pass and asked her to dinner, which was going swimmingly, and now she'd questioned him about sex. How in the hell was he supposed to have this conversation with her?

He turned sideways a bit and surveyed the yard. The night was crisp and clear, low humidity, still light out. He was at a loss, but he didn't want to lie to her or play her question off. He'd do anything for her, even fumble his way through this minefield they found themselves in.

He caught her gaze. "I do," he answered. When he swallowed, his throat dried up. What else was he supposed to say? Was she going to ask him about experience, what positions he enjoyed? Oh, man, he wasn't laughing anymore.

"And you're probably amazing at it?" Sasha said, on a huff, as if she already knew the answer and asked anyway. As if it were an offense on his part.

He damn sure didn't have a clue how to handle this situation. Cece would have him asking Alexa or Siri, but Connor was pretty sure the AI phone ladies, polite and intelligent though they were, wouldn't have a clue how to field his inquiry.

"You must be," she said. "I mean…you…" She gestured up and down his body. "Lure them in with that charming grin that makes your eyes sparkle, those strong arms, and…and women love you."

Yep, any humor left in the situation flew away on the soft breeze. *She thinks I have a charming grin. Yeah, and she also thinks I'm a major player.*

She quieted and tangled her fingers together, taking a huge breath. "Will you teach me?"

"I…about…" This time Connor couldn't hide the strangled sound. He was so far behind it wasn't even funny. What the heck was happening here? Her words sliced through their surroundings, leaving the atmosphere in his backyard one of piercing silence. They'd had one too many awkward silences tonight as far as he was concerned. *She cannot mean what I think she means.* He grabbed one of the water glasses he'd set on the patio and chugged.

"About good sex, attraction, how to enjoy it with someone. All that."

Connor choked on his water. God, he couldn't breathe, trying to get his lungs working again, clear his airway. He cleared his throat one more time and tried again. "I...I..."

"You know how to do it and you enjoy it. I don't. And that's okay. I might never. But if I had a...the right partner...you...because I...uhm...I feel all these things around you I've never felt..." She faced away from him as if to gather her courage. "Intimate, sexy things. I think."

Oh, darlin'. Could he just take her in his arms and hug her? She'd had so much bad in her life that she didn't recognize the good for what it was. Yet here she was putting it all on the line, risking so much.

"I thought, maybe if the person I was with wasn't Anthony, then..."

Ouch. Connor cringed. *She wants someone to teach her about sex who isn't her abusive, criminal ex-husband.* He'd lied earlier when he'd said he wasn't tangled up over *a* woman. Or partially. He *wasn't* seeing anyone, because he *was* currently tangled up over the one lady he probably couldn't have. And now that intelligent, fragile, beautiful creature wanted him, because she'd heard he was a player, to rid her of the damage Anthony Lucciano had done. Bile burned his throat. And, in an instant, the night burst into flames.

Her eyes went wide and she shuddered when she met his gaze. "Oh no. You're mad. I'm sorry. I..."

Shit, I scared her. The scene was racing out of control before he could even comprehend everything, before he could get a handle on his own emotions. His mind, his gut, his heart were twisted up in a knot of confusion. But she was upset and the most important focus right this minute should be her. He could untangle himself later. She sat down on the deck and was hurriedly tugging back on her sticky wet tennis shoes.

"Sasha, wait." He tried to help her, but she brushed his hands away. He crouched down next to her. "I'm not mad. Can we talk?"

"I know mad when I see it." She wouldn't look at him now, gesturing to his face while she signaled for her dog. "And the way your face cringed when I asked you, when I—"

"No." He shook his head and spoke softly, settling his features as he did so. Always worried about making her uncomfortable, he stepped back and put his hands in his pockets, when what he really ached to do was touch her, apologize for upsetting her, for being an ass. He wasn't mad at her, but any time he thought about her ex and the horror that beast had poured on her, he couldn't swallow down the rage he felt.

God knew what his face must have shown her in that moment. It wasn't her fault and he'd better be crystal clear not to make her feel that. Unfortunately, from the way she held her body stiff and closed off, he might have already lost. When Sasha shut down and disappeared, no one, not even Ellie, could break through her barriers. "I was surprised, Sasha. You shocked me."

She tagged her small purse. Braveheart stood at attention next to her, and Sasha backed up toward the gate. His heart raced. If she ran now, would they ever be able to talk this through? "Forget I said anything," she said. "It was stupid, I know that now. I'm sorry. Things in my head seem to burst out these days. I'm so sorry. What a fool I am. I didn't mean to ruin the nice night you planned."

She gripped Braveheart's leash and attached it to her dog's collar, with jerky movements.

His emotions yelled at him to follow her. His gut was still pissed off over her ex. Luckily, he had enough brain power remaining to stand there in the hot summer night and calm his racing pulse before he chased after her and made everything even worse. *But could you really make it worse? Is there a worse in this situation?*

His inner self was being a sarcastic asshole, but he wasn't wrong. A woman he'd been dreaming about for months was bold enough to ask for what she wanted. And she hadn't picked any old fool—she'd somehow felt safe enough to pose the request to him. And he'd spectacularly fucked everything up. Not simply her request, but potentially a hell of a lot more than that.

Kitten barked and raced out of the kitchen, galloping toward Braveheart, with plastic wrap hanging out of her mouth. The gangly mutt nearly knocked Sasha down with his energy before Connor got her under control. "You big menace, stop!"

"Oh shit!" Sasha knelt by Kitten's side. "Connor...I think..." She pulled the plastic wrap from Kitten's mouth then ran into the kitchen. When she came back to the open doorway her expression was full of worry. "I think Kitten ate the brownies. Connor, it's really unsafe for dogs to have chocolate or walnuts. We have to get her to Ellie's clinic now."

And right before his eyes, any hope of saving the date disintegrated into ashes.

Chapter Seven

Sasha was grateful Ellie was actually at the clinic when they arrived. With a new baby in the picture, her friend had hired more help at her veterinary clinic in Corvallis. She'd hired great people. Sasha felt comfortable around them all, but Kitten, biggest buffoon there was, was as precious to her as Braveheart. Even being upset, she hadn't hesitated to come with Connor to the clinic. What she hadn't expected was to rush into the veterinary clinic with Connor and the dogs to find her brother Jackson and baby Alex present this evening as well. She really, really didn't want to have to explain what she was doing with Connor to her brother, or to anyone for that matter.

How did one explain her complete ignorance and humility? She could see the headline now, *Best Way to Ruin a Date.* The article could write itself. *Admit complete sexual ignorance to a man you're attracted to and ask him to teach you about sex. Then watch the date crumble into a stinky heap of crap right in front of you.*

A date. Connor had called it a date. Why hadn't she realized that? *Because you were being dense and trying to deny it.*

Asking Connor about sex had made him mad. That was a curve she hadn't anticipated at all. At the worst she thought he might laugh at her request. A reaction she'd been willing to risk. She'd rather have had the laughter now that she thought about it. Because she'd never ever seen Connor Duggan mad. Worse, what she'd thought of as being bold, asking for something for herself, was exactly what had made him mad. That had hurt.

"What happened?" Ellie asked as she rushed out from the exam rooms.

"Kitten got into some brownies. An entire pan of chocolate walnut brownies."

"Oh, you poor thing, love bug," Ellie cooed to Kitten. "You better come with me. Connor, you too. This won't be pretty. How long ago did she eat them?" Ellie led Kitten and Connor through to the back.

"Hey," Jackson said from his spot on the floor. Baby Alex was on his back on a big cushion with two puppies licking his tiny baby fingers. Ellie's enormous calm Rottweiler rested by Jackson's knee, her soulful eyes never leaving Alex. Braveheart had cuddled up right next to them all. "You okay?"

Sasha let out an enormous sigh. *No. I'm not okay at all.* "Fine," she said. "Worried about that silly dog."

"I wonder if Kitten might be part cat. Nine lives and all that," Jackson joked. "She's had her stomach pumped before. Ellie knows what to do, and she'll take care. And Connor's a fool for that mutt. I think his love alone wouldn't let anything bad happen to her."

Sasha took a chair next to where the puppy-baby party was, trying not to let the embarrassment and exhaustion of the night slurp out of her in front of her brother. "Yeah." It was true. Connor made fun of his dog, but he one hundred percent adored her.

"He...uh, were you with him when Kitten got the brownies?"

Her face must have shown her utter lack of how to answer that question because Jackson laughed. "Hey," he said. "It's none of my business who you...uh..." He cleared his throat. "Date, or whatever."

Oh Lord, she almost rolled her eyes at how ridiculous her big brother was being, but he was so obviously uncomfortable that she took pity and simply listened. He'd lost over twenty years of big brothering. She had too. She supposed she could handle a bit. However, sometimes it felt so surreal being here with him. She still pictured the Jackson he had been as a child and it was hard for her to accept he was now instantly an adult.

But he was, although it wasn't instant. Rather that she'd missed everything in between. That loss, that sadness resting in the back of her heart, pushed to get out. It was always there, always waiting to overwhelm her again with every loss she acknowledged.

"Anyway, what I'm trying to say." He caught her gaze and gave her a small smile. "He's a good man. An amazing friend. The best actually. I trust him with my life."

Now her tears threatened again. One more unexpected twist of the evening. She'd thought she'd have to lie about her worst-first-date-ever, to Jackson, but he'd surprised her once again. However, now was not exactly when or where she wanted to talk to her brother about her dating life, or her begging-for-sex life. That awkward image had her cringing in embarrassment.

"How are you doing?" she asked, hoping to change the subject. It had been a shock last year when Sasha and her brother had been reunited after more than two decades. For both of them. After their mom had killed their dad in self-defense, then died in prison, Sasha had been whisked out of the country in a sealed adoption. Name changed, new life. The only part of her old life that followed her were memories and nightmares. She'd learned to shove those away, because the loneliness and fear had been too much for her five-year-old self to deal with.

Jackson had spent his life searching for her. They'd both endured so much, and now here they sat alive, healthy, together. They were friends and Sasha felt comfortable around him, but regardless of who it was, her social skills were still in the baby-bird stage. Four-month-old Alex was more adept at communicating his needs. It was better to ask Jackson about *his* life. *Bet he never fumbles date night, or anything, for that matter.*

"Exhausted," he said with a huge smile on his face.

Alex started to fuss. Poor baby scrunched up his face and let out a cry way too big for such a small being.

"Oh, buddy," Sasha said.

Jackson scooped him up and tucked him into the baby carrier on his chest. "Yeah, tiny man is not happy unless he's moving or attached to Ellie's breast. I mean...whoa, sorry, too much information. Gonna walk him down the block a minute see if I can lull him to sleep."

Okay, so maybe Jackson's not perfect at everything. She smiled as she watched him disappear down the street holding his son. He was such a great dad. Wow, so many emotions in one night. It was hard to keep up. She needed a long, long nap where she could hide and evaluate everything that had happened in the last few hours.

In her before life, before even Anthony, she'd flown through her days on fire, never too much thought or dwelling on emotions. She'd considered them an exhausting waste of her time. It had always been so much easier to ignore them. Then managing Anthony's moods and staying alive had taken precedence over everything else. Now here she was with Anthony gone. She was safe and alive trying to build a new better life for herself, but ignorant about so many things.

"Hey." Connor pushed through the swinging door from the back. "Kitten's going to be here for a bit. Thought I could walk you home."

"No, no, please. You should stay. I'm...we're going to go." She fumbled for her leash and hurried out the door with her dog, Connor following behind.

"Sasha, please. I'm so sorry about tonight. That wasn't at all how I hoped the night would go." Fatigue and worry pulled at his expression. "I'd like to hold your hand in the twilight, try to salvage at least part of our first date." She could absolutely not let him walk her home, to a hotel. He'd think, he'd *know* she had no clue how to deal with her baggage. Besides, why would he...after she'd made such an ass of herself, after she'd made him angry? Nope, she definitely had to go before her messy emotions spilled out around her.

"No," she said more forcefully than she'd intended. Connor stopped on the sidewalk. "You should stay with Kitten. I'm going to go. I'll be fine. It's still light out."

"I'd feel better if I knew you made it safely."

"I can take care of myself." She had to go, now. The tears were coming. Ha, now they spilled out everywhere, with no way to hold them back. "I've been taking care of myself for a long, long time." She turned away and headed into the warm evening breeze before he could follow her.

And wasn't she the biggest liar ever. She hadn't been taking care of herself. She never had. Her mother had died taking care of her. Her adoptive parents had done everything for her. She'd been so spoiled by them it was embarrassing. Then Anthony had *taken care* of everything. She'd let him, she'd let him hurt her. No matter how many times her therapist and well-meaning friends told her it wasn't her fault, the shame still oozed over her.

Even now, she'd survived, she was on her own, and she still didn't really know how to take care of herself. She lived in a hotel, didn't know when a nice man was asking her on a date, couldn't steady her feelings enough to talk uncomfortable things through with him. Instead, she ran away. There was so much *not* taking care of herself going on it wasn't funny.

Connor stood alone under the clear sky not knowing whether to swear or break something, two things he never did. Had he lost the chance of a lifetime? Not the sex part, although that was part of it, the ability to share something special with Sasha, a part of a normal life? An experience that could be full of pleasure as opposed to the only nightmares she'd known? And perhaps develop more than a friendship with this special woman? He hadn't even handled the conversation right, how was he supposed to handle the actual physical relationship with her? He couldn't have planned a worse date if he'd tried even a tiny bit. And now she completely closed up and walking home alone in sticky lemonade shoes, feeling embarrassed, hurt, lonely?

"Everything okay?"

Shoot! His best friend stood by his side on the sidewalk, Alex crashed out on his chest.

"I..." He tried to clear his throat, but it was tight and dusty all the sudden. "She...uhm, Sasha left." Captain Obvious right here. *Captain Dumbass, if we're being accurate.*

Jackson lasered Connor with the kind of focus that had made him a feared criminal defense attorney. "Brother, how long have we known each other?"

Yep, throat was dry as the desert. "Uh, long time." He sounded like a caveman who didn't know what language was. Connor could see the puzzle pieces fitting together in Jackson's mind. "I like your sister. Sasha," he blurted. "She...I...dinner. Well dinner didn't actually happen because..." *She wanted to have a sex talk.* "Kitten...and I..." Yep, better to keep his mouth shut. God he was sweating. This night was one long, epic uncomfortable silence after another. Bury him now, bury him in all his mortification.

"Ellie said you were tangled up over a woman." Jackson studied him, not giving an ounce. "Hmm."

What? What did hmm mean? Was it "You're no fucking good for my sister"? Or "No way Connor Duggan would ever be tangled up over a woman"? Or, what? It seemed an eon passed when Jackson gave him a small smile and gripped his shoulder. "Good luck,

Duggan." He faced where Sasha had disappeared up the hill and said, "I think you're going to need it."

"Wait." A breath rushed out of Connor. He felt faint. The events of the night hit him in the chest. "You, you're not angry with me? I mean I didn't tell you because I didn't really tell anyone, because I didn't think I should until I told her, and I wasn't sure she'd ever be ready. So I didn't say anything to anyone about anything. About liking your sister." *Whew.*

"Duggan. You're the best friend I have, not only because I don't let a lot of people in." He gave a wry smile. "But because you're a damn fine person. I know what it's like to finally find someone who's worth focusing on. And I trust you with everything important to me, including my sister. Hell, I don't know how to act around her any better than you do. Still feels like walking across hot coals sometimes, you know."

"Yeah." Connor was trying to quickly process everything Jackson said, and all that was left unsaid. The relief and pride at Jackson's belief in him washed through his bones. Connor couldn't imagine how difficult it must be for Jackson and Sasha to pick up a relationship after so many years apart and all the sadness scattered between them. He knew Jackson felt guilty for so much that had happened, even though none of it had been his fault. And Sasha, well, he suspected she had a lot of messy feelings around what had happened to them as kids in addition to her horrible marriage.

"You two doing okay?" he asked his friend. Connor found, messy or not, none of it scared him away. He wanted to know everything about Sasha.

"Better than at the beginning." Alex started fussing in the baby carrier. "I want her to be happy. I know I can't change the past, any of it, but I'm glad we get to have a future together. And Ellie helps make everything easier, better. She and Sasha have become close. I love that for both of them. I'm trying to follow their lead."

"Yeah." Alex let out another cry of devastation, poor little dude, and Jackson said, "I'd better keep walking. I'll be back to check on you and Kitten." And he walked off toward the park.

Connor sat down on the curb and took a deep breath, winded by the evening. He had been afraid to tell Jackson about his feelings for Sasha, probably because he hadn't really trusted himself. To know that Jackson believed he was a good enough man for Sasha was grounding and amazing at the same time. He glanced at Jackson, getting smaller and smaller as he passed Ruby's spa and The French Connection Bakery till he disappeared into the park. Then Connor slowly turned his head and gazed in the opposite direction, the one Sasha had hurried away in, and he realized she hadn't headed toward her apartment over the bakery at all.

He stood, his limbs tired from nothing but the fatigue of a shitty night, and headed in her direction for a few blocks. It was one of those perfect summer nights full of promise, a perfect night for holding someone's hand and going for a walk. A perfect night for kissing as the stars came out, for holding tight to that one special person. It had been so perfect he could almost taste it. But he'd ruined it. He wasn't holding anyone's hand and after walking a few blocks, he realized he had no idea where Sasha had disappeared to.

Chapter Eight

Sasha sucked up the tears as she walked home, using the exercise to purge her disappointment, breathing hard through the fast pace. She didn't let herself examine what had happened until she was alone in her hotel room, doors locked. She tossed her shoes in the bathtub and herself onto the bed. It was a lovely, quiet hotel room. No one could get in unless she invited them, her safe place. But she didn't feel great about it today. Instead, the walls felt cramped and stuffy, closing in around her. She'd barricaded herself into a home that allowed room for no one else and she was so weary of that.

She should have stayed with Connor and made sure Kitten was okay. *You should have stayed and talked things out with him.* But she'd fled, as she'd been doing lately, her default. Talk about embarrassing. Asking Connor to have sex with her, to show her how to enjoy it. What had she been thinking, asking him so naked a question? People didn't do that, God! Then she'd watched him recoil. *Dumb, dumb, dumb.* Would she ever be allowed to come out from the ugly cloud of her before life? Her therapist said it was her right to find happiness, to live a beautiful life. And she was desperately trying to.

People talked about one step forward and three steps backward. For her it was more like one itsy bitsy half shuffle *almost* forward and ten thousand leaps backward. She was forever climbing out of the pit, her past always chasing her. And she didn't want it anymore, any of it, the reminders, the ghosts, the lessons. Burdens upon burdens for her to carry.

She'd just left him and already she missed him. Missed their afternoon at the park, how Connor had looked when he met her in his backyard, joy on his face to see her, his laughter at her absurd three-way comment. She missed his delight over dessert. Even his gently concerned touch on her arm when she'd been about to take off. They'd been, or at least she thought they'd been, having a lovely time. He'd even gotten a laugh out of her. He'd been his wonderful, easygoing, funny self and she'd ruined it.

Regret was one thing it came down to a lot for her. But she'd been realizing over the past few months, regrets got her nowhere close to feeling free and happy. They were draining. She rolled into a ball on the bed, blocked her vision to her haunting memories of a different life and fell into a dreamless sleep.

When she woke, the sun had fallen. She peeled her exhausted body from the bed and dragged herself into the shower. After, she wrapped up in her soft hotel robe, wiped the wetness from the mirror and faced herself. Red puffy eyes, short hair slicked back. She fingered the pink scar on her throat that led down her chest.

One of the physical scars from Anthony fucking Lucciano. *He's dead. He's never going to hurt you again.* She'd spoken the words to herself daily, since the night Anthony had died. Almost one year ago. It had become her ritual. And even though it was the truth and had helped her in the beginning, now, she was tired of it. Tired of having that link be what got her through the days.

Weary, Sasha shook her head to try to stem more tears from falling. "I don't want this to be my routine anymore," she whispered to herself in the mirror. "I'm twenty-seven years old and I'm done. I have no energy left to give to that monster. I do deserve a beautiful life, my very own life."

Connor's face came back into her mind right before she'd left him. He might have been shocked or repulsed or angry, whatever he was when she'd propositioned him, but he had tried to talk to her, to apologize. Then she recalled the last thing he said, *"I'd like to hold your hand in the twilight, try to salvage at least part of our first date."*

No joke, it *had* been a date to him. And she'd so, so wanted it to be. Maybe they could try again. She could apologize and they could start over. It was time she focused on her present, no more using all the crutches she'd barricaded around herself.

"It's time to be brave, honey." She used the words of her friends, the words of her therapist, combined them into something that fit her, that she could say with truth from her gut, from her heart. "It's time to be brave, honey."

And for the first time she could remember, she smiled at herself in the mirror, a bit wonky and tired, but a smile none the less. *That sounds like a much better mantra than one about a demon. Yes, much better.* "It's time to be brave, honey."

Chapter Nine

The rooftop restaurant at Hotel Marisol was a gem any day, but on this epically perfect summer Corvallis morning with a clear view in three directions, mountains flanking the horizon, it was spectacular. Connor took a seat at the table he'd reserved. Sipping his water, he scanned the view. The city rolled out in front of him until it hit the foothills of the mountains in the distance. Not even a hint of pollution marred the peaks' stark and jagged stance today. He could see for miles. An entire world of new places and experiences awaited him. Maybe that would right his world. That was why he was here today, wasn't it?

It was quiet, a quiet that allowed him to think. The only sound was the murmuring splash of water as a woman swam laps in the outdoor pool that stretched out from the restaurant part of the rooftop. The glass doors were all pushed open today to expose the fresh air. Whoever had designed this pace had an eye for luxurious comfort.

Connor tugged at the dress sleeves of his shirt while he waited for the two business companions to meet him for breakfast. Not only was the hotel directly across the street from his business office, but it was definitely designed to impress. A long shiny black bar stretched out along one length while tables and chairs spread out, some inside, others completely exposed to the sun as they gathered closer to the pool. On a warm summer day, the outside and inside areas flowed together and became one.

He brought many clients here, no matter how much money they were going to end up spending, because he believed everyone deserved a bit of pampering. And Hotel Marisol had the best eggs Benedict, and the best blue-cheese burger he'd ever had. It was a toss-up which he appreciated more, breakfast or lunch. He'd have to be careful not to drool over the food during today's meeting.

"Mr. Duggan, great to meet you in person. Jeremy Rock and my sister, Amelia Rock."

The tall, attractive siblings of Rock Solid, a custom home-building company that had risen to success in the last few years with houses across the country and had graced every magazine from *Architectural Digest* to *Elite Homes* and *New Woodworking*, greeted him with firm handshakes and smiles. Their work was enviable. They had a waiting list over six months long for clients and it was because they did grand and stellar new builds with all the bells and whistles. They'd been courting him long-distance since December to come on board.

"It's so nice to finally meet you in person," Amelia said, rubbing his forearm. A cat ready to rub up against him. Connor pulled his arm away and busied himself with his napkin. "We're so excited to bring you on as a partner." Her voice was thick and suggestive.

From the attention Amelia gave him during the meal, she pictured him as more than a business partner. It actually made him nervous, the sultry eyebrow lifts she kept sneaking his way anytime her brother had his head buried in the paperwork. She had sleek dark hair and large blue eyes, a full mouth he might have enjoyed kissing in another life, but all he could see when he looked at her, at any woman these days, was Sasha. Connor gave her a weak smile, tugged at his tie and wished the meeting over quickly.

He found, as soon as they sat down and started talking business, that he was in no frame of mind for this today. Kitten was still at the clinic and Connor hadn't slept at all last night. Worry had been his constant companion. He'd texted Sasha to make sure she had made it home okay and she'd texted back a short *Yes, thank you.* It felt empty, hollow, so unfinished.

Two barks came from the pool area. Connor followed the sound. Braveheart moved from a spot in the shade and stretched out his paws to the edge of the pool where a woman ruffled his forehead before she turned back to her laps. *Sasha.* She was the swimmer. Nearly silently she stroked through the water, so smooth. She belonged there, a water nymph.

"Mr. Duggan?"

"What?" Connor dragged his senses back to the people in front of him.

"You'd move to Las Vegas by September to head up the company, and from there who knows, you could be working across the country if it's as successful as we project," Jeremy said. "We'd like to get rolling with the partnership as soon as possible."

"All travel would be included, and you'd have access to our penthouses around the country while staying in different states." Amelia's words were laced with innuendo.

A year ago, two, hell, for the past seven years Connor might have been seduced by this woman's proposition. In his old life. Now, with a clear mind and heart, he no longer recognized that life or himself in it.

He glanced at the pool again, drawn by the rhythmic sound of Sasha's hands cupping the water, the slight swish of her kick. She stopped again briefly to drink from her water bottle and flick her dog with a splash of water. The Boxer nipped at the spray and gave another quick happy bark.

"Connor?"

"Move to Las Vegas?" he asked. *I'm open to exploring options.* He'd tossed out those words on one of their conference calls a few months ago, when they'd suggested the partnership idea to him. It was right after Katie and the girls had moved out and his empty, lonely life in his too-big-for-one-man house stretched out before him like a desert with no sign of life or water.

He'd never cared for the acclaim and awards he'd received over his career. What he cared about was the feel of a newly framed wall, the scent of wood and stain, taking something so crumpled in defeat and resurrecting it to pure beauty.

But he'd been floored they'd sought him out. They'd appealed to his ego and his love of a challenge.

And honestly, he'd been restless.

This past winter, when they had first begun courting him, everyone around him had seemed to be high on love. His best friend, his sister, heck even Lachlan

MacGregory who Connor swore he'd never actually seen smile until Ruby Naylor cracked open his fortress.

Back when he'd been trying to deny all his feelings for Sasha. Because, after the hell she'd survived, she didn't need any man pawing around her. Because she was his best friend's sister, because...because. Emotion rolled over him in a wave so strong and so out of place, he could barely swallow. The desire to have his own soulmate was so fierce it cut his breath off.

"Yes," Jeremy said. "To our headquarters, as we talked about. You'd be instrumental in designing and building our new custom contemporary homes."

"Mm-hm." It was all he could do to mumble out a response. He aimed his gaze back toward the pool. The sunlight now blazed off the water, making the human swimming in it invisible. Nearly. Her arms reached out and over the water and rippled in the mirage. There one second, gone the next. Having him twisted around and upside down. Pretty much how he'd been since he'd met her.

The waitress refilled his water. Ice clinked in the glass. The scene around him felt stifling all the sudden, sweat beaded around his hairline. This brother-sister duo and their company were billionaires. It was the offer of a lifetime. An offer he couldn't even have dreamed of when he'd been a young journeyman carpenter learning his craft. Prestige, success, more money than he'd ever know what to do with. It was an offer he'd be an idiot to refuse.

And Connor Duggan knew he wanted nothing to do with it. He wasn't restless for more work, or bigger jobs building brand-new houses, or any penthouse perks this sort of acclaim came with. And with that thought the dry-hot air of Corvallis seared through him, filling his limbs with energy. Understanding, knowledge, honesty settled in his bones.

There was no fucking way he was moving to Las Vegas. Ever. Corvallis was his home. He was a homeboy, always had been, even when his dreams and heart had been shattered. Even now when his future was so undefined. But torture or not to be longing for a woman out of his reach, he'd rather endure that then leave this place, ever.

"We can send over the contract details via our lawyer and get everything settled —"

"Amelia, Jeremy," he interrupted them. "I sincerely appreciate your offer, but I have to decline."

Jeremy frowned and gathered his papers.

"I'm sorry if I gave you the wrong impression, but I have no inclination to leave Corvallis." Connor ignored his coffee and sucked down his ice-cold water. Pushing his chair back to facilitate the end of this pony show, because he knew they'd try to convince him, he grabbed the bill, said, "Safe travels," and headed to the bar to pay.

He didn't care if he came across as rude. He didn't even have the energy to waste making chit chat. He set his credit card down with the bill and made his way to the restroom where he leaned against the sink and tossed water on his face. He shrugged out of his suit coat and ripped his tie off. Business clothes sucked.

No, he had no time to waste. He'd been wasting the last seven years of his life. No, that wasn't completely true. He'd done some important things in downtown, construction-wise. He'd been a pretty good uncle. But he'd buried his heart and personal desires and left them there to dry up and wither.

"Everything okay, Duggan?" the bartender asked when Connor returned and took a seat at the bar. Wyatt was a friend of his who worked part-time for his sister Katie's specialty catering company. They'd grown up down the street from each other.

Connor breathed a sigh of relief to see that the Rocks had left. "Better now." Sasha stood with a Hotel Marisol towel around her, the same large, red, embroidered signature *M* that was on all the patio towels snaked around her hips. She playfully ruffled her dog's fur, leashed him and the pair walked away into the dressing room entrance. Out of reach again.

Connor was still unsettled, still empty and waiting for more in his life, but at least he was certain where his life was. Ha, his niece was probably right, being in touch with his emotions, positive or negative, was the only way to live. No more bullshitting his way through important things. No more flirting with leaving this place behind. An odd thought flicked at his mind. More stark white towels with the red *M*s sat neatly folded on each chaise-longue. Another stack of them rested in a large blue rolling bin.

"Can anyone use the pool, Wyatt?" Unease snaked under his skin, one image following another.

"Exclusive to guests, Duggan. You want to get a room so you can take a dive? Gonna be another scorcher." Wyatt chuckled.

"No, just curious." He tried to keep his tone, light, easygoing, the way people knew him. No reason to show his shock.

"Don't worry, we've got Ms. Kincaid covered. I know she's a part of your circle. Security is subtle but powerful here at the hotel. Your friend there" — Wyatt nodded to where Sasha had disappeared — "is the only one who uses it this early. She gets to have the pool to herself. We make special allowances for her, and we stay in the background so as not to scare her. We know her story. Whatever she needs, we're here for her."

Connor closed his eyes and tried not to growl. *She's living here. In a hotel. What the hell?* That was why she had been entering late the other night in the rain with her dog and her groceries. Why she had headed in this direction last night after Date Debacle Numero Uno. In fact, now that the pieces were fitting together, his memories clicked. He'd seen her more than once right near Hotel Marisol in the evenings when he'd been working late at his office. He'd thought nothing of it.

Connor added a large tip to the bill and nodded at his friend. Walking into the bright sunlight, he made his way around the pool. This pool was an oasis, a place one could imagine in a luxury spa in Bali, with all the potted plants and lush greenery growing up the glass walls, to the view beyond. The water was the perfect deep blue. Moroccan-patterned tiles shimmered beneath the surface. He stood where Braveheart had sat waiting patiently for his owner, and stared into the water's depths, searching for answers. *I thought she lived above the bakery.* They all did. She'd moved into the apartment temporarily last summer until she found something of her choice. As far as he knew, not one of his friends knew she lived in a hotel. He couldn't make sense of it.

The sun glinted off something shiny on the cement. Connor knelt down and picked up the locket. Opening it he saw two photos. One was the spitting image of Sasha from another era. The woman's hair hung past her shoulders, and she hugged a baby to her. It was faded a bit, but the woman's eyes were the same as

Sasha's as she smiled at the camera. The other picture was also of a woman, standing in front of a stunning Italian villa. Perfectly dressed, and not a smile anywhere to be seen.

None of this was any of his business, not the locket, not the fact that she lived in a hotel, but he couldn't shove away his curiosity and his worry for her. *Does she want to live in a hotel? Why hasn't she told any of us? Is she still living scared?*

For months he'd gotten small glimpses of Sasha's nature, or at least what she presented to the world. Slowly, since he'd met her, she'd come out of her cocoon, joined the group at dinners and get-togethers. Since she'd started working at The French Connection, he'd swear their pastries had become even more delicious. She must use those long, graceful fingers of hers and sprinkle on her magic goodness. She'd begun to relax and smile. There was one rare occasion last month when he'd even caught her smile aimed his way.

He'd lapped up every word or gesture she sent in his direction. He dreamed of her. She'd made his heart hum for the first time in a long time. But he was never going to be the kind of man to pressure a woman. And the last two encounters they'd had, she'd turned and fled.

Connor fingered the smooth surface of the oval locket. What he should do was give it to Ellie, the person Sasha was closest to, so she could return it. But that would mean betraying Sasha's secret of living in a hotel.

Sasha Kincaid was a mystery. She deserved her secrets. She deserved to live a brilliant life unafraid and she deserved her locket back. He'd have to find a way to get it to her without making her feel uncomfortable.

His mind zeroed in on Wyatt's words, *"Whatever she needs, we're here for her."* Damn. Even if what she needed was to be left alone.

Chapter Ten

Some might call it cowardice. She preferred conscientious, aware, paying attention. *All right, I am a coward, hovering around the door of the bakery, hoping he'll walk by, but it's all I'm capable of at the moment.* This morning Sasha had stopped at Ellie's clinic to see how Kitten was doing and she knew when the misbehaving dog would be getting her get-out-of-jail card this afternoon.

So instead of cleaning out the walk-in fridge, a job mostly no one enjoyed but somehow gave Sasha a huge amount of satisfaction, she was out front tending to the enormous flower planters that banked the door of the bakery. Discovering she had a green thumb, even a tiny one so far, had been one of Sasha's pure delights earlier this spring and summer. She babied and spoke to her flowers like they were her children. It felt as though they nurtured her soul in return.

But normally she didn't purposefully put herself in the middle of a busy afternoon of people meandering about the neighborhood when she focused on these plants. Sunday morning before most humans were even awake was her preferred time.

Hopefully it would be worth it. Connor was walking toward her from the park. He'd have to pass by her to get to the vet. See, stealth. *Oh, sister, you're about as stealthy as Kitten.*

"Hi," he said and stopped a few feet from her. This time his smile wasn't exactly there. It wasn't exactly nonexistent either. She couldn't tell what it was. She studied his face. Warm, open eyes met hers with a serious, intent look, but she kept getting distracted by his lips. Even now with his indiscernible smile, he made her feel a bit woozy, all that energy aimed at her. His quiet stirred her out of her daydreams. It was like he wanted to say something but was weighing his words, measuring her stability before he made a move.

"Are you okay? Is it Kitten—is she all right?"

His face softened at that, even his shoulders letting go of some of their worry. "Yeah. I'm on my way to get her now." Braveheart perked up from her nap in the shade.

Connor stood there. He didn't say anything else, but he didn't leave. Together, but separated, they were stuck in some weird in-between or unknown place. Something was off. And she knew it was her fault. She could feel his mind whirring. *Is he wondering if I'm worth the energy? With all my baggage.* She closed her eyes, confusion blanketing her now. *How to behave, how to behave.* That was another tick she'd been trying to rid herself of, but really it all always came back to that.

"I'm sorry I overreacted last night. I acted like a clown," she said.

"You're living at Hotel Marisol?" he said at the same time.

What? Sasha snapped her eyes open to see his penetrating gaze. *How does he know?* That feeling, that instinct she'd had that someone was following her...

"You." Her chest squeezed in on her heart, making it difficult to breathe. All the lightness of the breezy summer afternoon smashed as the pieces clicked together. "Someone *has* been following me — you." She stumbled and fisted her hands to hide the shaking. "Why would you do that? You know my past." She choked out the words. "Everyone knows... Connor...Jesus, why?"

Her dog was at her side in an instant, nudging her legs with his head. Reaching down to stroke his body and reassure him. She was so fucking tired of these stupid spikes of adrenaline, how they always left her feeling ragged and drugged out. They embarrassed her and she hated that feeling, especially in front of...this man who was so comfortable in the world.

"Sasha, it's not what you think. I wasn't following you. Please don't run. I mean you should...you can do whatever you want, but I'd like to explain."

Sasha focused on his deep smooth voice she'd come to appreciate, how the sound of it always felt warm and comfortable, a softness on her skin, a gentle breeze, and more recently a sweet caress in the dark. Now it was steady. She latched on to it and forced herself to pay attention.

"I wasn't following you. I promise. My office is right across the street from the hotel. In the rain one night a few weeks ago, I was leaving, and you bumped into me...didn't see me. It was that time after dinner at Jackson's." He put his hands in his pockets. "I..." He sighed, made to step closer, but hesitated. He rocked backward on his feet instead. "I was worried."

Oh, *oh*. She took some deep breaths and grounded herself on the sidewalk in front of the bakery. The sun was hot, but the shade cooled her. She fingered the tiny yarrow petals and felt the dampness of the wet plants seep into her.

"I happened to be at a breakfast meeting this morning. I have most of my meetings there at the rooftop restaurant if I can. It's a pretty spectacular place." He cleared his throat. "And you were…ah, you were swimming." He carefully moved a few steps closer and held out his hand. "You dropped this."

It was her necklace. A simple gold chain with an oval locket on the end. Nothing expensive or special, but it had delighted her when she found it at the antique store this past winter. She tried to control her shaking hands as she opened the locket. Inside she'd put photos of both her mothers. She always wore it against her chest, a talisman of sorts. *How did I not realize I'd lost it?*

"Is it special?" His voice was still deep and resonant, but full of caution. And she didn't want that from him, for him to see her as weak, to tiptoe around her. She was so fucking tired of herself. "I can fix the clasp for you, if you—"

"I'll figure out how to do it myself." She cut him off, took another deep breath, then added in a gentler tone, "I *need* to do it myself."

"Okay," he said.

"Thank you." She closed her eyes and tried to bring all her emotions under control. It was all she could do to force herself to stay standing there and not run away with her embarrassment. But her words kept getting stuck in her dry throat. "I'm sorry. Again. I keep saying that. And I don't even know what I'm sorry for."

"You don't have anything to apologize for," he said. "I would never intend to make you feel uncomfortable, but I might accidentally and it's okay for you to tell me when I do. I mean, take last night. I fumbled the entire evening. I'm pretty sure I didn't do one single thing right and I made you feel bad. After that most coaches might bench me, but I'd like to try again."

"With me?" she asked, stupidly.

"Yeah." He gave her his movie star smile then. "You and me."

You and me. Him and her. Connor and Sasha. He wanted that. *Do I?* She sure wanted to try. Brave couldn't mean getting scared off after one supremely uncomfortable date, and a misunderstanding on her part.

"Together?"

He nodded and smiled. "It can look however you imagine, equal, a partnership. I just want to spend time with you. And hopefully not spill sticky lemonade all over you."

"A partnership?" *You're a wealth of words now, parroting back everything he says.*

"Hmm." He scratched his chin. "Maybe partnership isn't the best word. It doesn't sound very romantic, but I'm sensing you haven't had much equality in your past...relationships." That cloud passed over his expression every time her marriage entered the conversation.

"Think about it." The sexy smile returned to his face. "I may be making a mess of my words, but I *can* think of other ways to bring romance to the equation."

"Oh." Sasha huffed out a laugh. How did he do that, make things so casual and comfortable, but at the same time with all his intensity focused on her, send pleasant shivers through her body?

"I'm going to grab Kitten, school her on how not to assist in ruining a first date, then drop her off at Katie's so I can head out of town for a few days." He reached for her hand, and she let him take it, watched his fingers play with hers. The warmth of his touch calmed her. It also sent desire running across her skin. *I wonder if he feels it too?* "Take all the time you need and maybe we could talk when I get back."

"Okay," she said. As much as she wanted to answer a quick yes, she did need time to think about it, about what a *you and me* looked like, a partnership. Because she didn't think she'd ever really had that, equality. She hadn't even been raised to believe in such a thing. It gave her all kinds of new ways to imagine the possibility of dating Connor Duggan. More importantly she needed time because she didn't really know what a relationship meant for her. If her dreams were the same as Connor's. Or if she'd ever be able to live up to his expectations.

Chapter Eleven

"Please tell me you haven't changed your mind!" Ruby shimmied and clapped her hands when Sasha walked into the salon the next evening. Ellie and the baby, Katie, and one half of the Ford and Noah duo had already arrived at Ruby's salon Spa La La. It was their monthly fun spa date. Ruby closed early on a Thursday evening, Katie brought a bunch of appetizers and they acted like teenagers, gossiping, snacking, laughing.

Sasha had only witnessed moments like this from afar during her own teen years. Her Italian parents had brought her up so strictly to act a certain way. She'd rarely been allowed to indulge in frivolous things. They'd considered most of Sasha's classmates frivolous.

She'd decided to grab on to her future, to be brave. Part of that included trying to relax and have more fun. She was going to have all the frivolous in her life now. As much as she could gather, for Pete's sake. Frivolous everywhere. Bring on the frivolous!

She also wanted her hair fixed. So she'd called and asked for Ruby's help. *It's time to be brave, honey.* Well, she might be able to say the phrase, but living it? *Wow, easier said than done. I could just turn and run back to the hotel.* Having her hair styled and beautified might have been the scariest part of the evening for her.

She'd been beautiful once, had been an absolute snob about it. It had been what had attracted Anthony at first. *"Her perfect skin and petite body are exactly what Anthony Lucciano is looking for,"* according to her mother. All Sasha's strict diets, exercise, contact lenses to hide her imperfect vision and expertly applied makeup had gotten her noticed by the wealthy businessman and she'd been elated. Now she recalled that immature, ignorant, shallow person and shuddered. She didn't want to know her anymore.

But hacking her hair off with dull scissors every month felt more like a punishment, and Sasha was also finished with punishments. The silence as everyone focused on her was a bit unnerving, but these were her friends. She gave a small smile to the group and turned to Ruby. "I haven't changed my mind. I'm done cutting my own hair. I was hoping you could work your magic."

"Noah is going to be so upset he missed this tonight, I'm texting him ASAP," Ford said, and ran his fingers over his phone to send a message to his husband. When he finished, he pierced Sasha with a look. "You need a drink or a hug, Sash, or both?"

A nickname. A tiny offhand gesture, but priceless to her. It purged an enormous sigh out of her. "I think a hug might help."

Ford was tall and lean, and he gathered her close as if she was something fragile and special. But when he hugged, he squeezed tight.

"You sure give good hugs, Ford." *Amazing*. Sasha held on. It was the first real hug she'd gotten or allowed anyone to give her since she was a child. Not even Jackson or Ellie, her closest people, had attempted anything more invasive than a side arm hug. And even that had taken months of getting to know them and feeling comfortable.

"Wow," Ellie whispered. Sasha caught her gaze in time to watch her friend wipe a tear from her cheek.

When Ford let her go, they were both smiling. And she decided she might as well go for it. She walked to her first real friend in the world and gave Ellie a hug, gentle so baby Alex didn't get squished. "Hey," Ellie whispered.

Sasha's throat was tight, and her words caught, but she pushed through. "Thank you for being my friend, for helping me this year, for sticking with me even when I wasn't...when I couldn't..."

"Hush. I love you. I can't ever know what you went through. You take as long as you need to do things. I'm so grateful you walked back into Jackson's life, walked into mine. I will always be here for you."

"My turn?" Katie asked and Sasha got a different but no less wonderful hug. When they were finished, she didn't feel the urge to run at all. She wanted to sink into their arms all over again. Years was too long to go without being touched in a gentle loving way.

"Do I get one too?" Ruby asked.

"Hmm." Sasha paused. "Maybe I'll wait to see how my hair turns out." She winked at Ellie and they all laughed.

"Oh, hugging people and throwing some sass." Ruby swirled her hand around Sasha. "I like it. Get over here, my darling, so we can begin. Short hair fits you. All we have to do is give it texture and soften the edges a bit."

Sasha took a deep breath, set her eyeglasses down and put herself in Ruby's hands. "I'm ready."

Ruby washed, conditioned and rinsed Sasha's hair with a dreamy herbal shampoo, placed a few highlights in and readied her back in the salon chair to wait while the color set. Ford gave her a fashion magazine and a glass of wine. And Sasha took the time to take in the joy and conversation around her. Warmth, luscious scents, friends, a comfortable chair, even something as silly and dare she say, frivolous as a fashion magazine. *Deep breaths, deep, deep breaths.*

While Ruby cut her hair, Katie gave her a manicure, painting her fingers a bright teal blue, and it was both frightening and lovely to have so much attention paid to her at once. "It seems as though you're having a moment, Sasha," Katie said. "Giving hugs, opening up a bit, letting Ruby have her way with you."

Giving hugs, letting Ruby. Sasha hadn't seen things that way, as though she were giving. It felt as if she were the one receiving it all, the kindness, the intimacy. But that was what healthy relationships were, her therapist had said, giving and receiving in a trusting place. Taking care of each other. Not belittling or putting each other down. These people had been boosting her up for a year and she had not been giving back. "I'm sorry," she blurted out.

"For what?" Ruby stopped cutting and rested her strong hand on Sasha's shoulder. Again, the warmth of a kind human touch seeped through her clothes and into her skin. And her body soaked it all up, so parched for kind touch she'd been, so parched she hadn't even realized it.

"For being so shut off and distant sometimes, unpredictable, for not letting any of you in. I…it…"

"That's not what you were doing, Sash," Ford said.

"It isn't?"

He shook his head. "Healing. You've been going through one intense healing process. You'll probably be on that journey for a while. You don't have to apologize for taking care of yourself." Ford had worked with foster kids for years as a social worker, before he pivoted and began an organization to help those kids who were coming out of foster care at age eighteen and had nowhere to go. "We're happy to have you in our lives and we'll keep showing you that. But trust isn't an easy thing to build back up after what you went through."

"But you all didn't hurt me or break my trust." It didn't make any sense to her. "Do you know…" The words came in a long stream. "Why I have short hair? My mother, in Italy, said women with short hair were unattractive. So once my arm had healed after Anthony died, I cut it, because I couldn't stand the thought of being pretty anymore. Pretty got me noticed by…well…"

Acid slithered up her throat and threatened to unhinge her. The hollow ache in her chest beat faster as the memories flipped around in her mind, little snapshots stinging back to life. She was trying to heal, like Ford had said. But sometimes understanding it all, the post-traumatic stress, the feelings of guilt, the ghosts, what she should do now with her life — it was all too much to bear. The weight was crushing.

Silence surrounded her. Inside, her heart pounded furiously.

"Here." Katie grabbed her wine glass before it fell from her shaking hands.

"Take a couple of deep breaths, honey." Ruby put her scissors and comb down and gently nudged Sasha's head forward. Placing warm hands on Sasha's neck, Ruby began a slow massage, working her way across Sasha's scalp and down to her shoulders. Sasha closed her eyes and tried to even out her breathing, letting Ruby work the tension out of her muscles.

"When I was a senior in high school," Ellie began in her sweet voice, "I had a horrible experience with the guy I was dating. And it took me years to trust people again, almost a decade to let Jackson into my heart. I was a disaster inside," Ellie said.

"Well, you had a horrible childhood with your monster mommy too, my dear," Ruby said softly.

"That's right, she broke your nose," Ford said. "I'd like to find her and break *her* nose."

Ellie patted him on the arm, "Okay, big guy, no need for more violence, but I appreciate that you have my back."

"She hurt you, Ellie?" Sasha raised her head.

"Yeah." Ellie nodded and smothered Alex's small hand with kisses. "It was a long time ago, but I go to counseling. Jackson sees a therapist too for everything he went through when you two were kids."

Her strong, stoic brother? "I had no idea."

"It's not easy stuff to talk about," Ellie said. "Is it?"

Sasha shook her head. "I'm trying to believe my therapist that I can get better, that I deserve goodness, but it's much harder than I thought." She rubbed her face and took the glass of water Ford placed in her hands. "Even tonight, something fun, and here I am nearly having a panic attack."

"Those are sneaky bastards," Ellie said. "But it doesn't mean you're not healing. Look at you opening up. Think about everything you've done this past year. And there's no shame in wanting to look pretty."

"You have all of us to lean on," Katie began. "You're not an obligation. You're our friend."

She took in the passionate, kind group in front of her. "Yeah," she said.

"Okay?" Ruby lifted her chin and met her gaze. "I'm almost finished with the cut. Shall I continue, or have you had enough for tonight?"

Sasha swallowed and focused on the here and now. "Keep going," she said, giving Ruby a small but honest smile. Exhaustion or relief, probably a bit of both, took over her body as she finally relaxed into the salon chair and let Ruby have her way.

"Here," Ellie said, handing the baby to Ford. "Your turn to hold my love muffin. I'm going to do Katie's toenails for when she gets to the beach next week."

"Where are you going?" Sasha asked.

"Leo and I are going to Hawaii for a whole week by ourselves."

"That sounds dreamy," Ford said. "Who's watching the girls?"

"My mom and dad are splitting the time with Connor. It'll be good for him. I think he's been lonely since we moved out. Or something. I can't put my finger on it. Maybe he's stressed with the huge offer he's contemplating."

"Offer?" Ford asked.

"Yes. A big name in construction wants to hire him to lead new builds around the country. It would be amazing, but I know the thought of leaving here and moving someplace new is conflicting for him."

Connor Duggan moving? Leaving this lovely place where he has family and friends, a whole community who loved and depended on him?

"Mm. Jackson said he was grumpy the other day," Ellie said. "Which I have to admit, I've never seen Connor Duggan grumpy."

"I think I need help," Sasha interrupted. "I...it's about Connor." The movement and sound stopped around her. She could feel it.

"You can open your eyes, you know, honey," Ellie said, gently.

Sasha shook her head. "Nope, I think I'll stay this way. All my bravery is used up for tonight."

"You like him?" Ford said.

Sasha squeezed her eyes shut even tighter but nodded. "My body is all shimmery around him...and other parts of my body keep having conversations with each other...my lips and my hands...about him, how nice he must feel, how, how..."

"Yes!" Ford yelled.

"I knew it," Ellie whispered.

"Sasha." Katie took one of Sasha's hands and held it between both of hers. "It's attraction. You're attracted to Connor."

Sasha eased the tension in her face and opened one eye a tiny bit to peer at Katie. The smile on her friend's face was warm and curious. "Is that what attraction feels like?" Katie's smile grew bigger, and she gave Sasha a nod of encouragement. *God, no wonder Katie's such a great mom. She has that calmness that makes me want to trust anything she says. That has me dying to spill all my secrets.* "I've never felt it before. I didn't know. Ugh, I'm a mess. I'm a ridiculous teenager in a twenty-seven-year-old's body. I've never felt attraction this intense before!"

"How do you feel about being attracted to him?" Ruby asked.

She gave an awkward half smile and wiped the random tear that had leaked out of her eye. "Confused, restless, hot. I ache to be around him. And I want to hide at the same time."

"Because you're worried?"

She took her time and thought about Ruby's question. "Only about making a fool of myself. But I guess I've already done that a few times. I sort of asked him to teach me about sex...and he got mad. Then I got mad. Then Kitten ate a pan of brownies."

"Wow!" Ford said. "We're definitely getting you in the salon chair more often. This is way better than therapy."

Sasha laughed and shook her head. It all seemed so ridiculous.

Katie rubbed her hand, drawing back her attention. "You know Connor would never hurt you, right, Sasha? He's a good man. Although getting involved with anyone who might be moving might not be the best step for you right now?"

Katie had offered it more like a question and Sasha didn't have a clue how to answer. Imagining this city without Connor didn't feel right. *But I'm not searching for a future with him, with anyone.* No. She cleared her head. In a way this information lightened her own worries. She just wanted to try to enjoy a casual relationship with a man. That might be all she was cut out for.

She swallowed back the tears that threatened. Tears that exposed all her vulnerabilities were always lingering under the bare surface.

"Let's deal with one thing at a time." Ford had pulled up a chair and was focused on her. "So you asked him to have sex with you?"

She nodded. "How absurd it sounds now. I've been having these feelings and I've been trying to take my life back, to make my own path. You all talk about how you enjoy sex and I wanted to see if I could enjoy sex too, so I asked him. But I think I made him mad. He said he wasn't. But his face was all kinds of angry."

"Do you think you could talk to him about it, clear things up?" Ellie asked.

"Yes. It's next on my new list." She took a deep breath.

"Your list?"

Heat flamed up her cheeks. "I made a Be Brave List. I'm tired of being strangled by my past or my fears or all the things I did wrong. I want to enjoy life and do the things that might seem too hard, or that I've never done before. There's so much I've never done. Self-care is on there. Coming here was first. Letting Ruby fix my hair that I'd deliberately ruined. Letting myself hang out with you all and have fun. Does that seem silly?"

Ellie shook her head and hugged Sasha's shoulders. "No, not at all. I love lists. And that one sounds perfect."

"I'll tell you something to add to that list," Ford said. "Kiss Connor Duggan. Because we all know, with his lips, he has got to be a master."

They all burst out laughing, even Sasha, while her cheeks flamed hotter. *Yes please!* Her lips cheered.

"I came as soon as I could get away from my clients." Noah rushed through the door. "What did I miss?"

"So so much," Ford said and fanned his face.

"Just Ford giving Sasha advice on kissing Connor," Ellie added, winking at Sasha.

His back to Noah, Ford gave Sasha crazy wide embarrassed eyes. She couldn't help giggling at him.

Noah wrapped his arm around Ford's waist and kissed his husband. "No one kisses as well as you do." He glanced around at the ladies. "But Duggan's lips were made for nibbling and sweet, sweet torture."

Ford smacked him on the chest. "See, exactly." And they all dissolved into laughter again.

Nibbling? Sweet torture? Sign us up right this instant.

"If he could hear you talking about him like this, he would be beet-red, dying from embarrassment," Katie managed to say, between laughs.

"Oh please," Noah said. "That man has swagger for miles. Trust me, he's aware of his kissing skills."

"Holy smokes, Sasha Kincaid! You look dynamite!" Noah stopped by her chair and fanned himself.

She peered into the mirror. "I do," she whispered. Sasha carefully touched her hair, turning from side to side. Ruby had added some deep red highlights and expertly shaped the locks around her head. Her eyes were huge behind her glasses. Even her smile had changed. "I have cheekbones."

"You have gorgeous cheekbones. You're a modern-day Audrey Hepburn, although your face is fuller. You look healthy and beautiful." Noah leaned in and side-kissed her face. "Breathtaking."

She took stock of her body and realized she wasn't scared at the thought of being beautiful again. Because maybe Ellie was right, that she was a different person.

Nerves still flittered under her skin, but some were of acceptance and excitement. "I'm definitely going to need more hugs," she said. And her friends gathered close and wrapped themselves around her.

Chapter Twelve

Years ago, in what now felt like someone else's life, when Nina had given Connor the engagement ring back and left him in a pile of dust after his brother-in-law had died, Connor got by on autopilot, helping his sister, making a home for his nieces, slowly disintegrating from grief.

Then he'd gotten drunk. He'd come to the bar and start with whiskey shots. The fire burned away any feeling he had left in him until he could float on a high. After that he'd consume as many beers as he could. Eventually a friend or bartender would pile him into a cab or their car and dump his sorry ass home. Fortunately, that phase hadn't lasted long. One morning, hungover at work, he'd nearly cut his fingers off on the table saw. It had shocked the stupid drinking out of his system.

Tonight, after his colossally disastrous week, he'd come to Lachlan's pub to drown his sorrows again, only this time with food. There was nothing a delicious meal couldn't fix. He sat at the end of the bar, nursing the one beer he allowed himself, and, unable to decide on the fish and chips with Lachlan's secret batter, or the clam linguini, he ordered both. Rocky Road Ice Cream Cake was on the dessert menu too, so he'd save some room.

Connor face-palmed and tried to scrub the dumbass from himself. There was no denying it. He was incapable of being a gentleman around Sasha Kincaid. First there'd been date disaster, where among every other misstep he'd embarrassed and upset her. Then instead of somehow finessing the fact that he knew she was living at the hotel, he'd barreled over her with the information and frightened her.

Luckily, he hadn't actually chased her away that time. She'd stood her ground and talked things through with him, kind of. He suspected there was so much more for her to unpack. Then he'd given her time and walked away. And he hadn't heard from her in almost a week. He'd also left her alone at the bakery, only grabbing a quick coffee two of the days, trying not to crowd her. Another reason for the double dinner—he'd been starved of Sasha's goodies all week.

"Dateless and desperate I see." His sixteen-year-old niece, Rosie, smacked him on the back and climbed up on the stool next to him. Leo walked up behind him, and Brie took the stool on his other side. It was uncanny how close to the truth Rosie was.

"Well, nice to see you too, my least favorite niece," he teased Rosie.

"Puuulease." She grinned. "You couldn't survive without my greatness in the world."

"True," he said. He gave each girl a hug and Leo a high five. "You humans joining me?"

"Picking up takeout," Leo answered. "Katie's exhausted and Cece couldn't find one single matching pair of shoes."

"She has fifty pairs. Where did they go?" Connor asked.

"Your guess is as good as mine," Leo said. "In fact, I'm not sure I really want to know."

"She's been tossing them off the roof patio into the backyard," Rosie said. "Trying to see if she can get them to land in the garbage can."

Connor and Leo shook their heads.

"Wow," Brie said when the bartender set down Connor's plates of food. "What have I told you about emotional eating?" She might only be twelve, but she was smarter than all of them combined.

Connor choked on his beer. "How could you tell?"

"Duh, it's me. Bet you ordered Rocky Road cake too, didn't you?" She tsked. "Without even waiting to see if you're full or not."

"Hmm." He studied her. "How old are you really? Come clean–thirty with a PhD in psychology?"

Brie giggled.

"Bet he has woman problems," Rosie chimed in.

"How would you know?" Connor turned to eyeball his other niece.

Leo chuckled. "Duggan."

"Fine, fine." He indulged his nieces. "But just because you're women doesn't mean you know *everything*."

Leo laughed outright that time. "Have you forgotten the seven years you lived with these ladies, my friend?"

"Never," he said to Leo. "But we can't have their egos exploding all over us. Okay, so emotional eating," he said over a bite of salty fish dusted with some genius lemon seasoning, while Rosie nabbed some fries from his plate. "Plus me alone at a bar equals women problems. Let's say you're correct. What does one ignorant man do about that, my wise sages?"

"Just tell her how you feel," Brie said as if it was the easiest thing in the world.

"Do you actually have feelings for a woman?" Leo joked. Connor was grateful for Leo's presence in his sister's life, his nieces', and he'd been a great friend to Connor, but damn that comment hit him as hard as Jackson's half teasing last week. Connor swallowed his food and took a long drag of his beer. The cold brew did nothing to ease the ache in his chest.

"Of course he does," Brie said, always defending him. "He's been waiting for the right one, someone worthy. So his heart doesn't get hurt again."

"Yeah," Leo said, serious now. He gave Connor's shoulder a squeeze. "I get it."

Leo did get it, better than Connor ever could. After Leo's first wife had cheated on him and had been killed in a car accident, Leo had sealed up his heart with super glue, until he'd met Connor's sister. Connor's problems were minuscule compared to what Leo had gone through.

The bartender handed over three large bags of food to Leo. "Hey," Connor said, acting affronted. "It feels like you people might be emotional eating too." He narrowed his eyes at Brie.

"Yes," Brie said, letting out a sigh of an exhausted know-it-all from explaining the ways of the world to him. "But we're happy-eating, not sad, lonely, trying to fill an eternal emptiness eating."

"Wow," Connor said with awe. This time he and Leo both laughed.

"Don't worry," Rosie said and gave him a loud smacking kiss on the cheek before she hopped down. "You won't be lonely for long. When we come to stay with you, we'll help you solve all your problems."

"Oh that's right," Connor said and gave Leo a nod. "You and Katie excited about your trip?"

Leo smiled huge. "Can't wait to dump these fools on you," he teased.

"Come on," Rosie scolded again. "You adore us."

"Let's get this food home. Time to feed my girls. Night, Connor."

He watched them go. And even though the bar was busy and noisy, they took all the warmth and love with them. He turned back to his food and dove into the pasta. With his mouth full of the delicious savory flavors of garlic and white wine, Connor decided he was perfectly fine with emotional eating. And dammit, full or not, he *was* going to order Rocky Road Cake, even if he didn't have anyone to share it with.

While he stuffed his face full of the warm comfort meal, he mulled over Brie's advice. *"Just tell her how you feel."* It sounded so easy, when she said it in her calm, knowing voice. And it did make sense. He'd have to figure out a way to do it gently and slowly, which could be difficult considering his heart had started beating again when Sasha'd walked into his life. How did one gently and slowly admit *that*? And he'd have to figure out how to be okay if she didn't want the same things as him. He took a deep breath. Yep, definitely going to be a dessert night. Potentially double desserts.

Chapter Thirteen

Well, she hadn't expected every one of her Be Brave Goals to go as spectacularly as salon night had. After all she had started with the easiest, or safest items, being surrounded by good friends, people she had grown to trust over the last year, even if it had taken her almost an entire year to believe in her instincts, to really open up to them.

Now she was jumping right into the most difficult item on her list. A week of thinking and psyching herself up hadn't lessened her nerves at all, but the fact that she hadn't seen Connor at The French Connection had her worried. He'd blatantly let the next move be hers. And while she respected it, she also missed him. Making the move was difficult for her. But she was here, and she wasn't leaving until they talked. The neighborhood was quiet in the early evening. A brand-new *For Sale* sign stood in Connor's front yard.

So he is moving. Sasha frowned. Honestly, she didn't know how that made her feel. It certainly cemented the fact that whatever this was between them should be casual. *Yes!* She cheered herself on. *I can do that. I can see if he still wants another date with me and try to enjoy wherever it goes.* She ignored the sense of sadness that pooled in her gut over the thought of him leaving town, and with another deep breath of courage, she approached the front door. Her palms started sweating, which wasn't great since she was carrying a container of cupcakes. But at least they weren't shaking, yet. That was usually a great indication she was headed directly into a panic attack.

You can do this. It's daylight. You're taking him cupcakes, for crying out loud. You don't even have to step inside. All these little pep talks she gave herself that had become normal over the year. They'd served her well. She'd been to this house before, many times, for dinners and BBQs when Katie and her girls still lived her. She'd never not felt safe here.

Sasha stepped up to the porch, and a switch flipped from the peaceful, lazy Sunday afternoon neighborhood to chaos. Screaming came from within. "I can't believe you destroyed my iPad!" "I didn't! I decorated it! Ow! Let go! Uncle Coco, don't let her murder me! I'll never make you another friendship bracelet ever ever!"

"Rosie, let her go!" Connor's voice boomed out. Kitten's barking joined the fray.

Before Sasha could comprehend what was happening or turn and run, the door burst open and a whisp of a red-haired child ran from the house — Cece, Connor's youngest niece, with his oldest niece, Rosie, in hot pursuit. Kitten bounded out next, sensed her pal and threw her body into Braveheart's, who eagerly leapt into play mode.

In one swift moment, Sasha lost control of her dog's leash and the treats. The loud splat of a dozen whipped mascarpone-cream-topped chocolate cupcakes hit the porch. "Oh, shit!" Sasha cursed. She'd completely forgotten to plan for the dogs' shenanigans.

The silence was its own kind of beast, like someone had muted an action film right in the middle of the climax. Not just muted, froze. No one moved or said anything. Slowly, the neighborhood came back into focus as a car drove down the block. The dogs chasing and play barking in the front yard drew Sasha's attention up. Rosie, her mouth opened in a large oval, gripped Cece by the straps of her overalls. Cece resembled a monster who'd been through a tornado and leapt out the other side to chase a hurricane, on purpose. To be fair, that was the sprite's M.O. Both girls stared at the mess, then back at Sasha, then at the open doorway.

When Sasha was brave enough to cast her eyes in that direction, what faced her wasn't at all what she'd expected. Connor Duggan, barefoot, wearing old jeans and a black T-shirt that had a sparkly rainbow unicorn head on it. Both shirt and jeans were covered with splotches of paint. Sasha nearly started to giggle. There was even paint in his thick brown hair, bright green, some pink. Hands on his hips, he stared down at the cupcakes, his expression that of a boy whose dreams had been absolutely crushed.

"You brought us cupcakes?" Cece wrangled out of her sister's grip and knelt down in front of the mess. "We'll still eat them, even though they're squished. I love squished cupcakes!"

"I'll put the dogs in the backyard," Rosie said, and, as she tugged the tangled leashes of Kitten and

Braveheart toward the gate, yelled, "Don't think I'm done with you yet, you little mosquito!"

"I'm not a mosquito!" Cece yelled back.

"Cece, hush now," Connor said calmly. He bent over in front of the cupcakes and carefully turned over the ones that could be salvaged. Then he took one, examining it as he stood, as if it were the holy grail. He peeled off the liner and shoved the entire thing in his mouth, leaving a mess of frosting around his lips. Such divine kissable lips. He pierced Sasha with such a hot intense look she'd require an encyclopedia to understand. *No, you don't—he's saying he likes your cupcakes. Mm-hm, does he ever.*

At that moment, Brie, the middle niece and Sasha's favorite, ducked under her uncle's arm and took in the scene. "Oh, hi, Sasha. Uncle Coco," Brie teased. "You didn't tell us you invited a lady for dinner."

He broke his gaze from Sasha and gave Brie a silly grin while he choked on his cupcake.

At that, while Brie broke out into a huge smile and smacked her uncle on his back, Sasha couldn't help it, she burst out laughing.

* * * *

"So, Uncle Coco?" Apparently the ridiculous nickname was Sasha's kind of humor because the gorgeous woman sitting next to him dissolved into giggles again.

He grinned. Damn, it was the prettiest sound he'd ever heard. She could mock him all day long, delight at his nieces' shenanigans at his expense whenever if it made her laugh that way.

"I never know what new nickname Cece is going to dream up to torture me with."

"That sounds lovely," she said with a wistful tone in her voice. "To have nicknames."

"Yeah, there have been some lovely ones, that's for sure," he joked and got another smile out of her. Maybe this was what he was meant for, making her smile. All those years of being funny, of letting humor be his way of communicating. He'd been practicing for this. When she laughed, the clouds disappeared after a long gloomy storm and the sun finally warmed him.

After having her cupcakes nearly destroyed, she'd stayed for dinner, almost had milk spilled on her, suffered Cece's three-point-five-million questions and smirks from the older two nieces, and she was still here. He didn't know what he'd done to deserve her company tonight, but Connor wanted to keep her forever, relaxed, laughing as the moonlight took over the sky. Everything felt right. She belonged here, by his side, in his bed, in his life.

This was the first minute he'd had with her alone. They sat outside on the back deck as fireflies danced around them. He leaned back on his elbows, watching the play of light. He had no idea why she'd even come tonight, hadn't yet had a chance to ask her. And part of him didn't want to ask and burst the bubble the night had surrounded them with.

"So, hey," he said like the tongue-tied idiot he was around here these days.

"Hi," she said then broke into giggles again. "Am I fourteen or something?"

"You?" He let out a laugh. "I'm the scrawny kid with acne and no mojo and the hot girl in glasses is paying me attention and I'm a mess."

"The hot girl in glasses?"

"Oh yeah," he said, his voice no longer teasing. "Hot, cute, so smart it's sexy. Talented hands." He took one of her hands in his and rubbed his thumb over each fingertip. "There's magical sugar in each of these. Maybe that's what I should call you. Sugar." He felt the shiver run through her hand. She didn't pull away.

"I wanted to apologize again," she said. "Or explain, talk things through like you suggested." Serious now, she fiddled with the collar of her blouse. The night hovered around them, heavier with the absence of humor, and he found he didn't mind. He was interested in every side of her, the uncharacteristic giggles, the patience with his nieces, even this serious nature of her personality, her demons, her fears, her hopes and dreams. All of it.

"You found my necklace and returned it and I…"

"I didn't mean to upset you."

"No." Cutting off his apology, she shook her head. "It's been a long year, and I thought I was doing better, but I still…I'm…I don't even know how to explain it. I started living at the apartment, but then…uhm, Bo needed a place to stay. He takes care of his sisters, and he can't…no one will rent to him. It wasn't a question about letting him have the apartment. You're not mad, are you? I haven't told Jackson yet either."

"Did you think we'd care?"

"You're the landlord and all and I should have…but then I got settled at Marisol. It felt safe, which I didn't feel at the apartment. Or I was still too hyped from everything that had happened I wouldn't have known safe if it was delivered to my door." Sasha let out a long sigh and gazed around his yard. "I think I just came to that realization right now. Huh."

She felt lost to him, and he wanted to pull her back.

"At the time, I craved the feeling of security," she continued. "And I love the pool. I feel so free in the water, Connor...I..." She waved her hand in front of him then rested it on the deck beside his. As quickly as she'd set it down, she lifted it up and tangled it with her other one, twining the fingers together in constant movement.

Taking a chance, Connor reached for her hand again and gently placed it back in his. To calm her nerves or soothe his, he wasn't sure. Her breath caught. She studied their connection and allowed him to rub his thumb over her fingers. "I like it when you do that," she said on a whisper.

I know, I feel it too. The spark, the current racing through their fingers, twining them together. "As far as I'm concerned, that apartment belonged to Ellie, even after Jackson and I bought all the buildings. She offered it to you when you needed a fresh start. You offered it to someone else as a safe place to stay. Can't see anything wrong with that."

"Is everything always so easy for you?" she said, her voice catching and breaking on the words.

Connor was glad for the dark then. *Is that what she really thinks? Is that what she sees when she looks at me?* He gave her hand a squeeze then pulled away. The truth hit him hard again. The punch kept coming. He should be used to it now. There wasn't one person in the world who knew him, fully, deeply, completely. That was what his friends had found in their partners, in each other. He ached to find it.

Unable to form the words, he shook his head, ran his fingers through his hair and let out a strangled sound. "No." He didn't want to burden her with the depths of his thoughts. He'd spent years putting on a façade for others. This wasn't the place to rip it down, let her see how uncertain of everything, how lonely he often was. He felt unhinged, exactly the kind of things he wouldn't burden her with.

"You must think I'm crazy, though? Living in a hotel?" Another hushed whisper as the night guided her words. She seemed to echo some of his internal battle. Was she interested in more than the funny casual guy he always was? Connor leaned his elbows on his knees and gazed across the yard. Maybe he didn't need to hide his whole self. Could he bare a small slice and still not scare her away?

"Crazy? Nah. Look at me, I'm still living in a house I bought for the woman I thought I was going to marry, who wasn't strong enough to stick by my side when my best friend got sick. I'm a master craftsman with awards from around the country and this behemoth is desperate for a gut job."

Sasha focused directly on him. A balm, a go-ahead to give a bit more. "And honestly, I don't have it in me to fix it up. Now that Katie and the girls are gone, this place means nothing to me." He met her assessing gaze with one of his own. "And I don't want to live in a place that means nothing to me anymore. So crazy? No. But...well, I don't think either of us is living their best life."

"No," she agreed. The night stretched between them, heavy now as the humidity and their admissions surrounded. "But you, you're moving on. Your house is for sale, and...you make everything appear so easy." Standing up, Sasha broke the moment. She walked out into the dark yard away from the porch.

He followed her. "Hey..."

She stopped and whirled around, resting her hand on his chest. He hadn't meant to get so close. He wanted her to leave it there forever, feel his heart beating underneath her palm. Neither one moved. When she met his gaze, a question passed over hers and she pulled away, leaving a hollow ache where her hand had been.

"You're right, actually. And I long for that, to live my best life, but, Jesus," she swore. "I don't even know little things about myself, let alone something massive like how to live a best life. I don't know if I enjoy butter on my popcorn, or if I hate shopping. I don't know if I'm the kind of person who leaves the dirty dishes for overnight. Or maybe..." She puffed herself up. "Maybe I prefer to be wasteful and use paper plates. Can you imagine such a thing?"

Connor didn't have a clue what was really happening here. But he was fascinated by her none the less, caught in her thrall. "I don't think the paper-plate police are going to come after you." He smiled, trying to lighten the mood, how he always did, with a bit of humor.

She gave a huff and poked him the chest. He could just throw caution to the wind, grab her hand and pull her in. Make their bodies flush together while she expelled whatever surged through her that he didn't quite understand. He wasn't feeling one bit humorous all the sudden at the image of her body pressed to his.

"Do you know those things about yourself? I bet you do. You love your popcorn smothered with butter and salt or doused in caramel. You hate to shop and...well, I don't know about the dishes since you did them tonight. Once doesn't give me an accurate indication." She listed off his truths as though she were offended.

"I'll have you know I'm an expert shopper," he boasted and got a small smile out of her. "But seriously now, I'm confused."

"All those little things that make up a person, a *whole* person I...I don't know them about myself. I don't know how to simply be, let alone live my best life. I'm not whole. Do you understand what that feels like, to not have had the chance to build layers of knowledge about yourself? My layers are all...are all...scars and tragedy. And fear."

Christ, he had no idea how that must feel. He wished she were in his arms then. He wished he could wrap her up and take her pain away. He wished it had never happened in the first place.

"I don't enjoy sex or even kissing. From my limited experience," she said with disgust. "And I want to. I should be able to, dammit!"

"Sasha, come here." He could try and she could pull away, but he needed to hold her and he sensed she needed the same. "I'd like to hold your hand, put my arm around you."

She paused and studied him, and his heart stuttered. Then slowly, she leaned into him and he tried to camouflage the sigh of relief that triggered in him. He pulled her close. *Finally.* Wrapping one arm around her waist, he brought her hand to his mouth. "Shhh," he whispered. "Seems to me you're already learning a lot about yourself this year. You stayed in the town your brother's in to rebuild a relationship. You've made friends. You take damn good care of your dog. You got a job and are learning how to bake, although it seems to me that might be a talent you were born with."

"I bought the bakery," she whispered and rested her cheek against his jaw.

"Whoa, that's the last thing I expected you to say. But that's awesome!"

"I…they were going to sell it. And it was the first place that felt like home to me after…well forever. And I couldn't let anyone else have it. I…I have money. His money."

"Shh. It's your money. You do what you want with it. Make yourself happy."

"I may as well tell you more of my secrets now that you know about the hotel. It feels freeing to tell someone, to tell *you*. I don't really know why I've kept it all to myself, except in the beginning of my new life it seemed important for me to have super strict boundaries, to have things of my own that no one else could have a say in. But to be honest the longer I keep the secrets, most of them, at least, I think it's out of fear. And I don't want to live my life out of fear anymore."

"Whatever you need. Keeping secrets or admitting them. But I can see what you mean about doing it out of fear. Probably not a great way for any of us to live. It sounds nice to have a person in your life who knows every last hidden thing." *I've never had that.* "It took a lot of courage for you to share the things you have with me." *And a helluva lot easier said than done, fool.* It had been a long damn time, perhaps *ever* since he'd bared all his truths to anyone. Self-preservation was a tricky bastard.

"Didn't feel brave admitting I hate sex to someone who's probably a sex god."

He chuckled, and some of the tension left his body. She wasn't only brave. She was so damn adorable. "Sex god?"

"Glad I can make you laugh," she pouted.

"Sugar, making someone laugh is a gift. And not many people make me laugh out loud. And if we're really going to talk about bravery, I think you win the award for showing up at my house again with chocolate treats despite my human and dog hooligans."

"Well, you ate them anyway."

He felt her smile against his cheek. "I enjoy all the sweet treats you make. I want to taste every single one."

Sasha stilled her body but didn't move away. The night's humid warmth pressed around them. "Are we still talking about my cupcakes?"

He barked out a laugh again and pulled her a little bit tighter. "I am talking about every single one of your sweet treats," he whispered and gently kissed her ear. "The ones you bake for me and the ones you keep hidden."

"Hmm." Her hand tightened in his shirt. That right there felt like one sweet treat, the way when she tightened her hold, she brought her body snug into his.

"Okay?" he asked.

"Yes...maybe we could try the kissing thing now." Her hands feathered at his neck, twirled through his hair. Her words surprised him, but her touch melted his concerns. She made no move to bring her face out from hiding.

He placed his lips against her ear, "That's a great idea," he whispered. He smoothed his hands to her hips, gently dug into her soft flesh. "I could kiss you like this." He teased her soft earlobe with his lips. She'd dabbed some scent right there beneath her ear. He breathed in. She smelled of secret rooms and stolen words laced in with all her sweetness. "Or like this." One gentle kiss against her temple. Her eyelashes brushed against his cheek. She braced against him.

Their bodies pressed together in anticipation, and he felt everything, her breath feathering along his skin, the beat of her heart, the way she stroked her fingers through his hair.

He leaned back so he could see her face. Eyes closed, lips slightly parted, cheeks flushed in the twilight, and he went from seducing to hard and needy instantly. Gone were all his good intentions. He rubbed her lips with his thumb, and she whimpered. Just as the back door opened and he heard, "Uncle Connor?"

Great timing, my little trolls. He wrapped Sasha up in a hug and sighed.

"Wow," she whispered.

I fucking know. He hadn't even kissed her yet and his body hummed with awareness. The intensity of it was worth the swear.

"Cece fell asleep on Kitten's dog bed again," Rosie said. "And Kitten is sitting on her face."

"Be right in," he replied, still holding tight to Sasha's warm body, which meant he felt the chuckle roll through her. Every single cell on his skin felt her body against him, wanted to join with her. Her heart raced next to his, her nipples were hard. Was she panting or was he? "Please tell me you'll let me take you home tonight?" he whispered.

"Uh-huh, sure," she said. "I'm a little dizzy. I think."

Chapter Fourteen

Sasha didn't know what was wrong, *or right*, in this situation, but she wanted to wrap herself around him and never let go. One whisper of his breath on her ear, one word of his asking her if she was okay. How in the heck was she supposed to answer that? Honestly. Was there such a place for *too much* truth? He'd barely kissed her, hadn't even touched their lips together, and her entire body felt electrocuted, eager for more. She sat beside him in his truck, silent again. Neither one spoke, but he held her hand and she could feel even there in his fingers how taut his body was.

And this wasn't like the other silences between them, uncomfortable in the sense of wrong uncomfortable. No, no, this felt agonizing in a delicious way. Nerves swirled between them. The night breeze stirred the air in the truck. The vibration of the wheels rolling on the pavement radiated over her skin, rumbling through her the way his kisses had. How he'd possessed her lips with his thumb. No one had ever told her about that, about the feeling of it, the power, both in her and in him. It felt like he wanted to own her pleasure, and that caused her entire body to light up with anticipation.

He'd parked at the hotel and was around her door, helping her and Braveheart out before she could collect her thoughts. What thoughts? Who was she kidding? There was only desire and she longed to fly on the wings of it.

"Floor?" he asked, never letting go of her hand. His gaze seared a brand into her skin.

Sasha reached out and pushed the elevator button and nearly whimpered again at the heat in his eyes. There wasn't one single smile of his to appreciate or dissect. Instead, his face sharpened into want. *It's attraction.* If that was what this was, she ached for more of it. How freeing and powerful to have such a man focus on her that way.

They stood in the elevator, that power shimmering around them and he stepped in, cupping her chin. "Want to practice more of that kissing now?" he whispered.

"Uh-huh." She nodded her approval and raised up on her tippy-toes to meet his mouth. Hot and smooth, his lips explored hers and she leaned her body in to feel more. More touch, more everything, to soothe the ache. But it didn't soothe—it wound her up and up so tightly. His kiss stayed gentle for a moment, or perhaps an hour. He gripped her head and touched her lips with his tongue, stroking the pad of his thumb along her mouth as if he were mapping the feel of her beneath his fingers.

"Connor," she said, angling in closer.

"Yeah." He pulled his head back and studied her. "All right?"

"I really like that." Watching him smile at her words took the breath right out of her. Her heart chased it as it flew up and away. The elevator dinged and startled them both. Connor gripped her hand and she led him down the hallway. Braveheart whined at her and pawed their door. She'd forgotten all about her dog. Forgotten how to breathe, how to walk, how to stifle her smile. The heat of Connor's body radiated over her skin as he stood close to her, connected. She used the keycard and let Braveheart in. Connor put his foot in the door so it wouldn't close, but he didn't enter.

"What now?" she asked. *Is that my voice?* She didn't recognize it. Somehow her brain was still working, a tiny bit.

"Now..." He grinned and raised an eyebrow. "If you want, we get to the goodnight kiss."

"I do want."

He held her tightly to him around her waist, bent her backward, touched his mouth to hers and succeeded in kissing the daylights out of her. Each kiss was different from the one before, better, sending heat surging through her, making her believe she could fly. He started slow, but not gentle, a savoring, as if he intended to taste every new spot he hadn't yet conquered. Little explorations urged her to return the favors and she did, nipping at his bottom lip, teasing her tongue to follow the path her teeth led with.

When she did, his touch turned all-consuming, devouring her mouth like it was one of Sasha's pastries made especially for him. As if her lips had his name branded on them, a beckoning, a *come here and taste me right now*. And just as he did her sweet treats, he tasted and licked like his life depended on it. It was nirvana, bliss. Greedy, greedy, hungry man.

She gripped his shoulders to hold on so she wouldn't fly away without him. So he would never leave, never stop giving her this high, until Connor's mouth zapped every rational thought from her head. He trailed his lips down her neck, kissing and biting and sucking, and she went boneless in his arms while every cell in her body pulsed with the need for more. More touch, more kissing, more biting. Then he found his way back to her lips, covering her mouth with his as he slowly lifted her back up. Speechless—he'd stolen her words, her thoughts. All that was left was the heat buzzing through her body.

Connor gently pushed the door open, leaning her against it. He wrapped his arms around her, soothing them both with his hand rubbing her back. His caress brought her down to reality. "Is that all?" *I want everything.*

He laughed against her skin. "Woman, you are going to kill me. *That* was out of this world, the best kissing I've ever experienced."

Oh. She felt weightless again and was grateful he held her up. "Me too. I think...I think you obliterated something in me, all my nerves and worry."

"Making out in a hotel hallway. Never done that before." His voice sounded rough and held a touch of awe.

"Me neither." She smiled. God, her smile kept growing. She touched her lips and her cheeks. Connor's gaze followed every movement. She could feel his desire. He took a small step back into the hallway, separating them. Without his arms around her, without his lips tasting her, suddenly acres spread between them.

"Don't you want to come in, though?" Her body was alive and he made her feel so cherished, all his focus directed at her, like *she* made him lose control and turn into a swarm of lust.

"You have no idea how much. How much I want to do so, so many things with you." Deep and mysterious, his words had turned. He cleared his throat. "But there's a whole list of things we need to do before I walk through that door with you."

The way he said it, so seriously, when so often he was casual and fun and lightness, caused a shiver of desire to race across her skin. She flipped through the possibilities of what he meant. "Oh." Her smile faltered. "You mean protection, condoms and such?" Practicalities, that was what he was referring to. *Hello! We appreciate a man who's practical about those things.*

"Hey." He nudged her chin up. "If we're going to do this, we're going to do this right. Yes, those things…" He grinned. "Are important. But it's not only about safety. There's exploration and fun to be had. Especially the *and such*. Now you're giving me ideas, images and goals to add to my fantasies of you, which makes me walking away tonight even more difficult. But…"

"Fantasies?" She leaned closer. How could she feel the pulse between them without even touching him? "Like more kissing?"

"Definitely more kissing, and not only your lips." He drew his finger over her cheek and she nudged her head into the caress. "This graceful neck," he whispered. "I love your hair. How it frames your eyes, gives me access to this part of you." He smoothed his hands over her skin, and she thought she might melt right there in the doorway.

"Ruby...uh...cut it."

"Mm." He smiled.

When his fingers trailed over her collarbone and finally, slowly, down her arm, she watched his eyes follow the path, like he was lost on the journey. Where would he go next? Which spot on her body would he caress? Finally when he'd finished teasing down her arm he took her hand in his, brought it to his mouth and let his lips linger.

She felt everything, every nerve, the slight lift of air twirling around them from holding the door open. Even the door at her back, solid, holding her up. Each little circle he drew on her skin hammered through her. And she felt her pulse alive and wanting low in her belly, between her thighs, places she'd never imagined a pulse before. She ached for him, for their bodies to be connected.

"Not just kissing, though." When he met her gaze, his eyes were hooded, full of greed, a hint of mischief. And she sighed. She could sigh right into his arms and have him carry her away on the feelings.

"Oh?" She didn't know if she wanted to stay here all night and have him swirl his wizard words around her or dive right into one of his fantasies, or one of hers. *Fantasies, yes!*

"I'm going to take my time, enjoy every second of discovery, all the things we deserve. And there are so many, many things you deserve. So many things to look forward to."

She didn't even mind the flush that crept up her cheeks because she'd begun to notice every time that happened to her skin, Connor's focus turned heavier, his eyes darkened. And she could practically feel him holding himself back from touching her. "Really?" What they'd been doing had felt spectacular.

He smiled. "An entire list of amazing things to imagine. There's holding hands." Connor held hers so carefully in his, the heat of his skin moving through hers, a comfort, a joy, a promise of more. "Flirting." He raised an eyebrow, brought her hand up and gave it one last kiss before he separated them. The man was probably born flirting with those moves and she didn't have a clue how to reciprocate. But she was flying too high to let her worry take over. "Secret gazes across a room."

He pinned her with that sharp intensity of his that she'd only noticed he was capable of tonight. He took a step away. "Anticipation." Her breath was the only sound she could hear, barreling through a tunnel. Another step back but his eyes held them connected. "Dating." Connor placed a hand on his chest. "Would you, Sasha Kincaid, like to go out with me one evening this week?"

She nodded. Tried not to leap after him and jump into his arms.

"What should we do on our date?"

Wait, what? She gripped the door and put her hand on her heart to steady the thundering. "I don't know if I know how to date." Anthony had only taken her out in the beginning, and now she could look back and see it had been to show her off. It had never been about pleasure for her. "After how I handled our first date."

"*You* were fine. I'm the one who messed up," Connor said. "Let's start over. We get to decide what we call a date, what we do, where we go. We can make it fun. We can make it sexy. We can make it ours. And you have all the control if you want it." His words cut through her freefall of concerns. "My bet's on you. I bet you're going to date the hell out of me. I bet you're going to drive me wild with your dating."

She chuckled. He made her laugh and flush with excitement at the same time. The way he teased her with his words and innuendoes. Wow. *I wonder if he'll tease me with his body, the way he does with his words. Ooh, honey, we sure hope so.* "I want to go on more dates with you, Connor." Wow. Now that smile of his could light the world on fire.

"I was hoping you'd say that." A slash of vulnerability flashed across his face. As if he thought she'd say no. Ahh, this man. She leaned against the doorway. He'd spiraled her up on a wave of desire and joy. She was giddy and alive. She couldn't wait to see him again.

"Goodnight, Sasha. Thanks for the cupcakes."

Sasha watched the hallway long after he'd stepped onto the elevator and disappeared. Then she floated into her room, let the door shut behind her, flipped the locks and grinned. She kicked off her shoes and twirled into the tiny kitchenette. Face flushed and happy, she fell backward onto the bed, running her arms over the covers, letting the fabric tingle along her sensitive skin. She brought her fingers to her lips. Connor Duggan could kiss. And she'd kissed him back. It nearly made her laugh. How silly, how bubbly she felt. Even when she got up to inspect her face in the bathroom mirror, to see the flush on her cheeks, the glossy sheen her eyes had taken on. She was a little rumpled in a deliciously wonderful way. She practically glowed with her feelings.

When her phone rang and Connor's name flashed across the screen, she tried to steady herself, bring herself back down to reality.

"Hello?"

"Sasha? It's me, Connor."

"Yes, hi." She blushed. And it was only a phone call. But why was he calling? "Are you okay? Are the girls okay? Kitten?"

He chuckled. "Yep. All four of 'em are crashed out asleep on my bed. It's the couch for me tonight, darn it."

How the man could sound happy about having to sleep on the couch was beyond her, except that was how he was, so, so easygoing. And he adored his nieces.

"Did they leave you a pillow at least?"

He laughed again. "I have a secret stash of pillows and blankets. I'm a quick learner."

"Oh." *Oh, that's all you can think of to say?* The quiet came through the phone. "I...you've never called me before." Months ago, Ellie had taken Sasha's phone and programmed all their numbers in, just in case.

"Now it's on our list." His voice was confident and vibrant in person. On the phone it seemed so much deeper or clear, with no other distractions to compete.

"Our list?"

"Mm-hm. Our list of things to look forward to. Late-night phone calls. Early morning phone calls. Goodnight calls."

He likes lists too. Even that silly thought made her blush.

Sasha climbed into bed and tugged her pillow to her chest. Braveheart curled up on her feet. "You already said goodnight." There was a smile in her voice because it didn't matter, she was delighted he'd called. He could say goodnight to her a million different ways.

He cleared his throat and his voice had lost its humorous edge when he spoke again. "Yeah, and part of me is saying that was the dumbest move ever. That I should have never let go of you, that I should have carried you in and…"

He took her right to the edge of need again. She ached for him. "And?" she whispered.

"Done so many other things on our list."

She could close her eyes and imagine him right there in the room with her, that was how focused he was.

"But I meant what I said about doing this right."

"This?"

"Dating you. Getting to know each other."

Gosh he was so confident. Her heart flipped over. This wasn't a part of her past, buried under the rubble. These images he conjured up were new and thrilling and lovely.

"Plus, I get to relax on my couch and listen to an intriguing woman talk me out of my loneliness. So, Sasha, how about a late-night conversation?"

She'd never in her time knowing him have pegged Connor Duggan as lonely, but she also didn't think she'd ever heard him be insincere. And everyone had hidden places they didn't share with the world. If talking with her meant he didn't have to endure his loneliness for the night, she was thrilled to do that for him. It added to the swirl of joyful emotions from their evening. And for the first time in her life, she drifted off to sleep talking with a handsome man who knew how to late-night conversation as good as he knew how to kiss.

Chapter Fifteen

He'd attempted to be first in line at the bakery the next morning, but getting three girls to school on time required the skills, focus and timing of an elite athlete, or a ninja. He'd done it before when the girls had lived with him. But oh, how foolish of him to think it was like riding a bike. It wasn't. Chaos ensued from the minute he walked into the kitchen from his early morning run with Kitten and found three nieces making three different breakfasts while simultaneously bickering and getting dressed all at the same time. He'd stood for a minute in awe of it all before he'd taken a deep breath and rushed into the fray.

Now it was after nine. He'd had his coffee, sweetened perfectly too, thanks to Brie who apparently could multitask like Glinda the Good Witch, make herself perfectly put together, kind and graceful while wielding a magic wand and turning the world around her perfect too. Or at least his hazelnut caramel latte, extra *extra* grande, she'd made for him in his thermos.

Mostly, the morning was a blur, as if he'd closed his eyes, gotten in position and pummeled through the gauntlet. His sister was a saint. All parents were. How in the beejezus did they survive that every morning?

He pulled up to his job site, dumped off his tools and checked on his team, which took longer than he thought because they were so awesome that they'd not only finished gutting the entire place, they'd had the engineer in to inspect the structure and had gotten the go-ahead to decide which kind of support beams they were going with. So, with enough caffeine in his blood to almost, almost tip him over into loopy, it was almost eleven when he walked into The French Connection.

He'd battled with what to do. On the one hand, he wanted to visit the bakery and see her, but they'd been up till after one a.m. talking. On the other hand, he didn't want to come across as stalker-ish. On the third hand, he didn't want to make her think he was ignoring her. Okay. He paused outside the door, took a deep steadying breath and ran his hands over his face. Potentially he'd had slightly too much caffeine. Because how many hands did he actually have? He needed to calm down.

Sweet caramel smacked him in the face and righted his world. It also made him realize how hungry he was. Of course, he was always hungry in this magical place. He filled his lungs with the goodness. Today it was something sharp and caramel, and that same comforting mixture of cinnamon and sugar. The yeasty humid scent of bread was ever present, but he also detected something fresh, herby and sharp.

There she is. Sasha was at one of the workbenches chopping tomatoes and cucumber and adding them to the blenders she had lined up. He stood watching her.

She caught his eye, quickly glanced back at her task, then slowly faced him again, this time with a shy smile. *Yeah, I feel it too, all loopy and high.* She washed her hands and came around the counter to meet him.

"Morning," he said.

"Hi," she answered. They stood there, two fools lost in the same dream, floating on the same cloud, caught in the same spell.

"You're staring at me like I'm a morning bun," Sasha said, and Connor laughed.

"I'm not sure how to answer that that won't get me in trouble, but you do look good enough to eat, if that's what you're referring to." He grinned as the flush bloomed on her cheeks. *So damn pretty.* "Am I drooling?" He wiped his mouth and got a laugh out of her.

"Here." She beckoned him behind the counter to her workspace. "I'm afraid we're all out of morning buns, but I do have a play on gazpacho for soup today."

"Gaz-what?" he asked, peering into the enormous bowl that sat in front of her. It was full of blended vegetables and...some sort of voodoo apparently. He was hit with a wave of sharpness, garlic, tomato— bright fresh flavors that had him salivating. Now he *was* in danger of drooling.

"It's a cold soup from Spain, although I make mine a little differently."

"It smells amazing." He might dive face-first into the bowl. "Can I have some?"

"Of course." She was already filling a bowl for him from another container. "It's better chilled. Go out to the back patio and I'll be right there."

She handed him a bowl and a spoon. And, careful not to spill this liquid gold, Connor made his way out through the back door. She joined him at the little bistro table next to a dog bed where Braveheart currently napped in the shade. In her hands were two bottles of lemonade and a basket of charred bread.

"It's pretty good by itself, but with the grilled bread, it's amazing," she said.

Overcome with hunger, Connor forgot all his manners and dove in. "Oh my God," he said. He hung his head over the bowl because the scent was as much a part of the experience as the taste. The chilled vegetables, lots of garlic, a spike of lemon or vinegar. "Good Lord, woman, you are a goddess." Dipping the crunchy bread with charred edges in was another experience altogether. He paused and caught her studying him. "You're not having any?"

"I think I've had about three cups already today, testing each batch."

"Mm. Your job sounds amazing."

"You're doing it again..." Her breath caught. "The morning bun look. It's like...like you don't care what I'm wearing or how awful my hair is or that I'm wearing glasses. That you don't give a hoot about my appearance."

Connor put his spoon down and wiped his mouth. He was sitting close enough to take her hand, so he did. It was shaking a little bit. Or maybe that was his. "Sasha, I think you're beautiful, and yes, people are often attracted to each other based on looks initially, and I definitely give a hoot about yours, but I don't think it's in the way you mean. When I see you, it's not your clothes I'm seeing, or whether or not your hair is perfectly styled that attracts me."

"It's not?"

He shook his head. "It's how focused you are when you're making bread, and nothing else around you seems to matter. I'm wondering how it would feel to have that focus on me. It's these graceful, powerful hands working hard to make special treats every day." He stroked the bones of her fingers. "I sneak glances at family dinners when you let loose a little with the ladies and, once in a while, I catch a giggle. It's the pure open joy on your face when you see baby Alex. How gentle and patient you are with your dog. Heck, even with my dog, who's pretty much a disaster." He stroked his thumb gently down her jawline. "It's this curve right here that demands I pay very close attention to it with my lips."

Sasha closed her eyes and nodded.

"It's the way your cheeks flush when I give you a compliment or touch you. And for the record, I think your glasses are hot." Her eyes shot open. "They magnify those gorgeous eyes of yours. And there's no way in heck that's a deterrent. Ever. In fact, and you can tell me if I'm making you uncomfortable, but I'd like to see you in nothing but those glasses."

Sasha turned her hand over and laced their fingers together. "Wow," she whispered. "You make me feel a lot of things, Connor Duggan. Uncomfortable isn't one of them, unless…uhm, you mean needy."

"Yeah." He brought her hand to his mouth because his body demanded he kiss her while her cheeks were rosy with attraction for him. Even though he was in dirty work clothes and showed up strung out on caffeine with an empty pit of hunger crawling at his stomach. "I think there's a lot more to attraction than just appearances, don't you?"

"Yes," she answered hesitantly. "I just can't believe I'm…" She gestured to herself. "I'm your type."

"I don't have a type." *I mean I do, if you mean you, then I have a very specific sexy type.* He took his hand back before he embarrassed himself with his fantasies. And so he could appreciate more of her amazing soup. Cold soup, who knew?

She grinned at him. Connor drank in her expression and marveled at how something so basic, so simple, so tiny could affect him so much. Too bad they weren't alone in a room with a bed. Heck he'd manage with a chair—she could sit on his lap while he worshiped her. "So you're an equal-opportunity flirt?"

He chuckled. His heart flopped around, basked in her teasing. Her grin, her touch, even her humor revved him up. "I guess you could say that. Something to that whole pheromone thing or the way we smell to each other. Maybe we're more like dogs."

"What?" she said with a touch of disbelief in her voice. "We like to sniff each other's butts?"

Connor barked out a laugh at that. It reminded him of that night on his back porch when he'd laughed so hard that he couldn't control it. Tears leaked from his eyes and his stomach hurt when he finally pulled himself together.

"You're laughing at me?" She didn't seem upset or wounded, more curious.

"You're funny. It feels good to laugh. But mostly, Sugar, I'm laughing at myself."

"Sugar, huh?" she said and studied him. "You called me that last night."

"Too corny?"

"I like it." She gave him a soft grin. "Ford called me Sash the other night, as if we were old friends, like I deserved to have a nickname. And it felt soft and fluffy. So does Sugar. I..." She fiddled with the collar of her shirt. "Names are something I think about a lot. My adoptive parents changed my name to Victoria when they got me. It took a long time for me to answer to it."

Connor put his spoon down and gave her his complete attention. "They thought I was traumatized from what happened to me," she continued. "And I probably was, but it was that they took away my name. That memory is stark and vivid in my mind. Even at that age it felt so weird. Everything changed quickly. Months later some switch flipped in my brain, and I was Victoria Garibaldi, living in Florence. I had to...I had to become her to survive, I guess. I was Italian and pretty and perfect. Everything my new mother craved in me. But in my dreams, I was still a little girl named Sasha whose real mom used to call her *pumpkin*. I often felt like two different people.

"When I married Anthony. I took on another persona. Again, to survive. Jesus." She rubbed her forehead and rested her hands against it. "When I got free, after his death, I changed it back to Sasha again." She swallowed and let out a deep breath, facing him with a small lift of her chin. An 'I dare you to challenge me.' "Sasha feels comfortable, like I'm taking part of myself back, or rebelling against everything I lost. But then...having someone, a friend, or you give me a nickname, all the pretty words you call me, it's even better than simply having a name. It makes me feel like I belong."

"I thought you were pretty the first time I saw you." He had to swallow back his own emotion as the hot waves of sunlight swirled with the serious nature of her admissions and settled heavy between them.

Sasha shook her head. "I had a cast all the way up my arm and half my head was shaved. I can't remember if some of my bruises were still there. But I definitely resembled more what the cat dragged in than human."

"I saw your wounds," he said. "I also saw a woman who had lost basically everything. More than that, a woman who had to endure what would have killed most of us. And I saw you being brave enough to find Ellie, to reconnect with your brother, to make a life here in Corvallis so you could try to rebuild a relationship with him. Your family."

"I remember you that day in the park." Sasha offered. "Standing away. I thought you were there in case I tried to hurt Jackson. You seemed so protective."

Connor remembered that day too. His heart had recognized hers from the first moment. It was such a feeling of rightness that it startled him. It narrowed down everything he was certain about in life to that pinprick clarity. He didn't know how to tell her that without freaking her out, but she'd changed him that day, for good. "I think I felt protective of both of you, right from the beginning. He's my best friend and I...well, I knew some of what you had been through from the news. When I looked at you that day, yes, I saw a woman who had injuries, who was thin and pale. I saw a woman who was lost, but standing. Something powerful happened in my blood. I knew...I knew you were special."

"And now? Do you think I'm still lost?" she whispered. "Especially knowing I live at a hotel and haven't had enough courage to be honest with my friends, and that I'm completely awkward when it comes to talking about sex, or most things, for that matter? That for every step you think I've taken forward, I take so many backward, that most of you never see? I don't *let* you all see."

"Absolutely not lost. You're finding your own way, as are the rest of us, but you've had way more hurdles, and you've overcome all of them, adapted each time. You had to build a new foundation to stand on. You had to start completely over, again, on your own. Every step counts, even backward stumbles, because that's how we learn isn't it? I think it's more about being in the present. And you are present. When you calm your dog, when you ask for something you want, like sex."

His heart settled a bit as she gave him a tiny smile. "You bake with a gift. Heck, you bought a business. You've warmed your way into the hearts of our friends so deeply like a piece had been missing and you were the only one who could fill it. You have a way with animals that almost rivals Ellie's, and your smile is the prettiest one I've ever seen. It feels like starlight on my skin when you aim it my way. I know you said you don't know who you are, but you're finding out new things every day. And it's stunning to witness." Connor cleared his throat, choked up by his own feelings.

"That...that was...wow," she said and slowly reached out for his hand again. Still so tentative. Each movement was monumental to her. It humbled him.

"Just...uh..." He wiped his face with his napkin and tried to thread his words through the dryness in his throat. "Guess I can be awkward too."

Sasha beamed that smile at him then carefully took his hand and raised it to her lips. "Not awkward," she whispered against his hand. "Tears can be beautiful.

That's what I think. That's part of my new foundation. You gave me a precious gift, Connor. Thank you."

Braveheart padded over and sat between them. Connor could swear the dog was measuring him with that steady gaze. Then he gave a bark and flopped down on his bed again.

Sasha giggled. "I've never heard that kind of bark from him. I swear he was wondering if every conversation between you and me is going to be super serious?"

"I'll take whatever kind of conversation I can get with you, Sasha. Serious, deep, funny, angry, frustrated, ridiculous, food related, sex related, even the quiet spaces. That's what hit me that day in the park when I first saw you, that this is a woman worth everything."

Chapter Sixteen

Connor: *Sasha Kincaid, would you like to go to the movies with me tonight? Or perhaps watch movies at my place?*

Hmm, Sasha was still buzzing with something unidentifiable — excitement, happiness, life? Connor had left her at the bakery to head back to work. He'd given her the softest kiss on her lips, his sexy, sweet grin and had held her hand through the kitchen and out through the front door of the bakery, boasting, in that silent way of his, that he got to be the one to touch her. And that wasn't all. He'd blown her world with his speech. If he really saw her that way. The facts he stated were true. She had survived. She did get up every day and continue, even when it was the loneliest, scariest thing in the world. Which seemed ridiculous since she had actually survived a true horror. But surviving didn't mean she didn't have doubts or insecurities or complete exhaustion from all of it.

"A woman worth everything." That felt both super special and scary. Because even though she was alive, she'd also been hiding, finding new crutches to get her from day to day. Hiding in her hotel. Hiding behind her job and not telling anyone she owned the business. Hiding behind her hacked-off hair and plain clothes. Hiding behind painful emotions.

She was aware of it all now, especially more so over the last few weeks. And she'd made itsy-bitsy attempts. But how to come out into the light, fully, unhidden…well, that was a different type of mountain she'd have to climb, and she didn't know if she was ready for it. *Every bit matters.* She wanted to believe that, and coming from someone like Connor, she absolutely could not take it lightly. *Can I be someone's everything? Do I want to?* Those were complicated thoughts that had been racing through her mind. Ugh! So many things to worry about.

Sasha took a deep breath and decided to be in the present and simply have a text conversation with a cute man who wanted to spend time with her.

Sasha: *What movies are playing?*

Connor: *You know it isn't really about the movie.*

How odd. Why ask her to go to the movies? Although, to be honest, she didn't even care that it seemed odd because Connor Duggan was flirting even through text. *Talented man.*

Sasha: *What's it about then, Mr. Duggan?*

Connor: *The popcorn. Of course. I think it's time we find out what kind of popcorn you enjoy, Ms. Kincaid. Warning, I'm prepared to bring my A-game. You may know the secret to melt-in-your-mouth cupcakes. But I, ma'am am an expert when it comes to movie snacks.*

Oh yes, he could flirt through text. Sasha smiled and tapped the phone to her mouth. She couldn't remember the last time she'd sat in a pitch-black theater. As she imagined it, it didn't hold that much appeal to her. She'd rather be able to see every second of Connor Duggan bringing his A-game.

Sasha: *Your house sounds good.*

Connor: *Would you like me to pick you up?*

Sasha: *I'll walk over. What can I bring?*

Connor: *Just yourself and that amazing dog of yours. I'm hoping we'll get enough sugar from the sodas I bought.* And he sent a string of emojis, dogs and popcorn and fountain drinks. The last one was a man and woman holding hands.

* * * *

When she arrived, Connor was sitting on the front porch waiting for her. He held Kitten by the collar. She let Braveheart off his leash and let him run to his BFF. Kitten waited on the porch, body shivering, until Connor released her with a command, which was nice because Kitten usually greeted Braveheart with a full-body tackle and kisses, and there had been a few close calls when Sasha had almost been included in that tackle.

"Wow," Sasha said. "I'm impressed."

"We've been practicing. Anything and everything to not scare the pretty lady away." He reached for her hands and set them both on his shoulders. Gently he pulled her in by her waist. "Hi."

Sasha stood still and felt his body alongside hers, the weight of his hands on her waist, the strength of his muscles under her fingertips. The skin on his neck beckoned, tan and corded, but his arms felt too lovely to move away from. She leaned in a little closer so their chests met and a current surged through her at the contact.

"Hi," she replied against his lips and got to watch in wonder as he closed his eyes, smiled and sighed into her, his entire body relaxing against hers.

It gave her the bravery she needed, and she moved one hand softly against his skin. *Warmth, pulse, softness.* She rubbed her thumb along the indentation of the top of his shoulder, stroked up until the barely-there scruff on his jaw tickled her fingers.

"Please don't stop," he whispered on a desperate breath.

So she didn't. She traced over his cheekbones and the delicate skin of his eyelids, smoothed the lines on his forehead, and back down to outline his lips, to memorize them as they were right now, full, barely parted, aching. She felt it too, so she wrapped one hand around his neck and touched her lips to his.

"Hi," she said again, her voice a whisper, and sent the tingles through them both.

When she did, he took advantage of her open mouth and took over, kissing and sampling her with his lips and his tongue. Featherlight touches from his mouth, while the hands holding her gripped tight, his body, so rigid against hers. The combination thrilled her, how he could be so needy and hungry and gentle all at the same time.

He ran his hands up her back and the heat from his hands on her bare skin electrified her. She could lie down right there and let him touch all her bare skin.

"I was wrong," he said through kisses.

"Huh?"

"You're the only sugar I'm craving tonight."

"Connor." She sagged against him and grinned. "I like your neck."

"Mm, I like yours." He sent a river of kisses under her ear and down her neck.

"Are we the most ridiculous people ever?"

"Maybe." She felt him smile against her skin. Until Connor, she'd never felt a man's lips against her neck, had no idea how stimulating it would feel. It made her lightheaded. It was wonderful.

He stood back and took her hand, leading her around through the backyard and calling the dogs to follow. It was a good thing he held her hand, keeping her tethered to the earth. She might float away otherwise. Which didn't sound like such a bad idea. How was he even walking, thinking straight? She'd have to take notes. On second thought, no. She'd rather see him so affected that he floated with her.

"Now." He put his hands on her hips again and steadied her. "Ready to check popcorn preferences off the list? I thought we could leave the dogs out here to play and wear themselves out. That way, hopefully the evening won't turn into a popcorn vet disaster or something worse."

"Right. Popcorn." She grinned. "Lead the way."

He smiled back at her, opened the sliding door and gestured for her to enter first.

"You did all this for me?" Three bowls of popcorn sat on the kitchen counter. Something sweet scented the air.

"Well, I did, but I do sort of love popcorn, so believe me, it was selfish too." He pulled a cookie sheet out of the oven and scraped piping hot caramel corn into a bowl. "Katie's recipe, not too sweet with a hint of salt at the end. It will blow your mind."

He set the baking sheet in the sink and turned to her. "But the most important bowls are here." He gestured to the counter. "One batch has only salt. The other two, I think we should salt and butter one lightly, the other a little on the heavy side of butter. Or we could go supercharged and use some of Cece's favorite toppings, sprinkles, chocolate chips, or cheddar and parmesan."

"Wow." She smiled. "This is much better than the movie theater."

"You can't know that yet." He tilted his head and studied her.

"Actually...I think I can. You went all out for me so I would know how I like my popcorn. I don't think movie theaters do that."

"No...uh...I don't think they do." Connor Duggan was blushing and it might be the cutest thing she'd ever seen. This man. He stopped and started her heart in a matter of seconds. He was so many things, cute, considerate, hot, steady, strong, embarrassed. She knew there were more things to discover about him and she was looking forward to finding each one.

She stood over the bowls. "How did you make so much anyway?"

"Popcorn machine. Katie's girls and I used to have secret contests where we'd put ingredients in brown paper bags, then we'd have to choose toppings without knowing what they were.

"Oh." She laughed. "I'm so glad you're not making me do that."

"Nah, we don't initiate popcorn newbies that way. Too harsh. They might never want to come back."

"And you want me to come back?"

"I do, very much," he said. "Besides. That's a different game. Tonight it's all about the best popcorn and movie experience."

I think it already is. And they hadn't even tasted anything or watched a movie yet. "I think we should do chocolate chips on one and, on the other one, lots and lots of butter."

Chapter Seventeen

Well, it was official. He was losing it, because now he was aroused over popcorn talk. "Toss or drizzle?" Connor asked. He had to get his attention focused back on the task at hand which was popcorn flavors, not kissing. He could tug her in close right now, see if she'd come to him, put his hands around her waist where they fit perfectly, then fuse his mouth to hers again, but then they might never find out which way she loved popcorn.

"What?" she asked, coming to stand next to him. The scent of her, sweet and soft mixed with the aroma in his kitchen, teased his desire into circles.

"Your choice, toss the popcorn in the air or drizzle the butter while I toss?"

"There's a science to it, huh?" She glanced up at him. Those dark green eyes through the lenses of her glasses—he hadn't been kidding when he'd said he wanted to see her in only those specs of hers.

"What?" he said. He was distracted by her lashes and again her scent swirled around him.

"A science to buttering it?"

"Oh…yeah. I told you…" He shoved his fantasy to the back of his mind. "I'm no amateur." He enjoyed teasing her. The cute smile she gave him each time that said she was aware of it and that she liked it. It stroked his ego more than was probably necessary, but he didn't care.

"Hmm, then I think you should do the tossing and I'll drizzle. Sound good?" she asked.

"Uh-huh." She was standing so close and gazing at him that it messed with his brain. He'd be lucky if he didn't toss food all over the floor. He fumbled for one of the large bowls of popcorn, handed her the measuring cup of melted butter and showed her how he'd gently toss it while she coated it in butter. When they were finished, he sprinkled it with salt.

"It smells amazing. I don't think I knew it smelled so good," she said.

"Wait till you taste."

"Do I have to wait until the movie's on?"

He shook his head and offered her the bowl. She grabbed a few pieces, put them on her tongue, closed her eyes and chewed. Jesus, he was now obsessing over chewing. It was the pure joy and interest on her face that got him. Her lips coated in butter didn't hurt. Then she moaned, "So good," and he was done.

She took another handful, and he watched her fingers go from the bowl to that sexy mouth of hers. "There's so much butter. It's so good. I thought we'd added too much, but now that I'm tasting it, it's divine." She licked her fingers and gave him a smile. "It's delicious. Salty, buttery? Mm. Connor?" She

Sara Ohlin

glanced at him. Her lips were parted, that was all he could see. Damn the popcorn.

"I really want to kiss you?" he asked and snaked his hand around her waist, so they faced each other, her warm soft body flush against his. "Right here." He thumbed her bottom lip where the butter shimmered.

"Before the movie or after?" she whispered, her gaze attached to his lips.

"Both. During too, if we decide to go for the whole movie-date experience," he whispered.

"I do," she said, and he didn't make her wait, didn't make either of them wait one second longer.

He brought his head down, teased her lips with his tongue, and when need shot straight to *must have now*, he ravaged her. He wanted to close her up against the counter, but he held her still, so she wouldn't feel caged in. She held on and kissed him back, met his hunger with her own. Yeah, who knew butter could taste so good? So damn good. Her chest rose and fell against his. And the softness of her breasts rubbing against him made him growl.

"God, you turn me on." He held her head steady while he explored her mouth. "I feel ignorant around you, and I feel like a beast, and I don't know which one you need me to be." He licked at the spot where the butter had been. Kissed along her jaw while she arched into him. Traced his fingers down her chest across the exposed tops of her breasts.

"I just need you." She panted and tipped her head back when he stroked her chest again, offering her skin to him. "Are there, are there other places you might practice your kissing on me?" He felt that in his groin. *Every damn where.* "Because I think...maybe you could kiss me right there where your fingers are teasing me. It feels so good."

"Mm." He walked them into the couch and sat her down. Kneeling down at her level, he carefully pulled her shoes off. Then he held her and lay down with his back to the back of the couch and her facing him. He tangled his legs with hers and even that was erotic, the bare skin of her ankles snaking along his. "We could kiss each other everywhere, anywhere. You tell me."

"Here, please." She carefully brought his head to her chest and offered that soft skin to him.

"May I?" He fingered the button of her sundress.

"Please. I think I might explode if you don't."

How could a person be flying and aching at the same time? The slightest touch of Connor's fingers brushing across the skin on her chest as he unbuttoned her sundress drew her up into the clouds and burned her down at the same time. It felt soft and erotic. It was gentle and not nearly enough.

When he stopped, she thought she might fall crashing to the earth but then he brought his lips to the same aching spot and *my God his lips feel even better than his fingers*. Or was it both? Where his fingers led, his lips followed. She gripped his shoulder and pulled him closer. Soft kisses on her chest, fingers trailing down, one button, another until he touched her belly, danced his fingers across and down and back up to toy with the edge of her bra.

"Take it off, please," she begged. And she watched him. He was so focused. He gave her one intense glance and when their eyes met, he sent her flying again, swirling up. Her breath picked up. Then he flipped the clasp and set her free. Arching into him, she tried to pull him closer. A shiver ran through her and it didn't stop as he brushed his fingers over one nipple. It was so hard, her breasts painful with need and standing at attention begging him to...

He kissed one, cradled her breast with his hand and fed it into his mouth like he was desperate for it. And his other hand stroked down her belly to her matching pink boy short underwear. Basic, nothing lacy or frilly, but they were pink. She'd allowed herself that small concession, trying to add in little bits of pretty without going overboard. She felt she might be tossed overboard now into the waves.

"So damn lovely, so soft," he said. "I finally found something worth swearing over."

"Wha...what?" She panted. *Please don't stop what you're doing. Ever.*

"Your skin," he said and kissed the tender skin of her other breast, circling her nipple with his tongue.

"Oh."

"So responsive to touch. You belong right here."

Yes, she wanted to agree with his confidence, but it was too much to focus on words when all her instincts urged her body against his. She managed to get one hand up under his T-shirt and she spiraled around again on the whirlwind of sensations, her stomach dipping and circling. His skin felt amazing too, hot and solid, all his muscles, tensed, working, even while he kept himself in control. "Can I feel your skin on mine?" she begged, struggling to get his T-shirt off.

Graceful and quick like a primed athlete, he tugged his shirt off over his head and flipped them so he was on his back and she was sprawled on him. The way his eyes drank her in made her feel powerful. He stroked his fingers up to the straps of her dress and her bra and so slowly dragged them down her shoulders. She felt every single scrape of his rough fingers on her arms, as if he'd stroked all the way to her core. He was twirling her up again, and she clumsily helped him get her arms free.

Then he put his hand on her head and brought her down so their chests touched and their lips met. He kissed her, drank her in like she was everything required to fill his body, his soul. She bent her legs and straddled him. Sasha delighted in this position because even with her dress still around her waist, she could feel every hard, tight definition of his body under hers, the heat of him, the hum of his desire for her.

She hadn't known what to expect when her chest met his, but it was hard and soft and wonderful, almost painful as she rubbed her body against his, her breasts rasping against his skin. She let out a moan.

"So sensitive," he said and ran the pad of his thumb into her chest. It scraped across her nipples and it was wonderful. His other hand started to roam, massaging her butt and with each caress, he pushed her body into his. She helped, rubbing against him. She sighed his name with the pleasure the way he took her higher. Then he slipped his hand under her dress and played with the plain edge of her underwear right by her tailbone, a spot that sent exciting shivers through her entire body. She needed a breath and buried her face in his neck while he stroked her body and talked her through everything.

"You feel so damn amazing to me, Sasha. How are you doing?"

She nodded into him and curved her body into his.

"Want me to touch you here?" He teased his hand under the lip of her underwear and the warmth of his hand on her ass was exquisite. His fingers caressed her skin.

"Yes, please. Do that. Whatever you're doing. I want to feel you touch me everywhere. I can't...I've never..." She nipped at his shoulder. Her core pulsed against his hard length. It started there, then spread throughout until her whole body began to shake. It was thrilling. It was unknown, driving up, up, up. He stroked his fingers around her stomach and down, teasing them in between the basic pink fabric and her skin. Nothing at all felt basic in this moment.

"Here?" he said and touched her folds gently, softly exploring.

"God, yes." Sasha moaned and he did it again.

And again until he increased the pressure a tiny bit and she was bucking against him feeling his cock, hard and erect rubbing against her through the fabric of his shorts as his fingers teased and performed magic. She was moaning then she was flying. She lost control and he sent her spiraling through the clouds crying out his name.

Chapter Eighteen

"Okay?" Connor's lips tickled her ear. It felt amazing, being this close to him when he spoke. The deep timbre of his voice sent shivers through her warm, relaxed body. She didn't even mind that she was naked from the waist up and pressed into his chest. In fact, it felt fabulous. Connor dragged a soft throw blanket from the back of the couch over them. Nope, she didn't mind this skin-to-skin business at all. *Should have put that on my list. Who knew?* Well, probably every adult but her.

"Sasha?" he asked again and gently lifted her head so he could study her eyes.

"Yeah." How could she not be okay? She was boneless and glorious. He was holding her close, rubbing her back under the blanket. She wasn't cold that was for sure, and neither was he. His skin burned so nicely under hers. But the cocoon he'd created by covering them and soothing her back with caresses was lovely. Her safe place to land after rocketing through the sky.

"I've never done that before." It would have been easier to sneak her face back into his neck, hide from all her truths, but Connor didn't seem to mind her rawness, her secrets. And honestly she was too blissed out to worry. So she saw his eyes widen when she said it.

"Done what? Just to be sure," he asked.

Lots of things. Begged a man to touch me. Tugged a man's lush mouth to my breast. Felt so desperate with arousal I didn't recognize myself. He doesn't want to hear all of that exactly. Or does he? She'd noticed his soft smile, one of her favorites, melt into his expression whenever she shared things with him. Even random tiny things that to another might have no consequence. "Had an orgasm given to me by someone else," she admitted. The real truth, the secret he couldn't have known simply by being present.

She didn't see surprise on his face, which was what she expected. Instead, his expression softened that way she adored. His eyes grew more vulnerable and open in a way that said he saw all of her and that he was glad she'd shared with him. Better, he didn't go backward, as she also expected, he stayed gloriously in the present with her. "So how was it?" And there it was again, the vulnerability on his face, mixed with care, with interest. His eyes said, *Tell me everything about you and I'll keep it safe.*

Her perma-grin grew to go with her flushed cheeks and humming body. It felt wonderful. "Out of this world. You made me fly," she whispered. She buried her face against his warm skin again, to kiss him, to breathe him in. His hands tightened around her at her motions. She pressed her hand to his face, ran the pad of her thumb across his bottom lip. He kissed at her wandering fingers.

"Thank you for making me soar like that," she murmured. "And for carrying me back softly. It's a good place to land, right here in your arms."

"Yeah." His voice was gruff. He turned his head and captured her lips in his. "Beautiful," he said. And it made her smile again and blush deeper, if that was even possible. She was pretty sure she'd reached maximum blushing a few minutes ago. Her entire body was a rosy flower in bloom.

"I think I ruined your popcorn experiment," she said.

"Nah." He snuggled in tighter and tangled his leg with hers as she stretched them out. "Popcorn will still be there. We got ahead of ourselves in the program."

"The program?"

"The date, the night, the list, whatever we're going to call it. All of the above. We went straight to one of my favorite parts."

"Kissing?" she said and smiled.

"Making out on the couch during the movie."

"I think we forgot the movie too." She giggled.

"Oh." He smiled. "Right. Got distracted. Guess we get to practice that too if you want. Making out during the actual movie."

"I'm learning there are lots of things I want to practice with you."

He hummed and there it went sending the shivers through her again. "Sounds perfect to me."

"So is asking a woman to the movies code for making out?"

He barked out a laugh and if there was a way to grab onto that sound and keep it in her locket next to her chest she would. It was dopamine to her brain. "No. But if it happens and it's as good as that, it's definitely a perk. We'll call it a list tangent or list adjacent, shall we?"

He kept making her smile. She hadn't been this giddy since she was a child, without worry. "So your list has things we don't know about, that we may discover along the way?" She liked that idea and was going to apply it to her own list.

"Yeah, what do you think?"

"I like it." She kissed him again, free with that too and it felt amazing, then rested her head back in his neck. "I need to go to the bathroom."

"Right." Connor reached down and helped pull the straps of her dress back up her arms. He flipped their bodies to the side, sat her upright and handed her her bra. "I'll finish putting the extra special touches on the popcorn."

She was correct—she was indeed flushed from her cheeks all the way down her chest. Sasha stood in front of the bathroom mirror with her dress back down around her waist before she put her bra on. Gently, she ran a hand over the skin of her chest, down to her belly, looking, really seeing her own body. There were scars, but there was more too. How much could a person change over the years? And could a person's being really withstand so much transformation?

She'd wondered that a time or two, but now the wondering felt different. *She* felt different, joyful. Literally full of happiness and awe at what her body could do, at what a good man with wonderous hands could make her feel.

Her flushed skin, her lips and breasts with rounded dark nipples, the indentation down to her slightly rounded belly. Shame and ignoring had been the way she treated herself for the past few years, trying to be barely aware. Then this last year, faced with scars and wounds, she'd had to take care of herself. She'd grown aware enough of how her body served her at work and on walks, or the simplest task of holding a mug of tea and letting the warmth seep into her hands. Swimming, when she felt free and weightless.

Now it was as if her entire being felt wide open and conscious. It was the flush, but it was more. It was all the curves and rounded parts, the bones, the sensitive skin, the muscles. It was strength and arousal and energy and orgasms and power. Her own body, her own beautiful power, pulsing and alive.

"All right in there?" Connor's voice and a soft knock. "Don't want you to feel awkward or anything."

"I'm good," she said, and she was. "I'll be right out." She fastened her bra and slowly put her clothes together. No sense yelling that she really wanted to be naked, to revel in the amazing feelings she was nearly overcome with. Although Connor might appreciate that. They could be naked together, because if her body was power and beauty, his was too. His was magnificent and she ached to explore it all. A small giggle bubbled up and out of her as she finished getting dressed. She was still tingling when she left the bathroom, with a smile that she hoped would never disappear.

Chapter Nineteen

He was placing the enormous bowls of popcorn on the coffee table when she returned. "Hey," he said. Maybe it hadn't been the best move to check on her while she was in the bathroom, but they'd shared something monumental for him, and he suspected for her too. The way she'd come so hard, so unabashedly, how all her skin bloomed into that deep rosy color, the smile on her face, so open, so trusting.

His heart had shifted in his chest when she'd gifted him that loopy grin afterward. His thumping immature organ had clicked into its true place, beating for her. He wouldn't have called it painful, or at least not in a bad way. More like he'd been coasting along not feeling much for the past seven years. And now suddenly, he'd exposed everything, torn away all the vines, thorns included, to feel love for this incredible woman.

But then she'd stayed in the bathroom, and he'd worried. Worried he'd hurt her, or he'd done it wrong or that her embarrassment had taken over.

"Hi," she said.

He studied her. The smile was still there, and when he held her gaze, ran his eyes over her body, flush bloomed on her cheeks again. He had enough of an ego to feel good about that. Even his own cheeks flamed with the memory of what they'd done.

"Sorry, I got distracted by…um, by all the feelings." She gestured to herself. "The good feelings that a body can, uhm, experience."

"Good." He loved how she didn't try to make her words proper or edited. "I like it when you tell me how you feel."

"Good." She nodded as they smiled at each other across the room. Two drunken fools, loopy on hormones. "It smells amazing in here. I'm starving."

Yeah, everything was all good. "The magic of popcorn. You get to pick the movie or show if that's your preference. Anything but home improvement shows," he said as the shudder raced through him

"Really?" Sasha stared at him, wide-eyed.

"No." He shook his head. "Tell me it isn't true. You're addicted, aren't you?" Lord save him from do-it-yourselfers. It was rampant these days, an epidemic. People watching shows and thinking they could fix a broken sewer line on their own. Or knock down walls without checking to see whether the damn thing was supporting the entire roof or not. "This is going to be a real problem," he teased.

Her expression was thoughtful. "I do like them. They always transform something ugly into something amazing. And I've been studying so I can find my own pile of junk and make it shimmer again. There's a property I'm trying to buy. I was hoping you'd help me."

"I'd be honored to help you do that, Sasha," he said. He loved building new structures, but his true love was making the dilapidated, forgotten buildings come back to life. It made him feel proud that she knew that about him, because at the end of the day, no matter how big his business got or how many rich people tasked him to build them something new and grand, it was the beaten down he preferred. Plus, he'd do anything for Sasha.

"Okay." She smiled. "Can I uh…have some of that buttered popcorn before I end up in a puddle of my own drool? That smell is killing me."

"Right. Make yourself comfortable." He gestured toward the sofa. Connor got their food and drinks settled, dimmed the lights and turned on a few of his lanterns. He didn't have any of the cute lamps his sister had, or candles. Next time he'd have candles.

"What are those?"

"Camping lanterns, in case you get scared. Or mood lighting." He winked. "Take your pick."

"Camping?"

He laughed again at the tone of her voice. He couldn't tell if she sounded shocked or was simply curious. Had she never been camping before? Now that would be fun to do with her. Explore some mountains and waterfalls. Kiss her on some hidden trails. Cozy up in a sleeping bag together. Watch the stars while he held her in his arms. She was prettier than any star he'd ever seen.

"You camp?"

"Yes, woman. I'm a manly man."

"But you're so pretty." She giggled. "I mean handsome, of course. And you always look perfect."

Connor rolled his eyes. "Pretty? Jeesh, I better work on my image. I cut wood, woman. I sand and build and wear a tool belt." He pounded his chest and got another laugh out of her. "What kind of man do you think I am?"

"You're tall," she said, smiling up at him. He laughed and it felt good when she teased him back.

"All right, smart Alec. Let's see what you picked and whether or not I'm in for some home renovation pain." He scooted next to her on the couch. "Remember," he said, serious now. "You have two tasks tonight — enjoy the show and decide which kind of popcorn you like best."

* * * *

Sasha startled awake with the cool nose of her dog pressed into her face. She blinked and took in her surroundings. The television was off. The camp lights cast an inviting, low-lit glow around the room. And she was surrounded by Connor.

It had felt so right, slipping into his arms to watch the end of the movie, or not watch it as she'd also slipped so easily into her dreams. Good dreams of a man holding her close, her body and her heart. Not demanding anything, just offering room for her to decide, with a good dose of encouragement. She smiled, remembering how he'd encouraged her with his hands, his lips, his words.

As far as dates went, now that she knew she could call this a date, it was fantastic.

She didn't know if everyone would label movies and popcorn on the couch and some heavy making out the epitome of dates, but she didn't care much what anyone else thought. It was her life and dreams now. And having had wealth and beautiful things beyond most people's wildest imaginations, having had a life that many might have seen from the outside and called spectacular, for her, special was how she felt in Connor's arms, protected, free, safe, sexy, precious, all at the same time.

"Hey." Connor's voice was rough and deep and sent shivers down her spine as he spoke against her head. They were stretched out on the couch. Her head rested on one of the soft side pillows. Connor slept behind her, her back to his front, his arm resting around her, holding her close. "You crashed out."

She remembered how he'd asked her if she'd wanted to stretch out beside him when she'd started yawning. And she remembered how she'd said yes without a hint of worry or concern. She sighed and ruffled Braveheart's head, scratching that spot over his eyes he basked in. *Starved for affection and cuddling, aren't we, love?*

Well, it wasn't a shabby place to be, cuddled close to Connor's strong body. Everywhere their bodies touched she felt his warmth, the hum of his blood in tune with hers. It was almost hard for her to believe she'd slept this way. "I'm sorry," she said.

"Don't be." He snuggled her against him. "You saved me from having to watch the guy who tried to bring the gas line into his house on his own without help from the gas company. He nearly blew up his house."

Sasha laughed. His arm tightened around her with the motion.

"It's late. Want to sleep over?"

She hesitated.

"No pressure. I'll take you home in an instant. Say the words. I like the idea of sleeping next to you, Sasha. Nothing else. It feels amazing having you in my arms. Feels right."

He echoed her thoughts. It did feel right, and so, so good. But he was wrong too. Her body still tingled from earlier. And now waking up in his arms, the masculine scent of him like a drug, the way his whispered words teased against her, thrilled her. But she wasn't sure how to express her desires. "I do want to stay." That much was the truth.

"Awesome," he whispered. He kissed her neck then helped her up. Then he led her downstairs to his suite. "I'll clean up real quick and let the dogs out. T-shirts are in this drawer and extra toothbrushes are in the bathroom cupboard, thanks to years of living with three nieces' shenanigans. I'll be back."

She used the bathroom and brushed her teeth and afterward she stared at herself in the mirror again. Flushed cheeks, slightly rumpled hair, clear happy eyes. All her uncertainties flew away. She'd been making her own decisions and choices for a year now. When she returned to the bedroom, she didn't use one of his shirts, but instead, stripped down to her underwear and climbed under the covers and waited for Connor to surround her again with his body.

Connor came in quietly. "Dogs are crashed out on Kitten's bed. You okay with that or would you be more comfortable with Braveheart in here?"

"I'm good," she said, not even trying to hide her smile from his thoughtfulness, from her anticipation, from the way the soft sheets felt on her skin, from how cute and sexy he looked with his own rumpled hair.

"You sure?"

"Yes," she said slowly and drew back the covers. And oh, it was fun to make him blush. She almost giggled at the sight. And when had she ever giggled in this kind of situation before? Never. *Ha! We've never been in a situation like this. I know, it's so exciting!*

Connor ran his hands over his face and stared at her again, serious, intent. "I really want to climb in there with you."

"That's what I'd like too," she said. "I decided I didn't need a T-shirt. And I don't think you do either. Maybe we could go without clothes all together. We could explore that idea when you climb in here with me."

"Sounds like you've thought about this?"

"I have. I've been thinking about you naked for a while. Is that bad to say? Is it rude or improper? I don't know, but it's the truth."

Watching Connor smile at her words was worth it to have said them. It wasn't his great big smile before he was about to laugh, or one where he was indulging her embarrassing actions. This one was heavy, if a smile could be, focused. His eyes sharpened and he whipped off his shirt and shorts before he climbed into bed next to her. Then he wasn't smiling anymore at all. His face was granite as he took in her body, dragged his fingertips down her arm, linked their fingers together and brought them to his mouth to kiss her knuckles. The gesture batted away the feather of nerves.

"You took your glasses off?" he said.

"Yes." He tangled their feet together, his leg brushing against hers and she felt the connection everywhere.

"Pretty with them on." He traced around her eyes with his nose, like he was learning her, scenting her, a soft nuzzle. "Pretty with them off too."

Connor gently kissed the corner of each eye. She closed them and leaned into the touch, into the feel of his nose dragging softly against her cheek, into the scent of him so close to her. He traced his lips down her cheek to the top of her lips and she didn't know whether to open her eyes and watch or leave them closed and simply feel. A shiver raced through her body, and she didn't know if it was from apprehension or anticipation. There was *so much* she didn't know.

But every cell in her body stood at attention for him, alive, waiting for his kiss. And when it came it seared into her as if it were necessary, as if it were a beginning. He took her mouth under investigation, her lips against his, learning them, tasting them. He teased her mouth open or maybe she gave it to him, desperate as she was for this, this exploration. But he didn't do anything more than that, didn't use his tongue, or his teeth. He danced and savored so, so slowly until she was panting against him, basking in the cravings that grew and twirled inside her.

"Is it okay for me to say I've been thinking about this too, about you naked?" He set her hand on his heart and placed his on her cheek, softly smoothed his way down the column of her throat to her chest, stroked the underside of her breasts with his thumb, making her body arch and seek him out.

She hummed. It was all she could do. She nodded, welcoming the flush as it bloomed all over her, feeling the warmth of his gaze take her from comfortable and a bit nervous to shaking with desire, hungry for more of this wonderful skin-to-skin contact. Her nipples threaded into sharp peaks with each pass of his thumb. Her breaths came heavier with each magnetic gaze he cast down her shape. Her body sang with each slide of his skin against hers. Naked suddenly felt amazing.

"You tell me if there's anything I do that you don't like. You tell me to stop, and I will," he said and continued his exploration down to her belly over her hips. Strong fingers from decades of hard work, surprisingly soft against her skin.

"'Kay," she said, and he gripped her leg and dragged it over his, locking them closer together, connected in that way she was seriously becoming a fan of. *I've never felt this connected to another soul in my life.* That thought stirred up her uncertainties.

When he nestled into her, she could feel his hard length against her pelvis through his boxers. The motion sent ripples of pleasure shooting through her body and down to her core. *Oh wow!* Everything was sharp and heavy, the way her body felt, the way her heart felt. All her vulnerabilities came crashing in. She closed her eyes and buried her face against his strong chest. The sensations were almost too much when combined with the emotions bubbling inside her.

Chapter Twenty

"Sasha." Connor hummed her name quietly, trying to soothe her back into their moment. "Hold on or let go?"

She wrapped her arms around him. "Don't let go. I'm okay," she said. "I mean I'm overwhelmed, but everything you're doing feels good. I...I'm trying... I don't know how to ease the flashes of insecurities that kept creeping up and tugging at my mind."

"I want hours and hours to discover this body of yours," he said. "But there is no rush, sweetheart. We can do this. We can sleep. I can take you home. We can watch more home improvement shows. Whatever you need."

She gave a soft laugh into his body and steadied her breathing to match his. "Can I touch you too?" she whispered against his skin.

"Absolutely," he said.

"I might not..." He felt each lingering flash of uncertainty glitch through her body. And he held on, continuing to trace a pattern with his hands over her hips.

"Stay with me, right here. In the present. It's you and me. Remember what I said, anything you don't enjoy, you tell me, even if it's ghosts trying to haunt you. You can tell me anything."

She focused her gaze on his. "I might not be very good at it, but I can learn."

Connor's body braced at her words, at the underlying secrets. He could see her ghosts, wished he could murder them for her. He forced his body to relax, and he shoved all his anger at her past away. He wanted her to stay in the present, which meant he had to as well. "We're learning together, okay? We're going to teach each other what feels good. I'll do my best to make it amazing for you, promise. And if it's not, we'll keep trying, keep learning. You can tell me at any time to stop or do something differently. You are in control. Okay?"

She nodded and he watched her face soften. "So far, I think this coeducation has been awesome," he whispered. He placed light kisses along her neck, teasing her there with his tongue right where her pulse beat like it was made for him.

She took a deep breath and softened back into his embrace. "I think so too," she admitted and let out a breathy sigh as he kissed her heart. "The way you touch me, the way you kiss me, light or demanding or silly, all of them are...I feel...you make my skin come alive."

"You're beautiful, here." He palmed her breast and circled over her nipple. "And in here." He kissed her heart again but didn't let up on the stroke of his thumb. "And the only thing that matters is you and me, right now."

"Yes." She breathed and stretched her body into his.

"You like me touching you that way?" Her body was speaking for her, arching into him, moving with him. He was focused on her, on everything about her pleasure. Every movement of her body against his had his blood racing, his cock hard, standing at attention. "I'm going to kiss you and touch you and keep finding things you enjoy. Sound good?"

"Mm-hm."

He smoothed his palm over her hip and down her leg, teasing her sensitive skin on the inside of her thighs, skipping over the neediest sensitive part of her. He would get to all her spots, discover every piece of her. "When I put my lips on you..." He spoke against the hollow of her chest and dipped his tongue in to taste her. She let her hands rake over his chest, and the rest of his sentence flew out of his head.

Her touch was fire and warmth and sparks. She closed her eyes and with slow tentative movements, let her hands roam and he watched her, watched as she drew in her power and let it take over her body, let it guide her. He'd never experienced such intense and careful exploration of another person's body, in giving or receiving. He drank in her softness, her scent, every sound she made. Each of them learning the other. He held back his own ferocious need to lose himself in her body. There was an entire landscape of things they could explore. And all the time in the world.

"I also have some items that we could play with." He rose up and nipped at her earlobe. "We could consider some of the 'and such' parts of the list."

"Oh?" she asked. Keeping them connected, he rolled them across the bed. She clung to him, eyes wide open. He searched their depths for any sign of hesitation, of uncomfortableness in her. When her toes caressed his calf and she kept him close, he took both as a sign to continue. He reached over and retrieved a box from his bedside table. He opened it and pulled out the contents. A box of condoms, a bottle of lube and a brand-new shiny blue and silver vibrator.

"Wow," she whispered. "Uhm…I don't think I have the full list, Connor." The blush rose up her cheeks, but her smile was there, languid, relaxed.

He grinned at her lighthearted, curious tone. "I don't know how things are going to go but I thought it best to be prepared in case we wanted some assistance."

"Some assistance?"

"Yeah." He kissed her lips, full and swollen and so damn tempting. "In the pleasure department. Toys, lube. Obviously we're going to have safety covered." He opened the box of condoms. "But there's so much more than that. There's fun and discovery, finding what feels good. To help make you wet." His kiss lasted longer this time as her heat spurred him on. She met his need with her own tongue, licking at his lip. "To help make it easier for me to slide home."

He tugged her leg higher around him and thrust his body gently against hers. He needed to be gentle for her, the thought pounded in his head. And Jesus, if he were any harder, he'd come right here all over her. "But mostly to help make you feel good."

"Home?" She was panting now, and he continued his exploration of her body. He teased her nipple with his mouth, the barest graze of his teeth, and she arched into him. She wasn't the only one panting.

"I imagine that's what it's going to feel like. The first time we make love." He placed a trail of kisses down her body. "The time after that. And…" He paused then from his position with his head between her legs, nearly lost in her arousal, in the feel of her silky skin underneath his hands, hands that were so used to rough hard work they had no right to be touching such elegance. His own insecurities swam through his mind.

"Connor, don't stop touching me, please," she begged. And with one phrase she chased his demons away.

"Every time we're together. Touching you feels like a memory, a homecoming, a place I belong."

"Uh-huh." She nodded. He placed his hand on her inner thigh, opening her to him. The blood rushed to his head, to his groin, to every cell in his body. Running his thumb slowly along her sensitive wet folds, she bowed up toward him. "Connor," she cried out. Her body shook and she gripped the sheets for purchase.

He studied her, conscious of every movement, every sigh, every plea. "Maybe we won't need any assistance." He toyed with her wetness, rubbed it over her folds, dared to tease his thumb inside her the barest amount. "Maybe we will. Sometimes it's fun just to play." *Nothing about this moment is play.* His heart thundered at him to focus, to make her his, to make him hers, to join them.

"Are we playing now?"

"Mm," he said. "Can hardly think rationally with you splayed out before me, but it feels more than that, so much more. What do you think?" He pushed against her swollen bud.

"Whatever it is, what you're doing right now, it feels so good, Connor." Without any insecurity she pushed her pelvis up, trying to find more friction against his hands.

"More?"

"God. Yes," she pleaded.

"Good. I'm going to kiss you now, here." He dragged his thumb across her wetness sending more delicious shivers through her. "Ready?"

"I…" She was shaking. "I have no idea, but I want to find out."

He leaned into her, drawn by her arousal and put his mouth on her core. With the last shreds of control, he licked and kissed and sucked at her, intent on bringing her as much pleasure as he could. He held the thundering at bay and feasted on her movements as she writhed against him and cried out for more.

"God," she moaned when he sucked and teased, his hands gripping her hips. She bucked up into him, again and again until finally she crested and burst into a million pieces, brilliant starlight lighting up the night sky.

Chapter Twenty-One

A rustling sound woke Sasha. Wind blew through the trees outside, furious, then settling down, shaking the leaves in an urgent message. The noise felt both soothing and urgent, like a wave racing onto shore, riding the crest up, up, up, then slowing back into the ocean on a soft ripple, down into silence, when it paused and stirred again to fall over the next crest. The breeze came through the open windows and flirted over her naked body. She breathed in the midnight summer air, humid and heavy and full of stories. She stretched her languid limbs, feeling loose and dreamy.

She was on her side in Connor's bed, facing him. He'd brought one of his camp lights in and set it on the bedside table. The low setting cast streaks across his body. Connor was asleep on his stomach, naked, with one arm under his pillow and one arm down by his side, her hand resting in it. She studied him. He was so gorgeous, the planes of his back muscles smooth and sleek, his hair curling at his neck, a smile on his face, even in sleep. She wondered if anything made the man unhappy. He lived in a bubble of joy.

Sasha inched closer and rested her head next to his on the pillow. He'd given her an orgasm that was, *whew!* Several over the course of the evening. She shimmied just thinking about how he'd made her feel. She barely remembered him holding her afterward, because she'd fallen asleep. Now she smiled, covered her face with her free hand and let out a small laugh. *Who even am I right now?*

"Hey," he said. And when she looked again his caramel eyes were wide open and his grin had spread across his face. He rubbed her fingers with his and brought them to his mouth to kiss them. Already, with one simple touch, her body pulsed to life again and she inched closer to him.

"I fell asleep," she said. *Duh.* She reached out to trace his mouth as he smiled at her ridiculousness.

"Yeah." His voice was husky from sleep or arousal, she couldn't tell, but it sang right through her like electricity, the wind picking up again. She felt that rustling in her core. Awareness, desire. *I'm so needy, so unfulfilled.* And uninhibited, she arched into that thought. At her movement he brought his hand to her hip and dragged himself so he was facing her, their bodies flush together. Her heart beat against his. Her nipples, already aching, grazed against his muscles. She tilted her head down. His cock was hard and heavy against her pelvis. Heat raced between them. The shiver ran through her, and the movement caused so many thrilling sparks to ignite everywhere their bodies connected. "Can I touch you?" she whispered into the night.

"Please." He traced light circles on her thigh. She reached down and wrapped her hand around his hard length. Connor hissed out a breath and tugged her even closer. The air outside whispered at a steady wave, sending ripples through the leaves, anticipation.

"You're so warm."

"Your touch is everything." He spoke each word as a curse, a good curse, and his words thrummed through her. She was achy everywhere. She needed their bodies to be more, closer, connected, more everything. She slid up slightly on the bed and moved his cock to her entrance. A stronger breeze swirled, increased, and she flew with the wind, used her power to control it, thrusting it out into the night to surround them and carry them up.

"I can feel you pulsing here," she whispered and rubbed his cock against her entrance, once, twice. "Oh, oh." He caught her whimper with his mouth with such insistence, an assault, tangling his tongue with hers, drinking her in. *Be brave, be brave, be brave.* The words pressed into her thoughts. "I want to know what it feels like when you pulse inside me." Midnight air kicked into a wicked dance, swaying entire trees into one another.

Connor brought his hand to where she played with their bodies and nudged her core in light flirty caresses. He pulled away and she thought she'd lost him. When he rolled back into her, he had the lube and a condom.

"Are we playing now?"

He brought her head to his and kissed her deep and hard. "Feels more monumental than play, doesn't it?" he asked. "You said before that sex sometimes hurt."

It had always hurt, before this. She stilled and focused on the powerful rustling from the wind, focused on Connor, on his words, his touch, his heart.

"I want to make it the opposite of that. Obliterate those negative memories." He gripped her hand over his cock and moved their hands in sync up and down. "It's you and me now, learning each other's bodies, right?"

"You and me now." She nodded.

He rubbed some of the lube over his cock. Now he felt smooth and silky under her fingers, but still hard and insistent. He thrust into her hand and there was power there too, in making him feel good. He nudged her hands away to roll the condom on, then gave her more lube to rub over him. All of it fascinated her, carried her along the wave. The rustling leaves sang to her blood, rushing her up, higher, faster. When he used some of the liquid to play with her swollen core, the orgasm slapped through her so fast she barely caught her breath.

"Connor," she cried and shook, thrusting her body into his hand, chasing the sensations. She was still holding his cock and he helped her line it up, teasing her with the tip. She grabbed onto his butt, and using him for leverage, thrust her body onto his. *Finally.* She let out a sigh, a moan, both wrapped up in each other. Finally he was deep inside her, the last ripples of her orgasm pulsing around him. She bucked against him again and again, partly conscious, partly letting her desire take control.

He held her tightly and drove himself into her while he kissed her. The sensations rose in her again and her core pulsed with energy. With each thrust and each kiss and the way his hands dug into her skin to keep her tightly connected. And when his entire body tightened and crashed against her, she rubbed against him in just the right spot until she spiraled up and over the top of that windy roller coaster again, riding the wave and crashing onto shore with him.

Their breaths mingled and mixed with the rustling of the leaves, and gently softened against each other. "Wow," Sasha said, breathless onto his cheek, where her face rested against his.

"Seriously," he responded. Every tiny and mammoth sound echoed through the quiet space and into her head. His breath, the rasp of her finger across his stubble as she stroked his cheek. The way his voice reverberated through her entire being. She drifted in and out of the aftereffects. "How do you feel?"

"Amazing!" She hid her head in his arm and squealed. And drank in the chuckle that rumbled through his chest into hers.

"Bath?"

"Mm, yes, please." She let him lead her into his bathroom, let him bathe her while she languished against him, let him towel her off and tuck her into bed against his side before she fell into a deep and trusting sleep.

* * * *

The next time her eyes opened, pale blue was beginning to lighten the sky. Dawn peeked through the windows. Connor's bedroom was in the basement, but one entire wall was made up of enormous windows and she basked in the view it let in. All the pink and lavender streaks in the horizon. The bright green grass and lush summer trees, the day peeking through. Bringing nature in.

His arm was still across her waist and when she moved, he tugged her into him. "Morning, Sugar."

"Hi," she said feeling both extremely satisfied and shy.

"Good night," he said, tickling her ear. "Amazing."

179

Yeah, amazing is putting it mildly. "Connor?"

"Hmm?"

"You asked me what kind of man I thought you were. You're a good man. You're the kind of man who makes people laugh, treasures the people close to him, you *are* tall." He laughed and nipped at her ear again. *Gosh, it feels good to tease someone.* "You're extremely handsome and capable and good at things."

"Keep going. I'm liking this." He snuggled with his words as good as he did with his full body, lined up against hers.

"And I haven't had many, not one to be exact, but in my opinion, you really know how to do movie night." His chuckle worked its way under her skin and made her smile.

"Best movie night I've ever had," he said and nuzzled his head into her neck, taking his time to kiss her there, his lips warm and searching, making her breathless again.

Her heart kicked up when he lingered there, like he'd discovered some wonderful new spot he'd enjoy spending hours investigating. It all felt so good, the kissing, the breathlessness, the cuddling.

"Thank you," she whispered. "For everything. For taking such good care of me."

"Sasha, it was my pleasure."

"Mm," she agreed and was rewarded with more of his deep laughter. Pleasure was definitely the correct word. She stroked her fingers over his arm and watched the day brighten outside. Her heart felt light and floaty. But her mind ran a marathon of questions. Was pleasure something that could last? *Honey, he can't bring you orgasms twenty-four seven. Oooo! Wouldn't that be delicious. Hush!*

Sasha tried to quiet the voices inside her body that were flinging out advice and ridiculous notions, and listen to the rational concerns in her brain. Of course pleasure couldn't last. And soon, he would be gone, but she wasn't going to worry about that. She was focusing on the present. And she was holding tight to this moment, right here, right now.

Chapter Twenty-Two

Lord. Not one week ago, she'd sprawled in his bed with him and called him a good man, listed his attributes, left his house on a cloud of bliss, her spirits high, her trust in him growing with every action he made toward her. She'd trusted him with her body in the most intimate of ways. The sex had been incredible. She was loving learning about sex. In the days since she'd never smiled or giggled so much in her life.

But today he was being absolutely stubborn, frustrating, and wrong.

"It's mine. I own it," she said again, crossing her arms over her chest, determined not to cower under the storm brewing on his face. She was done cowering. She thought he'd be excited for her. She certainly hadn't told anyone else she'd bought a property in near ruins. She hadn't told anyone any of the things she'd done with her money. She didn't relish talking about the money she'd inherited from Anthony. Or any of the other wounds she kept hidden. There it was, the truth of all her secrets, shame.

"Please tell me you're kidding, that you didn't really buy *this*?" Pure disbelief laced Connor's words. The tone wasn't any better. *Is he disappointed in me?* It was hard for her to tell. There were undercurrents, in his words. They were undecipherable to her and that pissed her off too.

"I did buy it." She'd almost answered uncertainly but had forced the courage through her words. She owned it. No sense prevaricating about it now. They stood in front of the house she'd paid actual dollars and cents for. Oddly enough it was right next door to the Art Deco mansion Connor and his crew were in the middle of restoring. On the other side of her property stood a grand old row of brownstones Connor had also restored. The park stretched out behind them.

It was one of many things Sasha loved about this location, that it was alongside the park in old Corvallis. The house was also in horrible shape, needing to be saved. It was only fitting he'd fix up this house too. She'd been eyeing this property for months. Once she'd even done something probably unsafe and snuck around to see the backyard, which was a pit of despair. It was the only fitting name for it. But cleaned up, it was large and long, a grand empty rectangle full of possibilities. And she had wild and fantastic dreams in her head for that backyard.

"I'm going to restore it and I want you...your company to help me." She'd already said the words once, a few minutes ago when they'd ended their walk here. She'd invited him on a date, and had been stupid enough to believe his delight in her would extend to this surprise! The surprise being the property they now stood in front of. She'd planned the entire evening out, a picnic in the park while the amazing high school jazz band played in the new gazebo Connor had built. Of course she'd stuffed the picnic basket with his favorites, morning buns included. And now to show him her house. Her very own place, pitiful state and all.

"No one can save that disgusting pile."

"I will," Sasha stated, standing her ground.

"You can't," he insisted. He faced the property with a strange expression. She kept sneaking glances, afraid of what she'd learn if understanding finally dawned. It was something she'd never seen on him. Anger, or disappointment, or both all rolled into one.

"It should have been burned to the ground long ago, but some selfish family members couldn't come to an agreement with their hated relative, so they've been feuding over it for decades now. It's been sitting, treated poorly, then neglected, rotting. Sometimes that's the worst crime when it comes to houses, the neglect, the not taking care."

Couldn't he see past all of that? Those issues didn't matter anymore. What mattered was what it could become, the potential of it all.

"No one can save this building, and no one should try. Bulldozers are the only hope for it now. You can't save it."

"Don't tell me what I can do." She bristled. Now *she* was angry. She'd lived enough lifetimes of everyone telling her what she could and couldn't do. Never again. It was one of the first promises she'd made to herself when she'd gotten Braveheart. She'd never been allowed to have a dog before and now she had the best one in the world. She might have more than one someday. An entire houseful of soft dogs if she wanted. She'd never had her very own place to live before either and this house right here, this was the one she'd chosen.

"And don't ever say something so ruined can't be saved. Everyone...*thing* I mean, *everything* can be saved, no matter how long it's been neglected or hurt." She barely got the words out before she had to get away. She'd promised herself she wouldn't run from him again, but she was furious and hurt, if she was honest. If this was what happened in relationships, she really wasn't cut out for them. She never should have shown him or had such high expectations of what he'd think. That certainly wasn't being casual, that was dangerous. Fine. She'd fix it up without his help. He was leaving anyway. What did it matter? What did anything really matter? She brushed the tears from her face, sucked in a breath and rushed toward the bakery where she could depend on herself.

Standing alone on the sidewalk, Connor gave a heavy sigh. *You screwed up royally. Again! How many times are we going to have to have this conversation with you, idiot? Ugh!* Connor took in the aftermath of one fabulous implosion. A wild west showdown and now the dust settled around him as he stood by himself. Feeling like the giant insensitive asshole he was. He'd handled his shock at her buying what he'd nicknamed the neighborhood cesspool with as much compassion as a disease. *Shit!*

It was worse than that. How had he not put two and two together? Sasha still thought she was a used, beaten-up pile of rubble that needed rescuing. But she'd already saved herself, she'd already rebuilt herself into a stunning bird taking flight, soaring over the land, powerful and light.

He was accustomed to giving her room whenever she needed it, but it wasn't a good idea to allow the hurt he'd splashed all over her linger. Connor headed after her. She rushed away with Braveheart toward The French Connection. He watched her open the gate to the small back patio of the bakery and he made his decision to follow her. When he arrived at the fence, he could hear her murmuring to her dog. Connor knocked. "Hey. It's me. I'm sorry. Can I come in and talk?"

"I don't really feel like talking now," she said, and he could hear the pain in her voice.

"I get that." *Dammit.* He rested his head against the wood. "I could do the talking and if you're still upset with me, I'll go." Please don't turn me away. I screwed that up pretty spectacularly." He'd beg if he had to.

"Fine." Her voice was clipped, but at least she'd let him in. He studied her face as he closed the gate behind him. She was upset but she hid it well. She faced him with that same hard stance as before, arms crossed, body held tight, chin up, smile erased. A battle-hardened warrior, beautiful, strong, but it stung a place in his heart that he'd been the one to cut at her vulnerability. He was an ass. That damn house had been a hornet's thorn in his ass and he'd completely lost his ability to tone down his hostility over it. Instead, he'd aimed it exactly where it didn't belong, and where it had hurt.

"I apologize for the way I reacted. I honestly didn't mean to hurt your feelings. I would never do that purposefully. I've been upset over that property for years. A puss-filled eyesore, getting worse over time, causing problems for the neighbors, attracting vermin. It's unsafe above all, not only structurally, but it's a health hazard and the family members have been miserable to work with. I guess I get a little overbearing when it comes to properties, especially that one."

"A little?" She huffed.

"I didn't know it had finally gone to auction and I was angry that you'd been swindled into buying it, into believing it's a simple fixer-upper. I was, *am* angry *for* you, not at you. I handled it all wrong."

"I never thought it was going to be simple."

Right. Get to the heart of the matter, you idiot. "Sasha." He took a step closer. "You are not that property." If he could only will the truth into her, make her see how far out of the ashes she'd risen. But he suspected it wasn't his job to prove that to her, whether he wanted it to be or not.

"Beaten down, treated horribly, alone, neglected." She tossed his words back at him, bitter medicine on her tongue. "All of those things are me."

"You might have been all of those at one time. And I hate that. But you are not any of those now. You don't need a renovation. You already saved yourself, dragged yourself up from the rubble, from tragedy. You dusted yourself off, which I know is a silly way to say what you had to go through to get to where you are. And now..." He made his way closer so he was standing in front of her, but not touching. She was still braced before him, protecting herself.

"Now?" she asked.

He lifted her chin so he could see her eyes. "Now you shine with your power and your beauty, your bravery. With grace and humor and kindness and compassion. With every single one of your emotions and actions. With those soulful eyes of yours."

"Hmph." A light flickered in her expression. "Doesn't feel that way to me," she said.

"Yeah," he said. "I can't make you see or feel things. I can only tell you what I see. And you are breathtaking and brilliant to me."

Carefully she placed her hands on his chest. A light touch, but a touch all the same. Forgiveness perhaps or the beginning of it. The fuse sparked between them again as she leaned in. That heat, that connection he felt the loss of when she wasn't near him these days. "I'm still going to redo that property," she whispered back.

Connor captured one of her hands and held it there against his chest. Brave and powerful indeed. He couldn't call her brave and expect her to back down at the first sign of difficulty. Of course he'd help her. He'd do anything for her, anything he was capable of. They might still have to tear the entire thing down, but he'd bring that up another day.

Her hand pulsed against his heart. "You still don't like the idea. I can tell you're angry."

"I'm angry at the former owners, the stupid, greedy family members letting it get to that stage. I'm frustrated you bought it without the most knowledgeable person by your side. I don't like it when someone I care about gets taken advantage of. You're angry with me because I was a complete jerk. I took out my frustration on you. And you have every right to be. We're both angry. That's okay. We can fight, we can even yell, although I don't yell very often. But if you feel the urge, go for it. I'd say you earned it. Aside from the fact that I don't want to upset you, I don't mind your anger."

"You don't?"

Connor took both her hands in his and leaned his body into hers. "Nope. In fact…" He walked her back against the warm brick wall, catching the last rays of sunlight. "It makes me want to kiss you?" His blood raced through his veins at the thought of pressing her body up against his, of letting all that power she possessed surge through her to him.

"What?" Gone was the worry, the pain, the anger. Those breathy sighs were back, the ones he loved, the ones he couldn't get enough of. "How strange."

"Not to me. Perhaps if it was a different kind of fight. But don't you feel it? Our emotions are high. You using your strength turns me on. You're all flushed. You're this bold vision and all I can think about is kissing you." The need rang through his mind, annihilating all other thoughts.

"Really?" she asked. She untangled one of her hands and touched his lips.

He felt the spark there, a burning. He'd burn for her. He nodded.

"I think you should then…"

And before she could finish speaking, he abandoned rationale and listened to the desire pulsing through him. He took her mouth, sought her power, wanted to anoint himself with it, fuse them together. She kissed him back, stole his breath with her lips, hot against his. Both of them greedy for each other. She gripped his shirt to hold him close. Unnecessary he would have said, if he could speak. He wasn't going anywhere except closer to her. He kissed across her shoulders and down to his favorite spot that made her sigh and moan and arch into him. Her hands roamed under his shirt to his back. "Connor."

"Yeah?" He took her mouth again before she could answer, then nipped at her lip.

"Is this normal?" She searched for his lips again. And he huffed out another laugh. Both of them trying to talk while kissing. He liked it. He liked it a lot.

"What?" He untangled her arms from his back and slowly, while dragging his fingers over the soft skin of her wrists, lifted her hands above her head. He needed to kiss her everywhere and he needed her to hold still. She had him so worked up, so turned on, so hard for her.

"This…this…this urgency, how my skin feels alive and humming all over, how I ache to touch you everywhere? Right now. Even though…or maybe especially since we were just fighting?" It did nothing to stem his own desire to hear her echoed words, to know she burned for him too, for this passion that was between them.

"I don't know," he said. He flipped her hands above her head in one hand and traced down her chest with his other, flicking the buttons of the top of her dress open, slowly, one by one. He placed a kiss between her breasts, lingered there, could feel the rapid beat of her heart. "Never felt this way before," he said against her skin.

"Oh, good." She was panting again, and he loved that look about her, completely undone. He watched her eyes as he flicked the clasp of her bra open, heard her suck in her breath. "Me…me neither. We can be…we can feel this amazingness, this unhindered together."

And that was all she said as he brushed his thumb over one nipple, already hard and waiting for him. She moaned and arched into him, carving that gorgeous body of hers against every hard and depraved part of his. But he was done going slow. He needed to watch her fly and soon, or he was going to lose it all over her.

He fused his mouth to hers again, continued rolling her nipple between his fingers. "Think you can keep your hands there?" He left them above her head, and she nodded. "Good." He smiled. God, she was such a fucking beautiful contradiction. Oversized, boring clothes for work, sleek black, cat-like anonymous at night and for him, these fucking short sundresses, flirty, flowery, soft. So fucking sexy. Giving him access to all of her right fucking now.

The sun was fading, and it cast a slash of light across her face. His sun goddess, that was what she was, lit up, purring beneath him, with her own passion. When his fingers made their way up the path of her smooth thigh and teased at her underwear, he found her wet, soaked through. "God, woman. What you do to me." He teased her with his thumb, snuck under the fabric and found that sweet little bud.

"Me?" She panted and thrust her pelvis into his hand. "You...you're doing everything." God she was sweet and sexy when her words were all breathy and aching. He was aching too. So, so much. "I want... I..."

"What? Sasha, what do you want?" He was pressed into her, his body pushing against hers. One hand cupping her breast, the other inside her giving his all to her swollen clit, he whispered against her ear, trying like hell to control his own body, to give her all of his attention.

"To touch you too." She writhed against him, gave him another sexy moan, seeking her own pleasure at his touch.

"Hmm," he murmured against her neck, snaking out his tongue to taste her right there where her pulse flickered and jumped.

"But I...this...what you're doing to me, is so... much." She was nearly incoherent and he was glad she let her body be at his mercy, allowed herself to be the sole focus. He wanted her touch with a ferocity, but giving her this was more important.

"You want this."

"Yes." She closed her eyes and nodded, her mouth hung open, unable to find the words, like she was tipping over the edge. "I'm so close." She echoed his thoughts, and he felt a thousand feet tall that he could give her this. That she felt powerful enough and vulnerable enough to take it.

"I…oh…I…" He followed his thumb with a finger, entering her, teasing her. And he took her mouth in his again, sucking and biting, as she exploded around him and clenched his fingers with all her power.

"Hey," he soothed as she fell apart in his arms. He held her up against the warm wall. Held them both up. "Okay?"

"I am so far from okay, it's delightful." Her voice was hoarse.

"Delightful?" He smiled against her skin as he spoke.

"I think I'm going to add this to the new list we're making together, so I can check it off, with checkmarks and hearts and smiley faces. Then…" She wrapped her arms around him and held on. God, he loved this, loved how open she was with him. He was so damn glad he got to be the one to see this side of her. It choked him up, suddenly, the idea that she hadn't had a chance to be this free with anyone in her life for a very long time. And it hit him that, although it was for very different reasons, he hadn't either. *We are meant for each other.*

"Then?" he prompted.

"I'm going to add it back onto the list so we can do it all over again."

He laughed and felt that squeeze his heart too, how often she surprised a full laugh out of him.

"I love it when you laugh," she whispered against his chest. She sighed and he felt her body go limp in his. He picked her up and carried her to the tiny sofa she'd set out under the awning.

"So does this mean you're not mad at me anymore?" she asked, and he barked out another laugh.

"I was never mad *at you*. More for you. Please believe me. And I should be the one asking you that. I really am sorry I bungled our date and your surprise. I had a piss-poor way of showing my anger about a situation. It was never about you. Do you think we could try again?"

"I'd like that." She lifted her head and put her hand on his cheek. "I don't enjoy fighting with you."

He captured her hand with his lips and kissed her palm. "Me neither."

"I don't like fighting at all. As you could probably understand," she said.

Shit, I messed up way more than I realized. He held her gaze and waited for her to share.

"But it felt...it was... right to get mad, to express myself."

And there it was, her words, a hint of uncertainty still. She'd given him her body, open and lovingly, her passions. But he was seeing now that was the easy part. It was her heart he still had to care for. He hoped he could show her that he was dug in to proving that to her, always. It had started last year and with every interaction they'd had since, or he was convinced she wouldn't have let him in this far. But he was seeing he still had a long way to go. Good thing he was in for the long haul.

"You should feel that way. Always tell me when I'm being a donkey's behind, or when I hurt your feelings. Please don't ever hold back with me. I will never hurt you the way he did." He refused to give the man's name presence in what he and Sasha were building together. This was their here and now. But he recognized her past would always exist, and to deny it wouldn't be healthy either. "I promise you are safe with me to be however you need to be. Always."

"Okay." She nodded and moved her hand to his neck. She'd found her way to his neck the other night in his bed too after they'd made love for the first time. She'd fallen asleep like that with her soft hand warm against his pulse. It had felt important. He loved the hell out of it. "I guess there is one thing that's not so bad about fighting with you." The lightness had come back into her voice.

"Oh yeah?"

"The apology part was pretty great," she said, and her cheeks flushed all over again.

"Ha." He chuckled. "One orgasm for each time I'm a doofus?"

She pressed her face against his skin and giggled. "That sounds awesome!"

"I think I can arrange that," he said and sat with his arms around her, while the light faded around them and the stars began to appear. She might be talking about the fight they'd had in front of the pile of rubble. He was picturing a bigger fight, the one for her whole heart, her trust, her love, and he thought he hadn't faced a better fight in his life.

Chapter Twenty-Three

"I'm so excited you're dating Connor!" Ellie squealed and gave Sasha an enormous hug. It seemed, since she'd stripped off the gloves and dug right into hugging her friends a few weeks ago, they doled them out frequently. And Sasha was not one bit sorry about it. *It's so glorious,* her body shuddered. *Isn't it, to be wrapped up safely in someone's arms.* "I knew it!" Ellie fisted her hand and raised it in the air for victory.

Ruby wiggled her eyebrows and gave Sasha a hug too.

"Knew what?" Sasha asked.

"Uhm..." Ellie tilted her head and gave Sasha a confused look. "That you and Connor would be perfect for each other."

She wasn't perfect for anyone. She let that comment disappear into the pit and focused on how her friends knew Connor had been attracted to her. "What?"

"Right." Ruby jumped in. "If the puppy-dog eyes and the drooling every time you're around didn't hint at it, his scowling protectiveness would have told us everything."

"I had no idea," Sasha said. "And I've never ever seen him scowl. What are you talking about?"

"Oh, darling." Ruby flitted her words away. "Of course he didn't let you see it—he didn't want to scare you away."

"Mm-hm," Ellie agreed. "I wasn't sure he'd ever actually make a move."

"So...so the whole 'tangled up over a woman' comment that day at lunch—you were referring to me?" Sasha asked. She sat down at the table where Ellie had set out an amazing assortment of sandwich fixings.

"I hoped so," Ellie said. She and Ruby joined her at the table.

"Wow. I was so...I was so flustered that day because I thought he had someone else in his life. Huh." She huffed out a laugh and remembered her embarrassment at asking him if he was already interested in a woman right before she embarrassed herself further and asked him to teach her about sex. *Although that wasn't a bad thing at all. I mean look where it got us. Naked and pleasured. And all the sex. With and without toys. So much playing.* Her cheeks heated at her libido's reminder.

"So things are going well?" Ruby asked.

"Yes," she said. She didn't know what to tell them or how to talk about it all. "He's...ah...wonderful." When she glanced up both women were staring at her with huge grins.

"Oh really?" Ruby said.

"That's awesome," Ellie gushed.

Sasha nodded, her face flaming again. "He's really good to me," she whispered. "You know with the listening and making me feel safe and the handholding and ah, the way he is in bed."

Ellie squeezed her hand. "That's how it should be. I'm so happy for you, and for Connor."

"I've been living at Hotel Marisol for the past eight months," she blurted out. "And I bought the bakery from the Heelys, the business part obviously, not the, uhm, building of course." There, she'd said it. She closed her eyes briefly and repeated her mantra about being brave and peeked at her friends. She'd been so stressed about telling them and it felt right to toss the words out there and see what happened.

Ruby glanced at Ellie, then both women faced her. Jackson had chosen that moment to appear in the kitchen with a sleeping Alex in the baby carrier attached to his chest.

"That's awesome about the bakery," Ellie gushed. "We...knew about the hotel, honey." Ellie gave a warm smile to Jackson.

Sasha met each of their gazes. "You did? All of you?" Apparently she hadn't been as stealth as she'd thought.

"Ellie and I sent you flowers a few times from Clare's shop," Jackson said. "Clare called me when she went to deliver them once and Bo's sister answered the door." Jackson took the enormous sandwich Ellie had made for him. "Thanks, beautiful." He kissed his wife on the cheek. "The next time I dropped you off at the apartment, I followed you to the hotel and talked to the owners. Not to interfere. I wanted to make sure you were safe."

"We all look out for one another," Ruby said. "That's what friends and family do, at least our group. We figured you needed that space, and you'd tell us when you felt comfortable with it."

"Wow," Sasha said. It felt good to tell them. And as she digested the information she found, it didn't bother her that they'd already known. Not anymore. "I didn't feel safe at first, in the apartment, and when Bo was looking for a place to live with his sisters, it seemed like a good coincidence. Probably too easy of one. But now, as I get healthier, Hotel Marisol isn't the right place for me anymore. I crave light and happiness, more color and my own home. I bought the old Stash house, to fix up. I don't know why I didn't tell you about any of it. Everything I've done since Anthony feels so strange and difficult. Sometimes not having to explain to other people makes it easier, I think."

"You don't have to tell us anything, Sasha," Ellie said. "I mean, we hope you'll feel comfortable enough to, but you're allowed your secrets and all the time it takes to trust people again."

"I told Connor my, uhm, secrets."

"That's good, Sash. He'll take care of them, of you," Jackson said.

Yeah. Sasha thought. *He's doing just that.* "You're not mad at me, any of you?"

Jackson smiled and shook his head. "Like El said, we want you to feel safe around us, but more than that, like you belong. Because you do."

"Okay." She nodded and reached for the Kleenex in her purse because that simple phrase brought on the waterworks of emotion again.

"Cry it out now," Ruby said. "So we can fix your makeup before Connor comes to pick you up for your date."

"Where's he taking you?" Ellie asked with an enormous smile on her face.

"And that's my cue to leave." Jackson took his sandwich and walked away.

"I don't know," Sasha said. "It's a surprise."

Ruby beamed. "Those are the best kind of dates."

Sasha didn't know, but now she couldn't wait to find out.

* * * *

Connor picked her up from Ellie's in his enormous old pickup truck that had seen better days, but somehow boasted coolness, like an ancient favorite pair of jeans. Her brain short-circuited when Connor and Kitten jumped out. Kitten raced off without even a nod in her direction. Speaking of old jeans, Connor must have come directly from work...wearing the sexiest pair of jeans she'd ever seen. Paint splatters and wood stain graced the thighs and one knee was ripped out. And *oh my* how they hung on his hips, and all the faded parts showcasing his butt and legs and...uhm, other things.

He planted his hands on those sexy hips of his. The smirk on his face gave a full-on hot flash. He knew what she was thinking. His white T-shirt and beaten-up old tennis shoes said casual, but there was nothing casual about the way he focused on her. She fanned her face as he approached. He wrapped an arm around her waist, snagging her and bringing her flush against him, like it was exactly where she belonged, as if he was compelled to tug her close.

"Hey, Sugar."

"Hey." She swooned in his arms and barely got the word out. *Good thing he spoke first or you wouldn't know what to say.* She could practically hear her aunties smirking too. Without thinking she brushed a finger against the one gracing his lips just then. *Mm-hm, smirks are absolutely fabulous.*

"You two have fun," Ellie yelled from the gate. She corralled all the dogs into her back yard then walked up to the front porch and linked arms with Ruby.

After lunch, Ellie and Ruby had helped her pick out a casual outfit, not the skinny jeans Ruby said looked dynamite on her. She wasn't quite sure she was ready for dynamite yet. Instead, she had on a pair of dark denim shorts and a cute white blouse that cut in at her waist, then flared out a bit. She'd paired it with her white tennis shoes, free of lemonade, and her locket. Ruby had clipped her hair back to the side for her with a pretty blue flower barrette. There, she felt casual and pretty.

"We'll visit with you guys another time," Ellie yelled.

"Yes, a dinner party!" Ruby clapped her hands with glee. "On my newly improved patio that is bursting with flowers and scents. It'll be so romantic. But for now, you two go and have fun." She blew kisses toward Sasha and Connor. Both women had huge grins on their faces.

"Ready for our date?" He broke into her thoughts, and she watched as his face softened into a smile. How did he do that? Bank all that sexy energy? She could ask him for lessons, but that didn't really sound fun. She pouted as he drew in his intensity. These days around him she was bursting with lust. Even thoughts of him had her adding the wrong amount of sugar to her pies this week. Way, *way* too much sugar. She'd ruined two batches of pie dough while daydreaming about him.

"I am," she answered and squeezed his hand. "More than ready." Two weeks had gone by since their first argument, slash make-up date. He was still all grumbly about her new property. Luckily, they'd had other things to keep them busy with him traveling to meet a client and her intense wedding season at the bakery. She'd made more cakes and mini cakes this week than she had in her life. They'd spent time together, grabbing quick late-night meals or sharing early coffee and pastries at the bakery, at each other's homes, in each other's beds, but this was their first official date since their argument date. He'd planned this one and aside from casual she had no idea what they were doing.

When they parked in front of the hardware store in downtown Corvallis, and he held open her door for her, she was still clueless and curious. On the drive he'd held her hand and avoided her inquiries, with jokes and laughter.

"Here we go," he said.

"Hmm." She gave him a quizzical grin, when he took her hand and helped her down from his truck. "The hardware store?"

"Can't rehab a house without tools."

"We're buying tools?"

"We're buying *you* tools. Unless of course you already have them? Everyone deserves their very own set of tools." She wasn't sure why she was surprised that a date with Connor Duggan, house builder extraordinaire, included a search for tools. To some it might be such a small gesture, but to her, well it almost took her breath away.

"Hey," he said and took both her hands in his, tugging her toward him and pulling her arms around his waist.

When she dared to face him, she saw the concern on his face. It was getting easier and easier to read Connor's expressions and that gave her a level of relaxation and comfort that melted the shield she held around her soul. He'd never once made her suspect him of being manipulative or two-faced. With Connor, what she saw was what she got.

"Did I mess up again? I thought you'd enjoy this since you want to learn how to do everything yourself, and well, I might not be able to teach you everything, but I can teach you how to build a house, or fix a house. It's not all that exciting, but it's what I know. It's who I am."

"I really, really like who you are, Connor." *I really, really want to know what lies ahead for your future. No.* She shook the thought away as quickly as it beckoned.

"Whew," he said and leaned his forehead down to hers. "Scared me there for a minute. Why the tears?"

She wiped the rogue tears she'd ordered to stay in her eyes, but apparently had no thought of obeying her. *You're being a dumbass if you think there is anything casual about how you feel for this man. Can you believe she thinks she'll be fine and dandy when it's time for him to leave town?* Sasha swallowed back the interruptions from her know-it-all libido and body parts. She wasn't allowed to contemplate that. This was what they had together, right here, right now. Connor had said so many times, the present. He would leave and she would move on. That's how it should be. Right here and now was more than she dared hope for, more than she deserved.

"Sasha?"

She could do this, focus on the two of them right now and ignore the unsettling in her stomach. She was a pro at that. "I wondered if you were still upset about the whole idea of that property."

"Damn," he swore, which was rare. But even now he did it in a calm, soft voice. "I really messed up that night, didn't I?"

"It's..." She'd almost said *it's okay.* Her old phrase. But this time she paused a second to think about it. "It was not a great moment. But you apologized and everything's been so good since then. It's just that I have some lingering issues with uhm, well, anger. He used to apologize after he hurt me."

"Darlin'," he whispered, a tortured tone in his voice.

"It's not the same, I know." Partly she wanted to reassure him. Partly she needed to explain her learning process. "People sometimes hurt each other's feelings and apologize in a normal relationship. I'm getting that."

"But you're still worried about it?"

She nodded. "I'm realizing that my issues don't simply disappear or heal up because my physical injuries are healed, or because he's dead. You know." *Yeah, and your relationship with this hottie isn't casual simply because you refuse to deal with how deeply you feel for him.* Sasha rubbed her forehead against his chest and tried to shush her thoughts.

"Yeah." He pulled her tighter and placed a gentle kiss on her head. "I am going to show you over and over again that I'm just me, no games, no manipulation, no false apologies. And I hope you'll keep giving me these ins to understand how you're doing day to day."

His hug felt good, the sun on her skin felt good, his words and his lips against her head felt good. Things didn't disappear, but she was healing more every day. "The tears were actually happy tears. You do show me who you are. Thank you." She lifted her head and looked at him, this wonderful kind man standing before her who enjoyed being in her space. And she almost couldn't believe she was here with him. Alive, healthy, or getting there, happy.

"So." She rested her hand on his neck, one of her favorite parts of him. Strong, warm, full of life, and yet vulnerable at the same time. His warm skin soothed her. The touch of him always did. "Are we including power tools?"

His face bloomed into that enormous happy smile of his. "Depends…" He raised one eyebrow. "Do you think we need more power tools?"

She laughed, wiggled her body against his, which was already hard for her. Goody, he was full of the same energy she was. She brushed away the heavy and got back to their date, where he was apparently going to walk her through the aisles of the hardware store, and she was going to have to control her libido. "Possibly," she whispered. "The first one you gave me is pretty awesome." Then she took his hand and led him into the store.

"Sasha," he whispered. "You're teasing a needy man, here." She wasn't. Or maybe she was. It felt amazing to hear the desire in his voice. Desire and flirting and fun, those were things she grabbed onto right now, while she shoved all the serious intruders into the darkness.

Chapter Twenty-Four

"Turn over." Connor's hushed voice trailed over the skin on her stomach. She was completely naked. They both were. Sprawled on his massive bed in the dark, with the low light from a few new candles Connor had set around the room casting a spell over them.

After buying tools, after a delicious dinner at Lachlan's pub, after kissing and holding hands up the walkway to his house and through the door and all the way to his bedroom without losing touch of each other. After trying to maintain the kissing while stripping each other's clothes off. And now, she'd lost all track of time, caught up in lust and sensations. He'd kissed and caressed every part of her body, luring her in with his whispered words across her skin.

She did as he asked, and slipped onto her stomach, rubbing her body against the sheets. "Connor," she begged. She was pliant and lazy and buzzing all at the same time. He could do anything to her. "You were right about anticipation." The night called for hushed voices and the kind of special attention for listening to each other's bodies. The sound of his hand brushing against her skin as he stroked her thigh. Each spot his lips kissed, the rough grate of his voice against her pussy before he'd savored her there, drove her entire body up off the bed with his tongue and mouth in worship.

His hands and his lips disappeared, and it was only his voice she heard now, shimmering along her skin. "Beautiful." She closed her eyes, tried to settle her body and waited, listened to his movements as he stretched out beside her.

He smoothed his wicked, lovely, powerful hands along the back of her arms, down her legs so lightly she nearly whimpered. Up again to her back and shoulders, then finally to caress her butt, to knead and make her moan.

"It's incredible." She spoke into the sensual space they'd created, lost in the dream world. That was what allowed her to act so free and wanton here with him. She felt not one nugget of nerves or fear. She felt pleasured and pampered and so, so needy. "Connor," she begged again.

"Hmm?" His answer, so patient, as if he had eons of time to pet her and bring her to the edge.

"I need." It was all she could get out, all the thought she could process, it consumed her.

"What, Sasha?"

"I don't know, it, everything..." His movement startled her then and, "Oh wow!" She let out a noise, half moan, half plea as he stroked her body with the vibrator. It hummed over her back and down to her butt, making lazy circles until he dragged it buzzing down her leg. "*God.*" They'd played with it before, but never this, never all over her naked body while she couldn't see, could only listen and feel.

"You like that?"

"Mm." She moaned into the pillow as he used the vibrator to toy with her body. She'd never in a million years imagined every speck of her skin could be electrified with an inconspicuous little toy. Another time, if she survived this experience, she'd ask him to do it while she watched, but now she embraced the feel of it. Sensations zinged through her body, through her imagination, pulsed in her core.

"Sugar, I think you're going to be very, very good at power tools."

"Connor." She was too high to laugh, but his name came out on a strangled grasp.

"Yeah," he said, bringing the vibrator, small but oh so amazing, right up between her legs, the soft skin of her thighs, and she gasped at how sensitive her skin was there. Her legs parted automatically, her body primed for its touch, for the vibrator to hum in her most private places, to make her come alive.

Connor rested one hand on her hip, warm and steady, guiding her, centering her. *I want to bring you pleasure.* The words he'd spoken earlier soared through her mind. A chant, heady with incense hovering around her, wrapping her up in the sensation that she was flying and floating and being pleasured. "That's good, isn't it? I can tell by the way your body responds to touch."

"*Your* touch," she whispered. Her words were a plea. *Please, more. Go further. Don't stop.* Her body felt torn in two. A current raced through her, sparked and lit, urged her to jump off the edge, while part of her resisted, knowing the feelings would end. *It's so good, so, so good.*

"I like knowing that," he whispered. "Does that make me selfish?" She grasped onto his words, the low hum of his own arousal. "Knowing that you're like this under my touch? Just the two of us together. I've imagined this, how amazing it would be. And nothing...*nothing.*" Now that sounded like a swear. "In my imagination came close to how beautiful you are when you're full of pleasure. Nothing prepared me for how watching you turns me on."

He tilted her head to the side and kissed her then, while his hands still toyed with her, using that vibrator on places she'd never put any thought to before. Ever. And what even was before? His movements, his touch, kept her intimately tuned in to her body in the present.

"Connor, please," she begged, trying to arch her body closer to his hands, to the movement of the vibrator, seeking all it could give her, even how it would ruin her finally, and that was okay. It was the kind of ruin she'd revel in.

"Gonna make you come," he growled as he placed the vibrator right near her pussy, but not touching, not yet. She sought it and he nudged it away. The tease. *He's such a good, good tease, isn't he?*

She stilled her body and waited for it. Quivering with need, she waited for him. And he rewarded her. The vibrator glanced across her aching pussy and she let out a foreign sound, half moan, half scream as her body jumped in response. He did it again, a barely there switch against her clit, then gone. She was shaking and moaning into the pillow, losing herself or finding herself, flying. And when he brought the humming vibrating pleasure back to her, she lost all control, all sense of time or place as she came in waves, moaning through the shocking exquisite pleasure of it all that wracked through her body and tipped her over. She was still shaking when he took his toy away. She heard the ripping of a condom package. When he began to coat himself with her juices, she was so sensitive it felt like she came again.

"Oh, God!" she swore as he finally ceased his pleasure-torture and thrust into her from behind and she exploded. How could she come again? She pushed back against him, wanting to feel how hard he was inside her. He wasn't gentle. He thrust deep and hard, over and over again, his body losing its grip on that last thread of control he always maintained around her. He came down around her, his body slapping against hers with each animalistic groan he pumped into her.

"You and me," he whispered into her ear as he kissed her and nipped at her there, kissing and licking, devouring her with his mouth and his cock. "Amazing. So damn amazing."

He stilled and she cried out, "No."

"Do you feel it?" he asked. He moved his hand under her body and palmed her breast. Her sensitive nipple beaded at his touch. Then he stroked the skin of her belly and all the way down to where their bodies met. He used his fingers to play with her clit, the weight of his body preventing her from doing anything but experiencing all of it, every ounce of wonderful, aching bit of bliss he seemed determined to wring from her body. It was glorious and otherworldly. Now that she'd dived off the cliff, she wanted to do it again and again, and again. "You." He rubbed her clit with his thumb, and she jolted.

"Yes," she moaned.

"Me." She could feel his fingers stroking himself, rubbing her clit, then back to himself.

"Uh-huh. Connor, please." She tried as hard as she could to writhe up against him, and he gave it to her then, finally. He gave her everything. Riding her with a frenzy while he played with her clit, his other hand still coveting her breast, his lips whispering oaths against her neck. All of it drove her wild. She screamed. She came in a flash, an explosion of fireworks, bursting into the sky around them.

Connor braced, held her to him, buried himself deep and came with such power she couldn't tell where one of them ended and the other began. They were as connected and entwined as two people could ever be.

"Christ," he swore and sounded surprised in himself. And she might have laughed again if she'd had one ounce of energy left. The man who didn't swear was completely undone, by her, by what they'd done together. He collapsed against her back and moved slightly to the side, but didn't lose his hold on her. His breathing was as rapid as hers. The hand that held her breast moved to her back, gentling her, or himself, perhaps both. "Jesus Christ." He nuzzled his mouth against her arm.

She wiggled her body against his, nestled her back against his chest. He wrapped his arm around her securing her tightly to him.

"I can't...I don't have words." Their bodies were sweaty against each other, and she closed her eyes to remember that sensation as well as the gruff awe in his voice. She didn't have words either. Only feelings at the moment. Soaring along on a cloud. "You okay?" And even completely obliterated, he thought to check on her.

She nodded. "I feel...I...you."

"Yeah." He chuckled against her skin.

"Sweet, sweet bliss," she said. "That's all I can manage."

"Good," he said. "That's what I was going for."

With featherlight touches, he dragged his fingers in a small circle right over her heart while their breaths slowed down, and their bodies came back to solid ground.

"What we just experienced..."

"Yes?" she asked.

"Was something special I've never...not in my life. Couldn't even begin to describe it."

"Good," she said and smiled into his arm as she hugged it to her. She echoed his words in her heart. Sex had never been this way for her. *This is way more than sex, honey. Way more.*

She snuggled down and decided to unpack that later when her brain cells were functioning again. Connor placed one soft kiss against her spine. "Be right back." When he returned, the condom was gone and he had a warm rag he used on her body. It felt so nice, and she knew she couldn't have made it out of bed to even take care of herself, the bliss fatigue was fierce.

Sasha felt him come back to bed again then pull the covers over them and wrap his arm around her. And she was out.

Chapter Twenty-Five

Connor was late. It wasn't out of the ordinary for him. Well, his family might say he excelled at it, but he wasn't late on purpose. Yet, he somehow always found himself rushing. He preferred to call it racing to be on time. Plus, he usually charmed his way out of any time constraints. But he hated being late for Sasha, and in fact this might be the first time he was. It turned out that falling deeply in love with his soul mate had him eager to be on time for her always. Or early.

To be honest, he wanted to spend every second with her. Too bad life interrupted and they both had jobs and responsibilities and couldn't stay tangled up in each other in bed. Next on the list was to see if she'd be interested in a vacation together far away from both their responsibilities.

He'd been stalled by some cool news for himself and some rotten news for her and now he had to find her and hope the information wouldn't devastate her. The bakery door was locked, but Connor knocked.

Braveheart came racing to the door, his loud bark and enormous body enough to scare most people away. The dog was more of a softy than anything else, but the illusion of a fierce guard dog was there, and that comforted Connor on Sasha's behalf.

She appeared from the back and the way she smiled at him wrapped around his heart and squeezed. *Damn, she's pretty. And she likes me.* The way his body reacted from seeing her through glass doors said she *more* than liked him. She had her glasses on. He'd finally gotten her naked with nothing on her but those sexy glasses last night. While he'd hooked his arms around her hips and brought her swollen pussy to his mouth, she'd gazed down her body at him, her eyes hooded and full of desire through the shimmery glass lenses, a professor giving instructions.

"Hi," she said and slipped into his arms. Her breathy sigh made him think she was picturing what they'd done last night too, and that she was excited to do it again. She was night and day from where she'd been last year at this point. The smug part of him wanted to believe he'd brought this relaxed happy side out of her, but his heart could see she was coming into her true self, shed of all her past abuses and chains from her own strength. "I was starting to get worried."

"I'm sorry I'm late. I got caught up in a couple of phone calls on the way over here or I would have called."

"It's only a quarter after." She glanced back at the clock. "And you're here now. I was doing some last-minute inventory."

"I try to get to you when I promise. I don't want you to think you're not important." He was a completely different man from last year too. Not that he'd treated people poorly before her, but she was front and center in his mind now. Always.

"Oh." She melted into his arms. "You've been doing an excellent job of making me feel important, Connor Duggan."

"In bed and out." He leaned down and whispered into her ear. Let his nose linger on her scent, the florally soap she used mixed with sugar and flour. He could walk her up against her baking bench and have his way with her right now. Peel her cute skirt and flirty blouse off, find all the secret places where she'd hidden the sweetest parts of her. All that sugar just for him.

"Mm-hm," she said. "Everywhere."

"Good." He held her close, cherished her touch. He straightened up, aware that they still stood on the sidewalk. And that he was about to ruin her good mood. "Go for a quick walk with me before we go to dinner?" He knew she loved the park, felt comfortable there out in the open area, one of her happy places.

At the *W* word, Braveheart leapt up and gave a woof. Sasha laughed and said, "We would love that."

She locked up and Connor took her hand in his, rubbing her fingers between his. One simple connection, being able to hold hands. It grounded him, set his heart to its steady happy beat. He hoped he'd never take it for granted even with all the other, one could argue, more intimate ways they'd connected.

"Busy day?" she asked as they strolled the winding path around the perimeter of the park.

"Packed," he said. "Like most days. It's great, having tons to do and diving right in to attack it. Got some news today." He stopped walking and led them to one of the new benches the community group had installed this spring. "The uh, city...uhm the city is, I guess, they're giving me an award." *Why the hell had that been so hard to say?*

"Connor!" She squeezed his hand and landed a smacking kiss against his cheek. "That's incredible! You're blushing. Are you embarrassed?" She scooted close, leaning her body into his.

"Ha," he choked out a laugh. "I think I might be."

"You say that as if you're surprised. I bet you don't get embarrassed very often."

"Never," he admitted. "I mean, jeez, I sound like an egotistical jerk. I usually don't…things…I let most stuff roll off me. Or I'm moving too fast to pay attention. Not necessarily great qualities. After Nina left me and so much changed, I used humor and work as ways to ignore all the hard stuff, you know. And I think that's okay to an extent, but not so that someone is ignoring dealing with stuff, you know? I mean me, so that *I'm* not ignoring the hard stuff."

"Yeah, I get that. Easier doesn't always work out in the end, does it?"

"No." He brought their hands to his mouth and kissed her fingers. Strong but delicate fingers, simple nails painted a see-through pink. *Pretty.* "I got some other news too. Here." He stood up and tugged her gently toward the part of the park that stood across the street from her house. He turned her to face it and stood behind her with his arms wrapped around her.

"Uh-oh," she said. All the happy drained out of her voice. *She knows.*

"It's not safe," he said. He could barely get the words out. This was monumental for her. And he didn't know how to soften the diagnosis. "We can't salvage it."

"None of it?" she whispered.

"No." He cleared his throat. Might as well get all the bad news out at once. "Water's been seeping into the house for years. The foundation is a crumbling mess. Termites have shredded a good percentage of the wood. The walls are covered in black mold. There's a scary amount of bats and bat poop inhabiting it. All the plumbing has to be replaced, according to new city codes, and the old wiring is a fire hazard. Not sure why the thing is still standing, but it's an illusion — it'll crumble as soon as we go in. Engineer says it's condemned."

"Wow." Disappointment laced that one word.

"You are not that house, Sasha," he insisted. "I can only guess how important this was to you. I can't know your thoughts or what you went through, but I know you now, and the state this house is in does not represent you at all. Life may have battered you again and again, but you've done so much more than survive. And you don't need anyone to rescue you or fix you up, because you've done all that yourself. You're amazing and powerful and special. I'll keep telling you this over and over until you believe me."

"I want to believe all of it. Some days are more difficult than others. There are so many things that still mess with my mind. Like you said earlier, it feels easier to shove them away, but they always resurface. And I don't like to talk about it a lot, but part of that is guilt that I let a man hurt me, that I slipped into his games and felt like I deserved it, that if I were a better, prettier, more well-behaved person, he never would have had reason to abuse me. I still feel damaged. That's the real crap. And that even when I do deal with the hard things from my past, they never really disappear altogether."

"I understand that." It took every ounce of control he had not to completely lose his shit for her. How could a man make a woman believe she deserved it? They stood together gazing at her house that wouldn't be her house for long. Secretly he was fine with razing the damn thing. She didn't deserve someone's neglected and crumbling diseased old memories. She absolutely didn't deserve to feel a shred of guilt over her past. She was worthy of the best of everything.

"So what do we do now?" She tightened her arms around his.

"We tear it all down." *Just like we do your guilt.* He wanted to say, but he knew, he knew it wasn't up to him how she healed, what parts of her past affected her or not. "Then we start fresh. New foundation, solid, something super strong that can hold the weight of whatever your heart can dream. We work with the best architect in the city and design a house that's everything you imagine. Then we build it, make it powerful and solid and efficient on the inside, like you. On the outside…well, there's no way we can make it as beautiful as you. But we can try. And there is one piece of good news."

"Oh really?"

"They've okayed the plans for a pool in the backyard." He couldn't give her her true renovation, but he could build her a new one along with the coolest pool she'd ever seen.

Sasha turned in his arms and hugged him, tilting her face up to his. "Thank you," she whispered.

He shook his head. "I crushed your hope."

"That's not your fault. And anyway, you helped me see a new vision. Thank you for doing that for me."

Again, he was too choked up to answer. He let his lips speak for him as he kissed her in the summer night that was both special and haunting. *I love you.* His heart jumped at the truth. *Tell her. Tell her.* But he was still holding back, not wanting to freak her out.

"It's a good thing we're going to Katie and Leo's," she said.

"Oh yeah." He leaned back so he could gauge her emotions.

"Because I think I need to drown my sorrows in Katie's delicious food."

"Yeah." He smiled and his heart settled. She was one helluva strong woman.

Chapter Twenty-Six

Sasha loved the old Victorian Katie and Leo had renovated. Perched above the city on the hill, overlooking Corvallis and the river, it was so stately and spoke of a history from long ago. But it was also newly renovated, and full of life and laughter with three girls.

Connor's dog and Sasha's dog added a bit of chaos until Cece lured the mutts outside with treats. It was noisy and messy, but it all felt right. It belonged. A house that had such a solid foundation it would always be there. And now, memories of Katie and Leo's family were seeping into the bones, adding to its story.

Aside from the amazing high ceilings, crown molding, hardwood floors, and the curvature of the grand front windows, the house hadn't retained much of the past. With a stunning modern kitchen, open floor plan and a lovely lived-in look, pretty but comfy. And right now, it smelled amazing.

She realized how hungry she actually was when they walked in and were hit with the scent of garlic and roasted tomatoes and saw the goodies spread out across the large kitchen island, especially Katie's famous crostini covered in tomato and feta. Jazz music played on their surround sound, Leo was opening wine and Katie, with her cute black-and-white apron on, was sashaying across the kitchen pretend-singing into her spoon mic while Brie smiled, and Rosie rolled her eyes.

Sasha wondered if a sixteen-year-old's eyes were permanently rolled with embarrassment when it came to their parents. That was one memory that brought a smile to her face—her at that age, secretly rolling her own eyes behind her mother's back. This house, this family nudged at her longing for normalcy.

"Congratulations, man," Leo said, shaking Connor's hand. "A well-deserved award. Corvallis owes its resurgence to you."

Sometimes she forgot how important Connor was, how necessary to his work, how many people sought out his expertise. He would leave here soon, and she would have to find a way to be okay with that. *It's fine, fine. I've dealt with much more difficult issues in my life. Having a few months with a wonderful man is something to be celebrated.*

Connor laughed at Leo. "Yes, I waved my magic wand and singlehandedly beautified and gave new life to downtown Corvallis."

Connor had a natural inclination toward humor. He was funny, but she rarely saw him use humor in a self-deprecating way. He was also blushing. Sasha reached out and took his hand. *This amazingly confident, successful man is embarrassed.* She wanted to offer him some of the same understanding and compassion he'd given her, even if it meant merely standing by his side.

He glanced down at her, squeezed their hands together then brought her in front of him so he could wrap his arms around her. But not before she'd seen the glimmer of vulnerability in his eyes.

"Leo's right, Connor. All humor aside. This part of the city is fabulous and alive again because you decided to take a chance on it and start fixing up all the battered buildings. Without those clean, safe and beautified spaces, we wouldn't have people wanting to move here, ground their businesses here. I am super proud of you. And you absolutely deserve an award."

Katie was so solid and sure of everything. If she wasn't also super nice and funny herself, Sasha might be envious.

"Thank you." Connor cleared his throat.

"Will there be a ceremony?" Katie asked.

"Yes, at the beginning of October, I think."

"Will you still be here then, or will you have to come back for it?" Sasha asked. *Oh no.* She wished she could suck the words back as quickly as they'd slipped out. She hadn't meant to ever ask him about moving. She didn't want to know a thing about it.

"Be here?" Connor asked.

"Oh," Katie said at the same time, saving Sasha from complete embarrassment. "At the Fall Chamber Night Gala?"

"Yes, at the Park Hotel," Connor answered his sister.

"I'm catering it! How awesome." Katie patted Connor on the arm. "Ooo, I think it's black tie or at least dressy." Katie swooned. "I'll have to stalk my closet and see what I have." Winking at Sasha she said, "Or we could all go dress shopping."

Park Hotel? Sasha tightened in Connor's arms. *Oh no.* She shuddered. *Calm down, honey.* A train roared to life and shattered her aunties' advice. *A black-tie event at Park Hotel is my worst nightmare.* Literally her worst night ever had been the last gala she'd been to with Anthony hours before he'd nearly beaten her to death. "No," she pleaded.

A memory sliced back into her mind. She was in the hospital bed. Voices came in and out as the drugs worked her over from unconscious to weird pain-filled floating states of being able to hear every single sound in the hospital room acutely. Like someone had turned the sound up on a microphone. "*I don't know why or how she survived. With the beating she took, she should be dead.*"

And a glitch back to the dance that night, the last time she'd danced in Anthony's arms when he'd smiled at those around him and whispered in her ear, "*I'll find out if you're having an affair.*" She hadn't been. "*And if you are. I'll kill you. I can do whatever I want, and no one will ever find out.*"

Her stomach churned and she wasn't hungry anymore. Katie's kitchen came in and out of focus. Sweat beaded on her forehead. The swirling of a long-ago dance slithered through her. Held captive in Anthony's cruel arms while the world glimmered clueless around her. She was spinning, lost in a vacuum. No sound reached her aside from the rushing fear and terror of that night. She gripped Connor's arms to try to untangle herself from him, a strange moan coming from deep within her body. "No. I can't!"

"Sasha? Hey!" Her mind flew back to the hospital. Sounds came to her acutely, loudly. Even the machines keeping her alive were yelling at her. Dizzy images pounded at the front of her mind and the kitchen lights blinded her. She had to get away…get out, before she…

"Darlin'." Connor's voice sounded so far away. The pounding in her head intensified.

"I'll kill you." Threats mixed with the music the band had played that night. She ripped out of strong arms and stumbled to the powder room behind Katie's kitchen, falling to the floor and dry heaving up every nightmare she'd lived through at the hands of Anthony Lucciano.

Chapter Twenty-Seven

It was minutes or perhaps hours, she didn't really know how long, when her arms finally loosened their grip on the porcelain toilet seat. Connor knelt in the doorway. Katie and Leo stood behind him. She pushed her body away from the toilet and sprawled on the cool tile floor, letting it calm her body.

"Can I... Is it okay if I put my hand on your shoulder?" Connor asked. Worry and concern labored heavy on his face. "I won't touch you if you don't want that."

She nodded, tried to answer, "Yes." But her throat burned with the attempt. He reached out slowly and rested his hand on her arm. With his other, he gently brushed her hair out of her face. She closed her eyes at the contact. His touch was cool against her clammy skin. All the energy drained out of her. She was here in the now, on a bathroom floor.

But the memory was ever present too. Moments like this and she felt as if she was surviving the attack all over again. And living through her nightmare—well, people saw survivors as amazing, as heroic, as strong. But to actually be one, to her, it ripped through her body without anesthesia. She experienced the attacks all over again. She knew it was shameful but when this kind of extreme attack blindsided her, she almost wished she hadn't survived, because the reliving of it all was so horrible.

"Here." Leo's deep soft voice stirred her eyes open. He held out a glass of water to Connor. Katie stepped in and ran a cloth through water in the sink. Connor guided Sasha up and cradled her spent, limp body in his arms. The rush of adrenaline and the episode had left her exhausted, sweaty and...ugh, she was all around icky.

Connor didn't seem to notice or mind. So much for her cute summer outfit she'd bravely picked out herself. Had she tempted fate by wanting to be pretty again? No, she shook her head of that thought. It was ridiculous. Connor handed her the water. When she took it, he draped the washcloth against her neck.

"We'll be out here if you need us, honey," Katie said.

Sasha attempted a smile, but it probably appeared more like a drunk carnival clown. Even her face was drained of all energy or the desire to pretend one ounce of anything.

"Wow, that was...hmm." She rested her head against him, unable to finish the thought or the words.

"Want to get some fresh air?" Connor asked, his lips against her forehead. He sounded wrung out too.

"Yeah," she whispered.

Connor lifted her into his arms. She hated feeling needy, but she honestly didn't know if her legs would carry her if she tried to walk right now. Her body was still hot and shaky. And it felt good to rest against him, to feel the soft fabric of his T-shirt against her cheek, smell the clean laundry scent of it. Simple, normal bits of life. She'd miss that when he left town, the calming scent of him.

He pushed through the screen side door to the wraparound porch and set her down on the enormous porch swing slash day bed. "I'm gonna get you some more water and be right back. Is this okay or is the swaying movement too much?"

"It feels good," she said. The gentle rocking motion brushed the air against her cheek. Katie had filled the grand porch with fun furniture and plants. Sasha breathed in the scent of sweet blossoms from a miniature citrus tree in a bronze pot. The scent always reminded her of Italy, the good memories. *Perhaps someday I'll go back.* It was rare for her, to have a positive thought about the past. So many emotions tornadoed through her right now and it was difficult to sort through them.

When Connor returned, her cheeks flamed in embarrassment. This was supposed to be a casual night with his family. And she'd pretty much tanked it. Not only that, but she'd interrupted their praise of him and the award he'd earned from the city, taking away all the attention from something wonderful about him.

"I'm sorry," she said.

"Don't." He held up his hand. He set water and an icy cold soda on the table beside her, climbed up and wrapped his arms around her. "This okay?"

Maybe she should be annoyed that he kept checking on her, but she was simply grateful. And his embrace was something she welcomed, the strength, the comfort, the safety, even the desire when she was in the right mental state for that. Being in his arms was so many things, all of them good.

"Yes. And I *am* sorry I lost it. You have to let me apologize, please. It's necessary for me to be able to express myself. We were celebrating *you* and I ruined it." Therapy had helped her realize that the way she felt was valid and it was perfectly okay for her to express those feelings, even if others disagreed with her or tried to dismiss them.

"Sasha, I respect your feelings absolutely, but you didn't ruin anything. Can you tell me what happened?"

"A memory." She closed her eyes to burn it from her mind, from her entire being, but it would always be there. "Of that last night with Anthony. The last time he hurt me. Hurt me the most."

"God," he whispered and laced their fingers together.

"We'd been at the Park Hotel for one of his charities." The words felt sour on her tongue. His charities that were all fronts for something else, something bad.

"Jesus, Sasha. Our conversation brought it back?"

"Mm-hm." They swayed gently. "And maybe from our earlier conversation too. He was on my mind, unfortunately." The temperature had settled down and the soft breeze played across them. She closed her eyes and leaned into him, let the comfort wash through her. *You're okay. He will never hurt you again.* "Sometimes my nightmares come in the daylight."

"I'm so sorry, beautiful," Connor whispered, resting his chin on her head.

"That one was particularly horrible. I'm going to have to call my therapist in the morning."

"Want to call her now?"

She relaxed another breath into him. "No, thank you. I'm going to require a long sleep before I talk to her." Sasha's vision was back in focus. Sounds of traffic and distant neighbors made their way to her ears. Even the voices coming from inside returned to a normal volume. She felt wrung out, but she was over it. The worst episode she'd had in a long time. She might even be a bit hungry. Connor would have to feed her, for all the energy she had left. She couldn't even muster enough to lift her arms and hold his to her, the way she loved. There was also the embarrassment times a gazillion factor of walking back inside and facing everyone after what had just happened.

This was certainly one of those times when she'd rather crawl into her bed, deep under the covers and hide from everything, the past and the present. The future wasn't something she'd let herself contemplate much, except for buying her house. Her poor house that couldn't be salvaged. The weight of that might have crushed her if Connor hadn't been by her side, if he hadn't made the alternative sound so lovely. *How can he be so amazing in so many different situations?*

"Is it all too much for you, my issues? I'm so fucking exhausted by it all, by the way it swings out from nowhere and backhands me." Her words came out harshly, her throat still raw from throwing up and from the whiplash of her memories.

"It's not too much for me, Sasha. Never. I..." He held her hand and turned so he was facing her. That steady handsome face of his gazed into her depths. "I am falling in love with you and that means every part of you. And I'm here for all of it. You can keep falling apart and I will be here every time."

Pain cracked open her heart, a breathless, good and also scary kind. Could she believe in love? She rested her head against his chest, felt the steady beat of his heart, willed his words and the meaning behind them into her own heart. What did she know about love? That people lied, loved with conditions, used the word as a weapon. That's what she knew. Or *had known*. She had to keep reminding herself all those versions were behind her.

But stepping forward into a new definition of love was the scariest vision she'd attempted to take a glimpse of. It was of that future again that she'd never let herself dream of. Worst of all, what would he do with his love when he moved away? He'd take it with him, that much she was certain about.

Chapter Twenty-Eight

I hope I'm not being too up in her space. Connor leaned against his truck outside a small building in downtown, not too far from his office and Sasha's hotel. Sasha was at her therapist's. It was Tuesday after their weekend when she'd had a horrible episode at his sister's. She'd volunteered the information about her appointment, said she might need a walk afterward. Evening walks were her favorite. They'd become his too, sharing them with her. She was going to call when she got home. But he hadn't been able to stand the waiting. He'd cancelled a meeting and gone in search of her.

And as much as he tried to balance showing Sasha how much he loved her without exhibiting stalker vibes, he'd also been there on Saturday night when she'd collapsed. During and after when her bones had turned to jelly, and she could barely walk or lift her arm to drink her water. If she was going to relive the nightmare again with her doctor, he'd worried about what condition she'd be in when she finished. His concern had snaked through his day and shot his concentration to hell.

There she is. His heart kicked up as it did whenever she was in his presence. She and her faithful dog who was glued to her side as they exited the building. She paused when she noticed him. Then walked right into his arms and face planted into his chest. "What are you doing?" Her voice was muffled against his body.

"Making sure you're okay. I was worried."

"I'm so glad you're here." She stayed there in silence, resting against him. "I don't think I have it in me for a walk."

"Yeah." He rubbed her lower back and gave Braveheart a gentle pat. "What can I do for you? Can I give you a ride home?"

She shook her head. "Can we go to your place and sit on your back deck? I could use a gallon of water and the dogs could play."

"Sounds good. Should I pick up tacos from Oaxaca on the way?"

"Oh my God, yes, please. I could eat a building."

He chuckled. "We won't let you go that far."

"Okay." She nodded, still closed in against his body and he gave a small sigh of relief, not wanting to freak her out at how worried he'd been. "Thank you," she whispered and placed a soft kiss against his chest. He closed his eyes and willed back his emotion. It was the most amazing kiss he'd ever received. When she pulled herself away and climbed into his truck, he rubbed the spot, trying to meld it with his body, trying to keep it forever.

* * * *

"She told me I'm not a crazy lunatic abnormal freak."

Connor held back his laugh. He knew she wasn't any of that, but now wasn't the appropriate time for laughter. But damn, she was funny, even if she didn't mean to be. Her tone of indignance, like she was upset her therapist had thought she wasn't any of those. He took her hand and kissed it. They were stretched out beside each other on the patio loungers. "Yeah? I agree with her, but it's probably nice to hear it from a professional."

"It is, but I think I'll have to keep hearing it, you know. I mean it *does* help to learn how PTSD affects people, how severe it can be, that I'm not alone, but I still feel like a weirdo."

"Well, we can be each other's weirdos. Sounds good to me."

"There is not one thing weird about you, Connor Duggan." Sasha huffed. "I don't even think you have any faults."

He did burst out laughing at that. "Oh, you haven't spent enough time with my family then. I'm constantly late, I don't pay enough attention to anything except my work, I'm too lazy to even make coffee…and those are only the ones on the surface. I could go on."

"Hmm, I haven't noticed those yet. Anything else I should know?" She teased him and it felt amazing, this relaxed intimacy they'd begun to share.

"I hate pillows. To this day I can't find one that fits me. I mean who even designs those tiny fluffy things? My nose is crooked and not for some cool reason like I got into a fight defending someone's honor. Mushrooms freak me out the way spiders freak most people out."

Sasha gave a small laugh. "I like your nose," she said.

It was difficult baring his soul to another person. He couldn't remember the last time he'd done it, if he ever had. With Sasha, he wanted her to know him just the way he wanted to know all of her. "And I let my charm and ego lead the way to distract people from seeing the real me because I'm embarrassed for them to see how lonely I am at times, or how shallow. I guess all that makes me more pathetic, than weird."

"I don't think you're shallow." The expression on her face was so serious, so pained. "How could you ever say that?" She took his hand and put it on her cheek. "You have so many depths, Connor Duggan. A person could spend a lifetime discovering them."

"A lifetime, huh?" He leaned over and kissed her. "That's what I'm aiming for." Little by little he'd started bringing up his feelings for her, about her, about their life together, how he saw things. He was prepared to wait forever for her to return the thoughts. He studied her face after he said it. She gave him nothing, not a glimpse of acceptance or distance. He hated that he couldn't tell where her thoughts were on the subject. But he'd promised himself he wouldn't push her.

He should be fine with the fact that she was here with him now, relaxed, hanging out, especially after the few rough days she'd had. They had one more potential hurdle to get through tomorrow and he wanted to prepare her. "One more tough thing to talk about. Then I thought we could go take a bath."

"Lay it on me," she said and closed her eyes.

"The demolition crew is ready to go for tomorrow." Her eyes sprang open. "Really? That soon?"

"I pulled in a favor. Thought we could wipe out that gnarly structure and envision what it could be."

"Sort of like ripping the Band-Aid clean off, huh?" Sasha yawned and sat up. She took his hand and led him inside, leaving the dogs behind. "In that case I am going to take you up on the bath idea."

His blood stirred at the image of her naked in the bath, her body brushing up against his. He was a lucky, lucky man.

"I've never taken a bath with a man before you." She flopped onto his bed and kicked her sandals off. "If it's anything like the first one, I'm spoiled for baths forever now."

It was amazing, the ability she had to make him rock hard in a second. His ego swelled again at being her first at things. He intended to be her forever. She brought out all kinds of possessive thoughts in him. He'd keep those thoughts to himself. Didn't mean he couldn't enjoy all the images they came with. When he walked into the bedroom after turning the bath water on, he climbed on top of her, felt the heat of her beneath him. She reached under his shirt and lifted it up, her fingers skating across his skin. He did the same to her, lingering on every inch of softness he touched. He tossed her shirt on the bed and lost his breath again. Her hair was tousled, her expression soft. Spread out before him, in her bra and skirt, pink bloomed across her chest. She rested her hands on his pecs.

"Hi," she whispered.

He leaned in so their lips barely touched. "Hi."

"Thank you."

He kissed her. "For what?"

"For showing me who you are."

"Hmm." He hadn't thought of being with her as showing her who he was in any purposeful sense, he just wanted to give her everything. He ached to press his whole body into hers, feel the way they fit together. But along with the soft happy content on her face was the unmistakable fatigue. "Come here." He took her hand and led her into the bathroom. She yawned and stretched her arms in the air, arching her body. She had no idea how sensual she was. And he knew he was in trouble when his heart flipped over, and his cock stood at attention at the display before him. *She's even sexy when she yawns.*

"May I?" Connor fingered the button on her skirt, and she flopped her hands down to her sides and nodded.

"You may. You may have to do everything. My body is wrung out."

"Mm." He kissed her graceful collarbone and removed her bra.

"That's what you've done for me."

"Pardon?"

"I've never let myself be this relaxed in front of another person, Connor. Free to express whatever I'm feeling. I want to kiss you, but I also really enjoy it when you take care of me. I'm not worried about what you'll think. And that all feels amazing. You have superpowers."

It was going to take super focus to keep things relaxed. His mind heard her, but his body was fueled by need and desire to mate with her, to make her his. "I'll always take care of you. In the bath and out." His bathroom was the one thing he'd upgraded over the years, putting in a massive shower and a tub with jets. He helped her into the tub.

"You're the last person I'd picture in a girly tub." She was teasing again. He loved the little lift of her eyebrow when she teased him.

"Girly my butt," he said. And she laughed. "Those jets can cure away all the labor from a hard day's work, make me feel like a man again."

"Hmm." She twirled her fingers through the water. "They do feel wonderful. Aren't you coming in then?"

"You sure? It's totally okay if you want to savor it and relax."

"You promised me a bath, with you. That's what I want."

Connor shed the rest of his clothes as if fire was licking at the threads and climbed in behind her. Her soft laugh went right to his dick. Hells bells, it was going to take more than superpowers to keep his hands to himself. Leaning her body back against his, she sighed and held on to his legs. Yep, he was going to need prayers. He hoped he remembered how. He took the soap and ran in across her belly and up between her breasts.

"Ohhh, that feels perfect," she moaned and arched her body in the direction of the soap.

Focus on her. Ignore your body. Right. Her body lit him up. There was no separating the two, not now, not at this moment. God, it was hard. *Wrong fucking choice of words.* She let out another moan and when she moved her butt slid along his solid aching length. He clamped a hand around her waist to hold her still. "Sasha."

"Keep doing that, will you? With the soap. All over."

It might have been a mistake to hold her steady. He could feel everything, the rapid pulse under her skin, the way her chest rose and fell, the vibration from her words, her pleas.

"I ache for you," she whispered, and his control began to slip. He brought the soap to her nipples, teasing them with it as he breathed in her moan. Again, he took the soap away, teased in and danced away. "Connor, more." He kissed behind her ear and nipped at her lobe as he dragged the soap down between her legs.

"Here?"

"Mm-hm." She nodded. "Oh." She tightened her legs around his hand. "Connor, it's too...I need too much."

"Let me give it to you." He spread her legs and stroked the soap along her thighs, brought it back against her core.

"I want you too. To feel you inside me. Please," she begged. "Especially... especially now that we got our tests back and we're both safe. You promised we'd get to play without condoms and I..." She rubbed back against him. "Can't wait to try sex with you bare."

And that was it, the leash snapped. He tossed the soap, gripped her and turned her over so she was facing him, her knees on either side of him, her pelvis rubbing against his cock.

"Put your hands here." He took her hands and placed them on the tub behind his head. "And hold on."

"'Kay."

Her eyes were closed, her body flushed. She writhed against him, lost in the sensations. He let her move, watched her. *I have never seen anything more beautiful than this woman right here right now.*

"Ready?"

"Yes." She nodded, almost with her whole body, bowing toward him and back, floating in the water, wrapped up in the feelings. He lined up his cock to her entrance, entering her little by little. It felt amazing. He placed his hands on her hips and guided her down over him, achingly slowly so she was there, finally, right where he needed her. "So good," she said and rocked against him.

Water splashed around the sides, and she did it again, using the tub as leverage. He kept hold of her and lost himself in her presence, in the power of her taking what she wanted and him able to give it to her. His blood, his bones, his muscles all hummed for her. She slumped against him and nuzzled her head into his neck.

"You...you'll have to do the rest. Feels so good. My body's so tired...lazy...tingling all over."

And Connor wrapped his arms around her, thrusting up once. So fucking tight she was around him. Twice, she pulsed around him, keeping him there, controlling him even while she cradled against him. The deep throbbing ache for her took over.

He held them tightly together, moved her hips while he drove himself up and into again and again until he felt her clamp around him. When she came, she moved with the water, waves crashing onto shore, onto him, whimpering into his neck. And he was right behind her cresting and exploding. The power of the water took him over. And they stayed like that, connected, coming down from the high, floating back out into sea, the motion lulling them both into peace.

Chapter Twenty-Nine

"It's a skeleton," Sasha said.

"Yeah." Connor beamed. "Isn't she gorgeous?"

Sasha chuckled. The man was head over heels gone for building her her dream home. He'd drooled more over the past few weeks of her house's construction than she'd ever seen him drool over sweets. Even her morning buns took a far, far second to how gleeful Connor Duggan was at constructing a house.

Foundation was poured, framing would be finished today and he'd said after that, things would move rapidly. It had already been fast in Sasha's opinion. Only three weeks ago they'd stood across the street at the park, holding hands while the bulldozers razed the entire thing and dump trucks drove it all away. Now the entire house was framed, and she could see through it, all the way to the backyard, to the swanky swimming pool the builders were glazing today. She'd have a pool before she'd have a kitchen, at the rate they were going.

It was a skeleton, but it wasn't *just* a skeleton. She could feel it, standing here next to him, the jubilation, the anticipation of creating something from the ground up, literally. And she'd been able to help as much as she could. She could add knowledge of nail guns, drills, table saws and how to frame a house to her skills set. And having been one of the bodies that had helped make it this way, she glowed too. It might have been a skeleton, but it was also the bare bones of a beginning. Her beginning.

Which was good because Connor had just accepted an offer on his house, and she wanted to glean his expertise on her project for as long as she could until it was time for him to move on. *Move on.* The words made her stomach upset and dragged a shadow over the bright morning.

"Yes, she is." Sasha tried to keep the despair out of her voice. "Thanks to you, I've never seen anything more gorgeous."

"I have," Connor said. Taking her hand, he twirled her in for a kiss. He took her breath away and she let him. She would soak up every second of his goodness to carry her along when he was no longer by her side.

He smoothed his hand over her cheek. "You okay? It's going to be amazing. I promise," he said.

It was getting more difficult for her to shove down her emotions regarding his impending move away. They never spoke about it, which just made her concerns increase and fester. *Ask him to stay. Tell him you love him. Yes, this is the epitome of 'be brave, honey'.* "I'm good," she lied and squeezed his hand, glancing back toward the structure so he couldn't read her expression.

"Once framing is done, we can wrap it with the exterior sheathing. After that, hopefully today, siding and roof. Wait till you see the transformation at that point. Not much you can help with today, but you're welcome to watch."

"Mimi from the historic society is meeting me here in a few minutes to take pictures of this stage before the siding goes on."

"Goody," he said and tickled her side, then grabbed her and nipped at her when she tried to laugh herself away. "I like having you here in my workspace."

"Mm." Sasha leaned into his embrace. "Speaking of goodies, you didn't think I'd come empty-handed, did you?" She could brush away the heavy thoughts for now, get caught up in his joy. She took the basket off the back of the bakery bike she'd ridden over.

"Be still my heart," Connor whispered. "Please tell me there are morning buns."

"Even better," she said and watched his grin.

"Better than morning buns? I beg to differ. There is nothing better." He nibbled at her neck again and slid his lips up to meet hers where he melted her with his kiss. Whew, the man should come with heat warnings. She should travel with a fan. "One thing in the world better than morning buns. This spot right here," he whispered and sucked her bottom lip into his mouth.

"Connor," she pleaded and with her last ounce of sanity placed her hand on his chest to still him. "Daylight, sidewalk, surrounded by people."

"Right, right." He shook himself and stepped a tiny bit back but kept a hold of her hand. "You do things to me," he whisper-growled and she wondered why why why they were standing in public and why they weren't somewhere private where she could strip for him and he could kiss her entire body, sucking and licking and nipping the way he'd just done to her lip.

"Sorry. Got distracted. You mentioned the blasphemy that was something in this basket of yours tastes better than your buns?"

"Connor!" She smacked his chest and couldn't help the laugh that bubbled out of her. His grin was all sorts of fire and flame teasing her libido. "You haven't tried my chocolate cardamom doughnuts. It's an experiment of sorts."

He took the paper bag from her and drew out a still-warm doughnut that had been tossed in a combination of sugar and cardamom. "Good Lord, woman, these smell like heaven."

He tore it apart and popped half in his mouth. Their eyes locked as he ate. His gaze turned serious. Then he licked his fingers, slowly one by one, and she thought she might combust right there on the sidewalk. He could do that to her, draw out her fiercest emotions to the highest, most sensitive off-the-chart levels, with lust and arousal. Have her willing to jump his bones right then and there on the sidewalk despite the public environment and his crew milling about. He still hadn't spoken an actual word of what he thought of her new creation, but he didn't need to. If the drunken pleasure covering his face was anything to go by, he was gone over the new doughnuts.

Connor tugged her back to his body and wrapped one arm around her. He gazed into the bag of doughnuts and back at her. "You are a magician," he whispered. "Please tell me…" He kissed her, softly, chastely. "Please tell me I don't have to share."

Sasha burst out laughing and watched the smile broaden over his face.

"Hey, Sasha. So sorry I'm late."

Sasha turned in Connor's arms. "You're not late. Hi."

Mimi stood on the sidewalk a few feet away. Before Sasha could move, the photographer brought her camera to her eye and snapped a shot. "Hey, Connor. Good to see you too. Another stunning project here. And the Art Deco mansion turned out amazing. Wait till you see the spread in *Architectural Digest* in the May issue. It's all Art Deco renovations across the country. Yours is the feature."

"Hey, Mimi. Good to see you," Connor said. "I'm sure your photos made it look a million times better."

Mimi chuckled. "Oh, Connor. You're hilarious. But it's nice to know your talent isn't overshadowed by your ego. Are those doughnuts?" Mimi let her camera hang from the strap around her neck and walked toward them.

The anguish that waved through his body had Sasha and Mimi both laughing this time. Sasha nudged Connor. "Go ahead and share, honey. I know it's hard. I promise to make you more of them whenever you ask."

Connor let Mimi take one then he walked backward toward her house and his crew, winking at her, gripping the bag of doughnuts to his chest.

"Wow," Mimi said and wiped a bit of sugar from her mouth after taking a bite of doughnut. She elbowed Sasha gently and led her gaze back toward Connor's retreating figure. "And double wow. Wait until you see the photo I got of you two. I hope you don't mind. I started snapping them as I walked up."

"Can I see them?" Sasha asked.

"Sure." Mimi wiped her hands off, then grabbed her camera and flipped back through the series of pictures she'd taken.

Sasha's heart caught in her throat at the happiness on her face, at Connor's bold, sizzling desire for her. She reached up and touched the screen. She'd never seen herself look that happy. She'd never *been* that happy before. *What am I going to do when he leaves? And Connor? He'll be fine. With his confidence and strength and absolute joy in life, I bet he doesn't even cast a thought behind him.*

"There is some serious love and chemistry zinging back and forth between the two of you. I waited to interrupt. But I was also worried about getting singed by the hotness."

"Mimi, do you think I could have a copy of this one?" Sasha asked. She'd keep it to remind her of the time in her life when she'd had love, even for the briefest of moments.

Chapter Thirty

"Hey, Sasha, can you join us for a few minutes or are you too busy?" Katie and her daughters stood ordering food when Sasha glanced up from decorating an anniversary cake. Sasha had kind of been avoiding Katie. *No kinda about it.* The gala was this weekend and as it crept up on her, she had a difficult time facing Connor's sister. Facing any of her friends who were attending the event.

She didn't relish disappointing people. Especially people she really liked. Not only had Katie become such a good friend to Sasha, with her steady, kind patience, she was Connor's family. Watching him over the last year with his sister and his nieces—how he cherished them, loved them, protected them, teased them, helped them—was one of the most important reasons Sasha had even let herself begin to trust him in her own life.

I know they're going to try to change my mind. Here it is, The Full Attack.

They placed their order and took over the best table beside the window. Sasha dragged her feet putting the cake in the walk-in and checking on her staff. When she met Katie and her girls at their table, they were laughing and enjoying cookies and muffins and tea.

"Sasha, these new chocolate cherry cookies are to die for," Katie said.

"They're not big enough," Cece said with a brilliant smile on her freckled face.

"Ha," Rosie said. "They're as big as your face."

"Exactly," Cece demanded. "Not big enough."

"I'll make a huge one for you next time, Cece. How does that sound?" Sasha asked. She certainly wasn't above trying to smooth things over with sugar. Even if there wasn't enough sugar in the world to make them forgive her for disappointing Connor.

"So, we had an idea," Katie began. "I know you can't go to the awards ceremony with Connor next weekend?"

That was one thing she appreciated about Katie, how forthright and honest she was. However, in this situation, the guilt made Sasha want to do what she did best, hide. Katie had been there when Sasha had collapsed hearing about the event. It had felt like walking right back in to relive that terror all over again, even though she knew rationally that the nightmare was over.

It had been two months since she'd broken down at Katie and Leo's house. And still the turbulent sick feeling churning in her gut wouldn't go away. Her *Be Brave* mantra shriveled in the face of walking back into the Park Hotel for another gala. She'd thrown herself into her house project, working alongside Connor and his crew as much as she could. The work had been thrilling. The exterior was complete and the interior moving at a clipped pace, faster than she ever could have imagined. Sparkly new fixtures had taken over her brain.

Now her home was almost finished. The upstairs with bedrooms, bathrooms and a large suite was completed. The kitchen would be done by Friday. They were hoping to get the back deck started this week. The pool was glorious. She'd already taken her first dip last week when they'd heated the water. And there was still lots of yard for the dogs. *Dog. Only one dog will be living there with me.*

Connor had said repeatedly that he didn't care at all if she went to the gala. And she believed him. It was the feeling okay with her decisions, feeling good about herself, that was still difficult at times. And this was one of them.

"We don't want you to miss out on the fun. Or maybe not fun for you. Shoot, now I'm rethinking everything," Katie said.

"Please tell me. I may not be able to go to the ceremony, but I hope you know how proud I am of Connor." She'd never realized how much it would suck to set safe boundaries for herself when it meant she had to let down people she cared about.

"Oh, please." Katie rolled her eyes. "We know that. And don't think for one second I'm disappointed in you. Even if I was, you could tell me to get over myself. We wondered if you'd enjoy shopping for a dress anyway, something special. You could surprise him when he comes home. Oh gosh." Katie covered her eyes. "I'm making a mess of this. We worried you'd feel left out and…"

Sasha grabbed Katie's hand and squeezed, and felt that simultaneous squeeze around her heart that had been so familiar these days. "Thank you. I've been so worried you'd be mad at me. Your brother is wonderful, but I...I..."

"You don't owe me any explanation, honey. None of us can know another person's traumas or triggers. It's so easy to let people tell us how we should behave, and we let self-trust and self-care go out the window. I absolutely respect you for setting limits. You are so strong, Sasha, a role model for me and my girls. I hope you know that."

"Yeah," Brie said. "And Uncle Connor has never been this happy. Are you in love with him?"

Sasha tried to mask her deer-caught-in-the-headlights face with a guarded smile. *Love?* She kept coming back to that word, contemplating it, rolling it around in her brain. Polishing a rock over and over again until it became something clear and smooth and shiny. If it meant being free and safe with a person to fully be herself. If it meant this giddy joy lived inside her daily. If it meant being in Connor's presence felt like being home. If it meant wanting to hold his hand and listen to his words. If it meant picturing her days ahead with him...a future, but that couldn't be. Again, she stumbled as her thoughts formed and swirled in her head.

"Brie!" Rosie scolded.

"She doesn't have to tell me. But I think she is. And maybe she wants to share with someone." Connor had called Brie his little sage and she was, seeing all the way into Sasha's deepest places. But Brie was wrong. Sasha wasn't going to let herself love Connor then watch him walk away. It only made sense to protect herself.

Brie faced Sasha again. "I'm just saying, you could tell me. I can keep a secret."

"I can't!" Cece said.

"Duh," Rosie said and rolled her eyes. *Like mother like daughter.* Sasha forced her smile and tried to join in their laughter. This right here was love, between these lovely humans. They'd been surrounding her with it since she met them. *Maybe I'm not so damaged and lost after all.* She stuffed her own heartache away, knowing she'd have to deal with it at some point, after Connor had moved on and she was alone again.

"I apologize for my girls. They have no concept of privacy."

Sasha could feel Katie's eyes studying her quietly. She gave a small smile and brushed her hand through the air. Swatting the topic far, far away, out of the door, out of town, floating away on the river.

"So," Katie asked, "does the shopping idea interest you, or give you dread?"

"Not dread so much as, well…I'd actually love to find a dress." And that was the truth. She liked Katie's idea of surprising Connor that night. She couldn't go with him, but she sure as heck could still celebrate him. "I still don't do very well at crowded malls or shops. Ruby and Ford have sort of been helping me improve my wardrobe a little bit, but they usually do the actual shopping without me and bring me things."

"Mm." Katie took a sip of her tea. "I think I have an idea."

* * * *

"It's a size twelve. I had no idea this designer made clothes to fit baby humans as opposed to regular humans," Ford said as he tried to choke back his laughter.

Sasha almost hadn't come out of the bathroom to show them this one, but even to her it was hilarious, how little of her it actually covered. *Handkerchief* would have been a more apt a name than dress.

Katie's great idea was how Sasha found herself two days later at Ellie's house, drinking guava cider with Katie, Ruby, Ford, Ellie and Natalie while Ford and Ruby brought out what appeared to be a night sky full of stars glittering around her. A million gorgeous dresses, or probably only twenty or so, in Ellie and Jackson's enormous bedroom, that Ellie had managed to also make feel cozy. The king bed was flanked by low nightstands and the bedding was a shadowy gray, with fluffy round pale-pink throw pillows, and the area rug was a soft shaggy white that felt delicious on bare feet. Ellie had added two oversized plush chairs with ottomans by the doors that lead to a private patio.

Her brother had lived here for years without Ellie, and Sasha could tell how such a monstrous home, made of stone and wood, could feel too cavernous and lonely. But now Ellie's warm touches were everywhere. Plus, there was so much love in this house it was almost ridiculous.

The chairs that Ellie and Katie currently rested on another soft area rug where baby Alex played on his tummy, teasing Ellie's Rottweiler, Buffy, who guarded the baby as if Alex were her very own pup. The other three hooligan dogs, Braveheart, Kitten and Chewy, were outside exhausting one another in the backyard.

Hooligan was a word she could currently apply to Ford as well, or Noah, who conveniently was at work again. Both men had gone shopping at Nordstrom with

Ruby to pick a bunch of dresses for Sasha to try on. Sasha had very much appreciated their thoughtfulness. However, the current dress she had on might as well have been made for a doll, based on how teeny tiny it was.

"It doesn't even cover my entire butt," she said.

Ellie's silent open-mouthed shock said enough, but in case it didn't Ruby was in tears from laughing. Katie, ever the voice of reason, muffled her laughter as she scolded Ford for his choice. Ford at least had the chagrin to look a bit embarrassed.

"Connor might not mind," Ford said, which started them all laughing again. Sasha blushed. Ford was probably right. *Although there is no way in hell I could ever wear this dress in public.* The fun and joy drained out of her. She'd never be wearing it in public, which was the whole point of today's shenanigans anyway.

"Hey, honey, we're not laughing at you. We're laughing at the ridiculousness of the dress and we're just teasing anyway."

Sasha waved Ruby's concerns away. "It's not that." The teasing felt good. She had no idea how much friendly joking from real friends could make her feel included. That sense of belonging blossomed in her every day here in Corvallis. And the full-belly laughter at some of the dresses felt wonderful. Crying from laughing wasn't something she had much experience with, and it was awesome. She tagged the floral print satin robe Ford had gotten her—he definitely scored points on that—and pulled it on over the handkerchief.

"Good idea," Ellie said. "We can't have you expiring from pneumonia. Here..." Ellie patted the chair cushion next to her. "Tell us what's wrong. I still hate shopping and trying on clothes although these humans usually make it fun for me."

"My body knows I can't go to the gala, but my heart is disappointed in me. It doesn't really matter if the dress looks good in public or not because I'll only be wearing it in the privacy of my home, or Connor's home."

"There's nothing wrong with that," Ford said. "It's a perfectly good reason to dress up. Date night at home. And Connor is going to be so surprised."

"Especially if she wears that tiny napkin," Katie said and got a few laughs again.

"I can't believe you all did this for me. I think I expected you all to be annoyed at me for not being able to go and support Connor."

"Oh, hush," Ruby said. "How you manage your traumas and your boundaries is no one else's business but yours. We think you're amazing. We love you."

"I was there when you lost it, when we were only talking about it," Katie said. "And I'm no therapist, but I think you're making the right decision."

"It was pretty horrible," Sasha said. Even remembering that night at Katie's and the memories it had dragged Sasha through was exhausting.

"I'm worried about how Connor will feel, like I'm letting him down."

"Did he seem disappointed when you told him?" Katie asked.

"Not at all." Sasha shook her head. "He was calm and serious and listened to me. He took care of me after my therapy appointment that followed the night at your house. He was almost mad when I suggested that by the time of the gala, I'd be able to go."

"Connor Duggan serious and mad? No way," Ford said.

"I don't think everyone knows those sides of Connor. How deeply he feels every emotion, including the hard ones," Sasha said, knowing it might be a risk to share those thoughts.

Katie smiled. "He rarely lets people get close enough to see anything but the humor and the work sides of him. And when someone is special to him, he does whatever he can to take care of them."

That suffused Sasha with warmth, washing some of the worry and guilt away.

"Okay, darling, there's one more dress. I think it's the one for you, and for Connor, if you know what I mean," Ruby said.

Sasha may have been exhausted but she loved how her issue of not going to the gala was no big deal to these people. They didn't judge. They tried to help her deal with her trauma in the best way for her. Friendship didn't come close to describing what they all meant to her.

Chapter Thirty-One

"Wow," Leo said and clapped Connor on the back. "So this is big-time."

"You deserve it, Duggan," Jackson chimed in.

"This city wouldn't be what it is without you." Even the man of few words, Lachlan MacGregory, had something to say about the evening.

The men stood surveying the ballroom at the Park Hotel. Connor was always amazed at how decorators could turn a large, open, mostly nondescript room into something glamorous and pretty.

"And on that note, my lady beckons." Lachlan left them and headed straight for Ruby who stood across the room with Ford and Noah. Jackson and Leo chuckled. Surrounded by her best friends, Ruby gave Lachlan a wave and he was pudding in her hands.

Leo had just arrived. Katie had been here for a while checking on her catering staff. Connor hoped she got to come out and enjoy the night too at some point. "I'm going to sneak into the kitchens and find the chef."

It was probably code for sneak a kiss, but Connor was grateful Leo spared him the details.

Jackson turned his way. "What's the scowl for? Is it because Sasha's not here?"

"What? No." Connor smoothed his face out. "I would never be upset that she's taking care of herself."

"Good." Jackson straightened his tie.

Connor studied his friend. His life was one hundred and eighty degrees from where it had been a year ago and it showed on his face, more relaxed, happy, full of love. It didn't mean Jackson Kincaid was one bit less protective of those he loved. One more thing Connor respected about his best friend, and even more so knowing that Jackson approved of Connor dating Sasha.

Hell, he wasn't just dating her. He'd fallen hard into love. The feeling dug deeper. The truth. That his life was finally settling down to right where it should be and it had everything to do with Sasha Kincaid, his person. "It's all this." He gestured to the room. "I don't deserve this any more than anyone else in this town who's been trying to get rid of the crime, make safe places for kids to play, providing food and music."

"Right," Jackson began. "You singlehandedly renovated most of the blocks in this neighborhood. Without your company making the buildings stunning and safe, the neighborhood would never have improved."

"I didn't singlehandedly do anything."

"You had help, you have employees, you even have me now, but you started your company on your own, from the ground up simply because you hated the horrible state things had fallen into."

Jackson was only partly right. Connor had also started fixing up houses because he loved the work. Then because he couldn't let any of the properties stay forlorn. Then to help his broken heart and his grief over his brother-in-law's death. Renovating houses and construction had been his everything. He'd never seen it as meaning so much to the town. Not to mention he had more important things, or, rather, people on his mind these days.

"You going to see her tonight?" Jackson asked. His voice had softened as his wife, Ellie, floated toward them on her own cloud of happiness, dressed in some shimmery long light blue gown that transformed her into the magical fairy she was. It had taken magic, Connor was certain, to warm Jackson Kincaid's heart. Well, not to warm it, to make Jackson believe that it wasn't cold and dead, that he had a reason for living.

"Yes, I'm going to her place at ten, or sooner if this thing ends early."

"Connor." Ellie's eyes sparkled with mischief. He wondered what surprises she had up her sleeve for Jackson. The two of them couldn't keep their love for each other out of their every expression. It might have been sickening if it weren't so adorable. Yes, Connor was skilled at recognizing adorable. Everyone around him in his life was presently adorable. His friends in love, his nieces, even his rapscallion of a dog. For the last few months, he'd even seen the adorable glimpses of Sasha, more and more as she let down her guard and grew to trust him.

"Ellie." Connor kissed her cheek. "You look lovely."

"Thank you." She beamed. "So do you. I can't wait till…I mean…you…I—" Jackson took that opportunity to kiss the stutter right off Ellie's face. Connor wondered what that was all about. Earlier Ruby had had mischief in her eyes too, and Ford had nearly been bouncing out of his skin at seeing Connor, like there was a secret everyone knew but him.

"Come dance with me, love," Jackson said to Ellie and swept her away.

He only had a few minutes alone before a couple approached him. *Oh shoot!* He'd dated the woman a few years ago. Correction, he'd had one date with her, but he couldn't remember her name, Kerri, Kelly, something. "Connor Duggan, it's so good to see you," the woman said. "This is my husband, Ian. He's a big fan of your work."

Whew, she was married. At least she wasn't hopefully going to give him a hard time. "Ian, nice to meet you."

"Connor Duggan. My grandparents lived here, and I used to visit them when I was a kid. It means a lot to see how you've cleaned up this place, the downtown especially. Great job."

This was one reason Connor wished for Sasha's presence, so she could hold his hand through all these compliments. He didn't do well with them, and her touch would have calmed his nerves. At least this one was attached to some good old-fashioned nostalgia. He could get down with that.

"Thanks, man. It's my pleasure. I love these old buildings." He was grateful when the emcee asked them all to take their seats. He never did remember the woman's name. After dinner, on his way up to receive his award, another woman he'd dated gave him a wink and a wave. The knowledge of how he'd dated women without caring enough to remember their names soured his gut. He knew the moment he'd met Sasha that she was the one and only for him, but that didn't excuse his too-casual past of dating and tossing women aside. He'd never been anything but nice—he just hadn't cared much to have them mean anything special to him, and that alone made him feel crappy.

Nina had done damage to his heart when she'd left him the way she had, but instead of taking responsibility for his own faults and fears, he'd allowed her desertion to be his excuse for being shallow, and worse, for believing he only deserved shallow relationships. He itched to get this evening done and get to Sasha. She made him whole. She made him study all the parts of himself. She made him become a much better man. It was that man he wanted to take into the future with her at his side.

"Congratulations, Duggan." Amelia Rock's voice was a snake slithering through the garden, making the hairs on the back of his neck stand up.

He straightened up from his lean against the bar. Again, his friends had recently walked away to collect their loves. *Damn timing.* Connor had been taking one last mental image of the night before he left. Despite being uncomfortable at receiving an award, he'd had a lot of fun. The ballroom was still full of people, most of whom he knew and a few he didn't. "*This is your town,*" Sasha had said. And he was beginning to feel that on a deeper level now that he had her in his life, as she made him really take in what it meant to have built a strong, lasting foundation. This was his town, his home, and Sasha Kincaid had made it all true for him. He couldn't wait to get to her.

"Ms. Rock. It was nice of you and your brother to come tonight."

She leaned into him, way too close for comfort. "There's nothing nice about it. We want you. What else can we do to sweeten the offer, Connor? We could head out and grab a drink together, somewhere less crowded. Talk things through." She reached for his arm and he stumbled back a step.

"I declined the offer once. That was final."

"Fine." She smirked. "Let's find a hotel room and fuck."

She stepped toward him again and he raised his hand, stopping her. Was that how he'd been, only seeking a night to satisfy an itch here and there over the years? He wasn't judging anyone. But he sure wasn't in that headspace anymore.

"I'm heading out. Have to get home to my girlfriend."

"Oh that's right." She cocked her head. "To the girlfriend who isn't here. I heard about her. Couldn't be bothered to show up to your amazing night. To celebrate your success. A bit selfish wouldn't you say, Duggan?"

He turned and, without a word, walked away. He didn't bother conversing. He wasn't Duggan to her. Duggan was for his friends, the people who knew him well, people who were close to him in a casual setting. And it wasn't his place to tell this stranger anything about Sasha's battles or her boundaries. It wasn't his place to try to make her understand. But it was really and finally time for him to leave.

Chapter Thirty-Two

She'd been dressed and ready and had spent the last hour letting her worries get the better of her. She'd straightened the living room, a task she'd already done twice this evening. The charcuterie platter Ford and Noah had helped her with was in the refrigerator, champagne chilling next to it. Everything was settled and in place. Except her nerves. Was Connor having a good time? Was he upset she wasn't there? Had his friends taken good care of him? How had the award ceremony gone? Would he even be hungry when he arrived? What would he think of her surprise?

Connor: *On my way to you.*

Finally, she thought as she read the text from him. Sasha turned the music on, got out the food and uncorked the bubbly. Then she dimmed the lights and got ready to wait some more. *Gah! Waiting is the worst!* He wasn't far, but she'd been waiting all day for her surprise, hoping it would work, hoping it might take some of the sting out of her not being able to walk through the Park Hotel on his arm.

She'd thought about showing up at the last second when she was taking out her dress. But then hives had bloomed all over her chest and abdomen. She'd climbed into bed, wrapped her hand around Braveheart and let the beating of his heart calm her into a fitful nap. As panic attacks went, it wasn't bad. But as far as going to the gala, it had pretty much sealed the deal that she couldn't do it. Her body had given a vehement no and she had to listen.

She was grateful the hives had disappeared, and she was excited to see Connor and hear all about his night. Braveheart barked and wagged his tail, letting her know it was someone familiar on the porch. Kitten was spending the night with Connor's nieces, which meant a calmer night on the horizon.

When she opened the door and saw him, her breath whooshed right out of her chest. He was stunning. Every time it hit her, no matter how hard he'd been sweating at work, whether he was tired, serious, funny. But she'd never seen him in a suit. Gray with a white dress shirt and no tie, the strong column of his throat on display. Almost relaxed in his dressed-up demeanor. Completely devastating.

When his eyes locked onto her, his body braced and his smile fell away. She didn't know whether to move forward or take a step back. *God, what happened?* Was he upset, was he hurt, were her hives back? She fingered her neck as if she could stop the onslaught if they returned.

He stepped into her, nudged the dog out of the way and shut the door, all without taking his eyes off her.

His caramel irises had turned heated and serious as he raked his gaze over her, slowly down her body. Her heart sped up and her breath was short. "Hi," she whispered.

"Mm." Was that the beginning of a smile? *Why am I so nervous?* Something seemed off. Her pulse spiraled out of control. *There's nothing calm about this night at all.* She turned and walked toward the kitchen. She had to move, do something. "I wanted to surprise you when you got here because I couldn't you know...go with you."

He gave a small shake of his head, closed his eyes for one sharp second, then burned her with the force of his fixed stare.

"Here. Are you hungry? I have some snacks." She set the tray on the gleaming marble island in the kitchen.

Connor glanced at it. He took a cracker and tossed it into his mouth. He followed that with a grape, studying her while he chewed. *Is it hot in here?* "And I...um...I thought champagne was...would be nice, to celebrate. Unless you...unless you're done celebrating and too tired? You might be too tired. I hadn't thought of that," she said to herself as she set the champagne glasses gently on the counter. Her hands were shaking and the last thing she wanted to do was break glass all over herself.

Slowly, he shook his head.

No, he wasn't done celebrating, or no, something else? Did he want to dance? She hurried over to the stereo and raised the volume. "Or we could dance?" There it was again, a hint of a smile and a small growl. Was he growling? "Say something," she whispered. "Is something wrong? You don't like the surprise? I...I..."

God, was she going to hyperventilate? This wasn't supposed to happen. This was not what her friends said would happen.

"Sasha, Sugar." Connor stalked toward her and took her in his arms. "Shh." He tucked her head into his body, holding her close. "Nothing's wrong. Why would something be wrong?" He let her go, barely an inch and pierced her with that same dark gaze he'd had at the door when he'd first seen her.

"You're not saying anything."

Connor took her hand and nudged her around in a slow, slow spin. "I'm stunned speechless." His voice matched his eyes, potent, powerful. He seemed on the very edge of something astounding.

"Oh," she whispered. The rest of her words disappeared with her nerves.

He wrapped both hands around her waist and tugged her close. She placed her hands on his neck and held on. Something was happening here, and she wasn't quite sure what, but it felt monumental, life-changing as it moved through her. She needed to hold on. Touching him eased more of her worries. The feel of his skin beneath her fingertips always did that to her, calmed her, warmed her, made her feel safe. There was something else tonight and safe wasn't exactly the word she would use as the heavy air circled between them.

"You did all this for me?" He swayed them together, really together, and she caught her breath.

"Mm-hm." She rested her head against his chest. His heart raced too. *How can he remain so cool on the outside?* "I thought we could have our own special celebration, the two of us, so I could show you how proud I am of you. There's charcuterie and champagne and…I picked a dress too."

He stopped their dance. His face was pressed into her head. She could feel him take a deep breath, feel his body physically straining against something. But what? What was it?

She pulled away. "Connor, something's wrong. I can feel it."

"No." He stepped in, cornering her against the sofa. "This…" He gestured to the food and drinks. "You did all this for me, and I really appreciate it."

It didn't sound like he appreciated it. It sounded like he was… *Needy? Honey, he's all kinds of hot and bothered for you.* Connor traced his fingers over her collarbone, back and forth as if he'd never seen it before. He dragged his hands down her body. over her hip, sending delicious shivers through her.

"Thoughtful." His voice was its own caress too, hoarse and…

She swallowed.

"But none of it matters. I just need…" He trailed his lips along the column of her neck.

"What," she whispered, caught in his heady gaze, wrapped in his deep voice. "What do you need, Connor?"

He snapped then, at the breathy plea in her voice, as her body melted under his touch. Connor tugged her hips to him and kissed her. He'd intended to take his time, skimming his mouth over the soft skin of hers, making her shudder under his touch. But his skin heated immediately at the contact. And he went from careful to ravenous in an instant, pouring everything he had into that kiss, tasting her, demanding everything she had. Like a magician she was luring him in, and he couldn't do anything but fuse himself to her. She was so damned special. Everything she'd done tonight to surprise him.

But everything she'd done was on the periphery. He'd tried to listen, tried to pay attention, to eat her food, notice the nice champagne she'd purchased, but all his senses were laser focused on her. The tantalizing edge of her perfume danced around him. Her hushed voice drove him wild. Her curves in that goddamned dress molded to her body. From the top that graced her shoulders, the sleeves that came to her elbows, and all the way down as it ended right below her knees. A haunting green to match her eyes, some sexy fabric showing not much skin, but molded to her, displaying her body in a way that to him was pure sensual. He wanted to caress every scrap of that dress. Or rip it off her.

His desire to spend forever staring at her was eclipsed by his craving to possess her body under her hands, make her burn for his touch the way he burned for her, ached for, couldn't breathe but for her.

Their lips tangled and she tasted like every dream he'd imagined, while her essence, her everything invaded his senses. "I need you. Only you," he stated, and held her away for a minute so he could take one last look at her. Goddess that she was standing before him. A powerful witch. Those high fucking heels that brought her to his height. "I'm going to burn this image of you into my mind."

He took her hand and twirled her again. Fuck, the back was almost better than the front as the fabric dipped low, exposing glimpses of her bare skin. And when he brought her around to face him and saw the flush rise on her cheeks, he brought her body into his. "This dress is dynamite."

"You like it?" The wispy sigh told him she was as far gone as he was.

"I love it. God, woman. And now, I'm going to peel every last scrap of it off you. This is where my night begins. Right here with you."

"Really?" she asked as if she couldn't, didn't dare believe him.

"You're where everything begins for me. *The rest of my life, the rest of our lives starts right now.* You with me?"

She nodded. He gripped her head and brought his mouth back to hers, sampling, imagining, holding back for one more second before he let loose all his desires. She stepped away and took his hand, leading him toward the bedroom. "Maybe you could help me with the zipper, then?"

He followed her. He'd follow her everywhere. Her bedroom was lit with candles, the light turned low. She turned in his arms and he granted her wish, sliding the zipper down, smoothing his hands over the exposed skin, leaning in to kiss one shoulder blade, then the other, taking power from the shiver that ran through her body. He helped her step out of the dress, followed her down to the bed. Urgency roared through him. He dragged her sexy black bra up and feasted on her breasts, loving how her body moved and writhed under his touch.

"Connor, I have needs too."

"Good." He kissed a path down to her sexy emerald underwear, which he promptly discarded, along with her shoes. He thirsted to be skin-to-skin, with nothing else between them.

"I need you naked too," she pleaded, echoing his thoughts.

He shrugged out of his clothes and watched her in the twirling lights as they set her skin on fire, all her glorious skin, her scars, her muscles and soft curves, the flush that rose everywhere he touched her. He stroked her skin, starting with her neck and down to her nipples, rosy and swollen and standing up for him. He paid them attention and drank in her moans as he did. He fused his other hand to her hip and held her steady while he made circles with his thumb, dipping closer and closer to her inner thighs, watching her smolder under him.

"You need me?"

She nodded. "So much. I ache for you."

"Where? Here?" He tugged her toward him and placed a kiss on her lower belly, sucking at the skin, taking what he wanted from her.

"Uh-huh."

"Here?" He stroked his tongue lower to the insides of her thighs.

"Yes. There, everywhere, please, Connor."

He brought his mouth closer, gently teased her pussy with his thumb, watched her eyes flutter shut and her body bow toward him. "Here," he said and it wasn't a question anymore when he fused his mouth to her. All her sugar was here waiting for him, seducing him, making him wild. When he sucked on her clit, she cried out, gripping the sheets with her hands.

"Please do that, exactly that way," she commanded, and he obeyed.

He stroked and sucked and brought her higher, his cock growing harder with each whimper, each time she cried his name. He loved discovering what worked for her body. And it had been a few months of glorious discovery. He loved that she was no longer worried about telling him exactly what she wanted. It meant he could give her pleasure, make her lose control. He gave one last stroke, and she came, her entire body shaking in his arms, his name on her lips.

"I need you, now, please," she begged and grabbed at his arms. He climbed over her, drew a path from her navel to her mouth with his hand. His thumb graced across her lips. "Inside me," she whispered.

"Now?" he asked.

She nodded. He nudged his cock at her entrance. "Not too sensitive?"

"No." She arched her pelvis up to him, seeking that same connection he did. And he gave it to her, thrusting into her wet pussy, still pulsing with her orgasm.

"Pure beauty," he said, watching her eyes, hazy with lust. He pulled out and drove back in, barely maintaining control. How could he when she met every intention with her own, her body wild and free.

She wrapped her legs around him and he bit back the curse at how good that felt. When he buried his face in her neck and lost control, drilling into her with every aching lust-filled thought, his body, his love, she wrapped her arms too, finding purchase on his back.

"God, you're going to make me come again, Connor. Don't stop."

Right, any chance to make her come again was a challenge he accepted. He pulled her leg higher up his hips and angled and he didn't stop.

"Oh. Oh," she moaned and clamped around his dick, the movement bringing him an instant closer to losing it. Her body braced around him, and when she exploded again, this time he was right there in the ruins with her, losing everything he had to this woman, his soulmate.

Chapter Thirty-Three

Who knew a person could feel exhausted and elated at the same time? Sasha closed her eyes to the sunlight and reveled in Connor's arms around her, well, not only his arms. His entire body was tangled with hers in sleep, like he meant it, but not too tight that she couldn't get away. He was always providing room for her to feel uncaged. Maybe he was preparing her for when he left.

"Morning." His muffled words against her skin made her dream of languishing here forever, force him to stay with her in this tiny bubble of pure joy. *Forget the rest of the world.*

"Hi." Yes, definitely stay right here in this warm embrace where nothing could intrude, where she could focus on her body and not her emotions. Every limb and muscle felt gloriously used and tired from sex. Not just sex. Amazing, earth-shattering, mind-blowing sex multiple times with Connor Duggan. She shimmied herself closer into his hold. "I never got to ask you about the ceremony."

"Fine with me." He nuzzled his head beside hers "It was boring."

She laughed. "Boring?"

"Yep, nothing compared to what came after." He kissed her neck and dragged his lips to her earlobe. "Now that's what I call a celebration."

"Mm." It was her turn to purr.

"I realized something last night."

"Oh?" she said and played with his fingers. He had scars too, from work, from machines. One thumbnail had split down the middle.

"You are the only thing I need. None of the fanfare or awards mean anything to me. You came into my life and blew everything to smithereens, made me realize what's vital, what I've been missing. It didn't just occur to me last night...but..."

Is he nervous? My Connor Duggan, struggling to express himself?

"I want to spend the rest of my life with you, Sasha Kincaid." He turned her body so she was facing him. "We can take it slow, but I want to marry you, plan a future together, spend the rest of our lives getting to know each other and celebrating." He grinned his happy boyish grin and quirked his eyebrow.

"What?" she blurted out and pushed against his chest to give herself some room to breathe. *Marry?*

"This isn't official. I plan to make the proposal special, something you deserve, but I want to marry you."

"Marry? No," she whispered and shook her head, that one word a sharp edge slicing open her soul. *Do not freak out over this, deep breaths, deep breaths,* she told herself. *Oh, honey, it's going to take a lot more than deep breathing to help you figure this one out.* She could be calm about this. It was simply how things were for her. "I can't get married again. Ever."

"What?" His body tensed up and his joy turned to confusion.

"I can't, Connor." She sat up, dragging the sheet with her. "After...after Anthony..." She was finally getting to the point where she could say the bastard's name and meteors wouldn't come crashing down upon her. "That I would never let someone have that kind of control over me again. I'm never getting married."

"Sasha, not all marriages are like that..." Connor placed his hand on her shoulder.

His touch felt too hot. Everything was too hot all the sudden. *God dammit!* When was she going to be done with these panic attacks, these crappy adrenaline surges that knocked her down hard?

"You can't change my mind, Connor." She made a weird shake-nod with her head. Her head didn't know what to do or how to expel the suffocating feeling. "I...this is nice but..."

"Nice?" His voice pitched low. He threw his legs over the side of the bed and stood. "What did you think we were doing here, all these months?" He threw his arms out.

"I...I..." She tightened her hold on the sheet and looked around, anywhere but at him, at the storm brewing on his face. So much weight forced itself on her lungs. She was drowning and she didn't know how to bring herself back to the surface and find air. "Seeing each other? Getting to know each other?"

"You sound like you don't know." His voice rumbled. "Are you asking me?"

Am I? Something was definitely wrong now, but this wasn't the same as last night. Last night he'd been lost for her. "We are enjoying each other."

"Is that *it* for you?" There was a tone she'd never heard in his voice now, stone and sharpness. He was guarding himself, when he'd never held back in front of her before. "I thought we were building a life together."

Alarm bells rang in her head. *A life together?* She was building her own life. He was leaving…what was he talking about…he was leaving. She couldn't get married. And it would…it was going to hurt when he left…she couldn't…she couldn't do that.

"But you're moving…going away. Your new…your new job… Katie said…the…the big company hired you." She flailed her hand in the air.

"I'm not going anywhere. I never was. I turned that offer down."

"But your house…I…I thought you were…" She couldn't make sense of anything.

"Wait…" He paused, put his hands on his hips in that way she normally loved, when he was readying himself to pay every ounce of attention to her. "You've said that before, about me leaving. Have you been thinking that this whole time we've been together?"

Do not answer that! a chorus of aunties yelled at her.

"Yes," she said, instantly feeling as though she'd said something wrong with her truth. *Oh, girl, you have no idea.*

"So, all this time, all of this…" He gestured between them.

He sounded so far away from her, as if he were in pain and she couldn't reach him. Every word a slice.

What had she done? She'd only answered his question. She didn't understand.

"Every moment we've spent together, every second I've been falling in love with you, you've been going along with things expecting me to leave?"

"Well...I...yes. I don't understand why that's so bad, you...you're really angry with me. I thought I could enjoy you while..." *Until you decided you didn't want me anymore.*

"Enjoy me?" He choked out his words.

"It's okay. I don't need..." Words fell out of her mouth, being expelled at random and she had no control.

"Okay?" he yelled. Silence echoed around the room. He took a step back and calmed his voice, holding out his hands to barricade himself. "*I* need you."

"Yes. I know I heard you last night. I —"

"Not just for sex, Sasha," he bit out. "Here." He pounded his heart. "In my soul. I need you in my life. And goddammit I know you're strong enough to do everything by yourself and you're so fucking brave and amazing, but I need you to need me too."

No. She shook her head. She didn't. She was incapable. Baring her deepest wishes for love and connection, for someone to cherish her, to want to keep her. Her entire life people had either been okay with leaving her, or they'd tried to chain her, control her. It had never done anything but shatter her heart and her soul. No one really needed her, he was wrong. And she would never depend on anyone again in that way.

"I don't... I can't... Connor." She was shaking her head when she said his name and flinched at the way his face turned to granite in front of her, as if she'd become a stranger right before his eyes.

Unrecognizable. The pain that sliced through her at that look was worse than any she'd had before, real or imagined. Instantly she wished she could undo it, but she didn't know how.

The ringing of his phone cut through the tension. He ignored it, staring at her with his face void of expression. She'd never really been unable to read him, even when she thought she couldn't, she realized suddenly as things shattered around her. She'd learned every day a little more about him from his openness, his blank honesty? But now? He was a statue. His phone buzzed again and rattled against her nightstand. Something jarred his attention. He stared at his phone as if he'd never seen it before, then picked it up. "It's my sister. She'd never call me this early unless something was wrong."

He turned from Sasha and answered his phone. "Katie?" Sasha watched his body flinch. He reached up and gripped the doorframe between the bedroom and bathroom. "Jesus Christ. What? Okay. It's okay, shhh. I'm leaving now. I'll be there."

"Connor?" Sasha held the sheet and crawled across the bed toward him. "What is it?"

Connor turned and the anguish on his face took her breath. "I have to go. Brie's been in a car accident. They had to..." His voice broke. "They had to cut the car apart."

"Oh my God." Sasha stumbled forward and wrapped her arms around him. He was so cold, like stone. His precious niece, his favorite. "Let's go to the hospital right now. I'll go with you."

"No." His voice was a sharp slap to her face. Worse. She'd felt real hits before. "It's okay." His tone quieted a bit, but then it slipped back into that bland dismissal.

She felt her heart being torn out of her body. "You don't have to go."

"Please let me. I…" *I love you*. It hit her with the force of a brick. She rubbed her chest. How could she really know it was true? How could she trust it? Her heart hurt with its intense pounding trying to tell her something and she didn't know what. Connor had turned and was tugging on his suit from last night. Sucking in a deep breath, she shook off her fear and her own selfishness. His family was counting on him. She pulled away and hurried to gather some clothes. "I can't drive you, but I can be with you, whether you want me to be or not."

"I can't do this now. I don't know how you'll get home if I…if things are bad." Braveheart thundered into the room. He dug his head into her hip, always able to read her heavy emotions. "Your dog needs you. And I…I'll call you."

Sasha stood frozen in place until the door slammed and she slumped on the bed, all her energy, all her joy from last night, from the last few months, wiped out in a foolish instant. All her hopes and dreams shattered on the floor. *What have I done?* She curled into a ball on the bed and hugged her knees to her chest. She didn't cry. She was in too much pain. This time it was a pain she wasn't sure she could get over.

Connor raced to the hospital, the drive a blur, his heart in a pummeled heap at the bottom of his chest. *Brie, Jesus Christ! Focus on Brie*. Right now, nothing else mattered. The drive was surreal. He sped, unconcerned with getting a ticket or even being unsafe. He had one goal, get to his family. It wasn't until he entered the waiting room and saw Leo and his other nieces that noise and sensations crashed back into him.

"Leo," Connor said.

At the sound of his voice, Rosie stood and fell into Connor's arms.

"Hey." Leo's voice was gruff. "Katie's with Brie now. She has two broken bones in her left leg, at least one broken rib and a concussion. They were worried her back might be broken, but...Jesus..." Leo couldn't talk. He took a few deep breaths and wiped his eyes. Cece sat in his lap with her arms around his neck. She was stiff and quiet, and she patted his cheek.

"It's not broken," Rosie said, tears streaming down her face. "They just came out and told us a few minutes ago. "It's not broken. It's not." Rosie's tears drowned out her words and Connor held her tight. "We thought—"

"Yeah." The air bled out of him. He wasn't sure how he was still standing, but it was what he did for his family, his girls. It was what he'd always done. The words came on autopilot. "It's all good, honey. We'll get her healed up, right? We're all here."

Connor ignored the aching hollowness in his insides. He wasn't prepared to deal with his own life's implosion, not now, not ever. He'd get through this by taking care of his family, the way he'd always done.

Chapter Thirty-Four

"Where's Sasha?" Connor and Katie watched Brie while she slept. A long, intense day of waiting and sitting with Brie had finally darkened into night. It was late, but Connor had no idea of the actual hour. Leo had taken Rosie and Cece to drop them off at Jackson and Ellie's. Connor would have done it, but Cece wouldn't let go of her hold on Leo, and Connor didn't know if it was for her own comfort or Leo's.

Connor had asked Cece to take special care of Kitten when they picked her up too. Hopefully that would allow his youngest niece to snuggle down and relax. Leo was going to return with food for them and clothes for Brie since the surgeons had had to cut hers off her. *Jesus Christ, Brie.* He palmed his face with his hands, trying to rid his brain of the what-ifs.

"I thought...last night, well that she might be with you this morning," Katie said. "When you came to the hospital."

He'd numbed his emotions, but now he had to walk through the destruction, speak it out loud, feel his bones scraping against his skin. At least with Nina, she'd disappeared and ghosted them all, but Sasha was a part of all their lives. He couldn't pretend she never existed.

"Connor?" Katie studied him. He wasn't sure what she could read, but he *was* sure it wasn't anything good. He couldn't mask his pain. "Hey, what happened? And don't you dare tell me nothing. Brie's going to be okay and yet you still look like someone died."

Connor bent over and rested his head between his hands. He was a mess. Here he was in his niece's hospital room. She'd barely survived a horrible accident and he was the one who might puke. The night, the morning, everything came barreling forward, smacking him in the gut. It was all too much. "She doesn't want to be with me."

"What? Are you crazy? You're all she wants. Well, not all. I mean there's independence and safety and a happy life, but..."

"I asked her to marry me last night. I mean this morning and she said she's never getting married again. She was appalled that I even asked. Worse than appalled. I don't know what emotion exactly but it certainly wasn't happiness."

"Oh, honey. I... No, no...are you sure? There has to be more to it than that. Look at who we're talking about. Perhaps you should try to see it from a different perspective."

"There's pretty much only one way to take that kind of refusal. She thinks, thought...she thought we were 'enjoying each other until I left town with the Rocks' job offer."

"Hmm." His sister studied him. "You're sure it isn't more?"

Connor didn't know how to answer, barely knew how to speak at all.

"You know," Katie spoke softly and carefully like he was the wounded bird who required tending. "I love you and I want you to be happy and have everything possible in life. I was thrilled when you and Sasha got together because I can see how happy you make each other, and you both deserve a heavy dose of wonderful but..."

"But you were worried I'd get my heart broken again because I sure know how to pick 'em."

"No." Katie shook her head. She patted his arm in that tender, loving, you-poor-idiot-man way.

Well, he'd passed Idiotville a while ago, apparently. Back when he'd told his heart to go ahead, dive off the high dive and do a back flip into love. Instead, he'd bellyflopped big-time. It didn't just sting, it sucked the breath right out of him. He was sure he'd have dark purple bruises on his chest if he peeked.

"I suspected," Katie began. "Being with Sasha might be both the easiest relationship you've ever had, the way you two really take the time to see into each other and how wonderful you are at taking care of people. But also, the most difficult relationship of your life."

"Because our dreams are on opposite sides of the spectrum? I wouldn't exactly call her 'not wanting to marry me' difficult. What can I say to that? Worse, she'd gone along with this...whatever we had between us with the idea I'd leave anytime." The acid from his tone did nothing but burn his own tongue. He hurt for Sasha living that way as much as he hurt for himself.

"Hmm. You're upset now and all worked up because of Brie, but I think when you've had some time, you might be able to talk things through with her. Think about what Sasha's been through," Katie implored, squeezing his arm. "She carries so many scars with her. That's what I meant by difficult. You have to be strong enough to wade through the minefield of her ghosts, to walk by her side, to support her, to ask her to support you. I know you're up to the challenge. I guess the question is do you know it? And..." Katie flicked his arm.

"Saying she can't marry again doesn't mean she wants to live without you. She's survived one trauma after another, Connor. She's taught herself to expect the least amount of goodness. That's all going to take a lot to undo. Did you ask her to consider a future with you, to accept the fact that you are not leaving her, give her the time to imagine it all?"

Connor let out a long sigh, exhausted to the core. His entire body ached from the emotions and adrenaline of the day. He felt worse than if he'd run a marathon and passed out at the end from dehydration. "Why are you always so calm and levelheaded about these things?"

Katie managed a tired grin. "Older, smarter and prettier. I got them all."

Connor chuckled. "I don't think you left any adjectives for me."

"Listen, I was an absolute mess when I got the call about Brie this morning. I don't even know how we got to the hospital. Thank goodness for Leo. You were there when I drowned my sorrow in work after John died. I lose my ever-loving mind when Mom gets on her high horse about how I'm raising the girls. You *know* I'm not levelheaded all the time."

She gestured to Connor. "Thing between you and Sasha is much easier for those of us not in the relationship to see. But at the same time, you know her best. You are the one she trusts and loves, honey. Any of us can see that. I wonder if she even recognizes it as love. She's had years of unlove. You have to decide if marriage is the most important thing to you. Or, if giving Sasha whatever she needs can fulfill you in return. Whatever the outcome, you have to try, you have to give her a chance. You both deserve that."

* * * *

He didn't know whether to find it ironic or one more addition to his stupid life that he was now in a hotel room, Sasha was living in her dream home and they weren't speaking to each other. It certainly wasn't humorous.

After he'd left the hospital on Saturday, he'd gone straight to sign the closing papers on his house, leaving him a lighter man in terms of housing baggage, and a wealthier man when it came to his bank account. Also, the unhappiest he'd ever been. Although that had nothing to do with the home he'd just said goodbye to.

At least he hadn't had to meet the buyers. He'd heard enough about them to set off all his annoyance alarm bells. Young, newlyweds—okay, so maybe he was jealous—and, worse, do-it-yourselfers. They had the dumpster waiting in his driveway for the instant they got the keys and could start the demo. They probably even had matching renovation T-shirts and colored safety goggles. *How fucking cute.*

After becoming homeless, which surprising took only about fifteen minutes, he'd picked up Rosie, Cece and Kitten from Ellie and Jackson's, taken them all home to the grand house on the hill and stayed with them for two nights until Katie and Leo could bring Brie home. Katie had begged him to stay longer, but he was, for the first time in a long time, no fit company for anyone.

"Nothing good will come from brooding," his sister had said, but he thought he might start giving lessons on brooding. He was that damn good at it.

He thought the quiet would help him think. They'd happily offered to take care of Kitten for him, and even his dog hadn't seemed to care. Correction, Kitten was concerned about Brie. His furry canine had sprawled on the floor right under where Brie rested. His dog had taken her crazy excited shivers down a few notches and wherever Brie got moved to in the house, Kitten had followed, quietly patiently hovering, one more worried parent.

Boy did Connor get his quiet. A sterile, haunting silence all alone in a nice, impersonal hotel room. Houseless, dogless, loveless, appetiteless. Jesus, he was an overdramatic jackass. But he fucking hurt. There was a reason he hadn't ever sworn that much in his life, because nothing, *nothing* had hurt the way his heart hurt now.

Sasha had called him twice over the weekend to ask about Brie and see if they could talk. Both times he'd let it go to voicemail, too much of a coward to face the truth, that their relationship might be over. That for her this was just them enjoying each other's company, when for him, it was life or death.

He rarely heard her voice on the phone, as their relationship had been mostly in person. Secretly he'd also let it go to voicemail, hoping she'd leave messages so he could have them and listen to them if she decided she was done with him. He'd be done with him if he'd walked out on himself like that. *Good Christ, I'm talking about myself and my feelings in third person now.* Her voice was beautiful, but she'd sounded as lost as he felt.

Sitting in a chair that was too small for him, taking in the city lights below while the world beneath him continued on in laughter and madness and love and hate and beauty and heartbreak, and him alone, outside of it all made him realize how badly he'd messed up. He knew he needed to talk to her. *Not just talk, asshole, apologize.*

He'd bared his heart then taken it away at the first sign of injury. That wasn't who he was. That wasn't one iota of how powerful his feelings were for her. Now he'd have to find a way to be vulnerable in her presence without flipping out on her. Do what he'd been doing, show her he loved her unconditionally and give her the freedom to make her own choices. Then he'd hope like fucking hell she chose him.

Chapter Thirty-Five

"Are you sure I can't get you something to drink, Sasha? Wine, tea, water?" Katie asked.

Sasha shook her head. "No thanks." Polite words spilled out. She was surprised the rough waves of bile roiling in her stomach didn't come up and embarrass her. They'd been churning, threatening for days now.

She sat on Katie and Leo's deck around the firepit, surrounded by warmth and love. Katie and Leo were snuggled together on the loveseat. Beside Sasha sat Ellie and Jackson. Jackson held Ellie's hand, while baby Alex slept on his shoulder, content to be still for once. Ruby was walking around the deck babying Katie's flowerpots while Lachlan traced her every move, and Ford and Noah stood against the house, holding hands. Natalie and her crew were coming in a bit with the pizza. Everyone important in her life was here.

Everyone but Connor.

She noticed his absence now like an open wound, painful and bleeding out. Where was he and was he ever going to want to be in her presence again? Was he ever going to talk to her, listen to her, hold her hand, kiss her?

Work hadn't helped. She'd barely been able to make one loaf of bread before she'd had to run from the bakery at the thought of never feeding Connor her sweets again. Walking in the park had only reminded her she was alone, and that it was her fault. Even her aunties had been oddly silent. She felt them hovering. She wondered if they'd turned their backs on her too. *We haven't. We're waiting for you to figure things out. Only you can do that, honey.*

She should be happy, relieved, elated. Connor's nieces were all safe and alive. Cece lorded over the backyard, sneaking the dogs crackers and making them do tricks in return. Rosie was cuddled next to Brie, playing a new game on the Nintendo Switch Leo had gotten them, Brie's casted leg propped in front of her on a cushioned chair. Well Rosie was doing the playing. Brie looked happy but exhausted as she rested her head against her sister and sipped hot chocolate. Sasha gazed up. It was a perfect autumn night, a black canvas full of stars.

And she was broken.

One week since Saturday, since Connor had left her to go to the hospital, since she'd spoken to him at all. One week since she'd made the biggest mistake of her life. She did love him, yet she'd blasted him away out of fear. Her old nemesis coming back to taunt her. The pain hadn't lessened. In fact, she felt worse now than when she'd upset him that morning in bed and the realizations crashed down around her. Marriage had been her trigger in that moment, she could see it now.

Everything else had spiraled out of control after that. And she didn't know how to make it right.

When Connor had repeatedly not returned her calls, she'd broken down and called Katie to see how Brie was doing. These people had become like family to her. Not *like*, they were family, and she wasn't prepared for that to end. Katie had invited her over and of course she'd brought treats.

She'd had to wipe away her tears when she saw Brie on the deck wrapped up in blankets, tired but alive. She didn't know everyone else was going to be here, and she didn't know if being surrounded by all these wonderful people while her heart was a pile of ashes would hold her up or break her. Because they all embodied such deep love. She did, in fact, have great role models in her life of unconditional love, of people who had risked their hearts and found happiness. That was what she'd secretly dreamed of for her and Connor. She wished it hadn't taken her blowing everything up to face it, to share it with him.

"You still haven't talked to him?" Katie asked quietly.

Sasha shook her head again. This time she wasn't capable of any words.

"Have you tried calling him?"

Sasha nodded. She fingered the soft blanket on her lap. How easy it would be to run home, hide in her bed till the pain subsided.

"He's being a dumbass," Katie said. "He'll come around."

Sasha ached to believe Katie, but her heart hurt and without being able to talk to Connor, she didn't know what else to do. Beg? Not only had he avoided her calls, he hadn't come into the bakery for his coffee and morning buns, hadn't texted her, hadn't been at the park for his daily play time with Kitten. The worst was yesterday when she'd walked by his old house and seen the new owners inside already tearing it apart. He'd disappeared into thin air, shredding their relationship to pieces, never to be seen again. Perhaps he really had left without saying goodbye.

Silence greeted her as the gentle conversations around her stopped momentarily. Katie's eyes grew wide.

"Hey."

Sasha whipped her head around to see Connor standing in the doorway, his arms full of wrapped gifts and flowers. His hair was curly and messy, and he looked worse than she felt. Dark bags under his eyes signaled he hadn't slept much either. Her heart stopped for an instant wondering if this was it, when he came to say goodbye. But then she saw the gentle smile and the way his eyes, clear and powerful, pierced hers. And a tiny flutter stirred in her heart.

"Uncle Coco," Brie said softly.

"Mama says you're being a dumbass," Cece yelled.

Connor gave a small grin. "Well, she's usually right."

And Sasha breathed the tiniest bit easier. *He's here! Here's your chance to apologize, tell him you were being an idiot. Hush, it's not her place to apologize. She doesn't have to get married ever again if she doesn't want to.* Her aunties were back. Maybe there was hope yet.

"You shouldn't have brought me all those gifts," Rosie said.

"Ha ha," Connor said. He set the packages down by Brie and gave the flowers to Katie, along with a hug.

Sasha watched him, her heart fluttering with hope until he made his way to her. "Hi."

"Hi?" She studied his face.

"Can we talk?"

She nodded.

"Would you like your friends and family to stay, or would you rather talk in private?" Now she was worried again. Was he going to end things with her, is that why he suggested she have a support system present?

"All right, my fools." Katie stood. "Natalie's crew and pizza should be here any minute. Let's go inside and eat. You two enjoy the fire and uh, come in and join us if you want."

The mention of pizza was all it took to get everyone moving at warp speed. Even the dogs followed the mayhem.

"Are you giving her the gift?" Cece yell-whispered as she walked by.

"Hush, you," Leo said to Cece and nudged her inside. He lifted Brie into his arms, and in a matter of minutes, Sasha and Connor were alone.

"You look cozy," he said.

He towered above her and if she had to guess she'd say he was nervous. Nervous didn't being to describe her. Nervous was the calm ocean water. She was the swimmer lost in the riptide, waiting to see if he was going to dive in and save her or let her drown.

"Sasha." His voice was a harsh plea. "I am so sorry for how I behaved, for walking out and pushing you away. I...I... God, I hope you can forgive me and we can—"

Sasha scrambled out of the blanket and threw herself into his arms. He braced at the force of her body hitting his, wrapped his arms around her and held on tight. When he sat them down, she breathed out, finally, all her worries and fears.

"Hey." He soothed her, rubbing circles on her back. "I'm so sorry I hurt you. Are you crying?" He pulled gently out of her monkey embrace and cradled her head.

She wasn't crying, she was sobbing and hiccupping at the same time. Her eyes were puffing up and she couldn't control the snot. And she didn't care about any of it because she was right where she was meant to be. "Christ, I messed up."

He snagged the tissues from the side table and handed them to her while he kept that warm caress on her back.

"I thought you were done with me, with us, with this." She gestured between them. "I messed up so badly and you wouldn't answer my calls and I couldn't find you anywhere. It scared me," she whispered, and face planted into his chest.

"Never." He squeezed her to him again. "I never want to be done with us, with you. I got scared too and hurt. I closed up and acted like a jerk. Then I didn't know how to fix it. I…was so afraid I couldn't."

"No. I owe you an apology too, Connor. That's why I've been trying to call you. I hurt you. All this time I thought you were leaving town, taking that new job, so I told myself I could only have you for now, that I wasn't going to get the future with you, that something so beautiful wasn't mine for the taking. I convinced myself. It was easier than believing I deserved a love like yours."

"Sasha." He crushed her to him again. "I didn't stay and let you explain or try to understand where you were coming from. But then Brie got hurt and…well, I've been trying to figure out how to apologize ever since my brain started working again. I let my fear get the better of me."

"Yes." Sasha nodded. "I get that. I thought I was done living in fear too, but I think I was letting it guide me. And the biggest fear I could imagine is losing you."

Connor tilted her head up and rested his forehead against hers. "I should have said, I love you, Sasha Kincaid. You are my life. I want to spend my days with you. What do you want?"

Now when he said the words, she opened her heart and let the love seep in, let herself believe in it, deserve it. "I don't know if I can ever get married again, Connor." She whispered the words that had nearly broken them a week ago. "I trust you. I love you. I want to be with you, to be your family, but I still have a lot of work to do on myself and my issues, and I don't know if I can get over my fear of marriage after what I went through. Can we…"

She swallowed and wiped a fresh batch of tears that seemed to be never ending. "How can we make it work, if your dream is marriage and mine isn't? You shouldn't have regrets. You're wonderful. You should have everything your heart desires."

Connor wiped his thumb across her cheek and cupped the back of her neck so their eyes met. "My heart belongs with yours. It's that simple. I don't need rings and marriage. I don't think I ever really did. I stupidly assumed, like the dumbass I am, that all women want that. And I lost my marbles when you hinted that this thing between us wasn't serious. Because for me it's everything, you and me together. I let my hurt feelings come between us without being mature and really talking it out with you. You're so amazing doing everything by yourself. It's awesome to witness," he whispered. "So damn beautiful."

Sasha choked back how that made her feel.

"There is a part of me," he continued, "that wishes you needed me too, but the more I thought about it, I realized that doesn't mean marriage. It means this." Connor reached in his pocket and pulled out a small gift, wrapped in pretty pink paper.

Her hands were shaking as she unwrapped it, trying to save the paper so she could tuck it into her journal later. It was a locket, an antique silver heart attached to a leather string. She opened it up and inside was a picture of her on one side and their dogs, Braveheart and Kitten, on the other.

"It's for me," he said. "The girls helped me. It's so I can keep you close to my heart, to care for you, to cherish you."

That set her tears loose again. He'd asked his nieces to help him find a way to tell her he loved her.

"You'd wear a heart necklace? It won't...ah...it won't mar your manly reputation?" she teased and melted at the grin that formed on his face, the secret, intimate one that was full of love and all for her.

"I'd do anything for you, Sasha. I just want you, that's all. The girls helped me with another gift too." Connor reached into his other pocket and drew out one more present. It was a small square box. "It's not an engagement ring," he said as he opened it to reveal a brilliant ring with a shimmery dark green stone set in an antique gold setting. "I wanted you to have something gorgeous and the color reminded me of your eyes. It's tourmaline, green tourmaline, and it signifies everything I see in you, grace, beauty, strength, power, love, healing. You should have all the pretty things in life, Sasha. There are no strings attached, no conditions. I love you."

"It's…so…" She couldn't speak. He took her breath away. "It's stunning."

Sasha took the ring out and held it in her hand. She put it on her finger, then latched her hands around his neck. "I love you too. I love you so much, so much it scares the hell out of me."

"Last week, I got scared too and pushed you away. I promise not to do that again." He kissed her, making promises in that heartfelt Connor Duggan way.

She pulled back and rested her face against his chest, drew her hand along his neck to feel his pulse beating against her fingers. "You closed on your house. I saw the new owners."

"Yeah, it happened faster than I expected."

She sat up and met his gaze. No hiding anymore. "Will you come live with me? You and Kitten and me and Braveheart all belong together."

His eyes sparkled when she asked him. "You sure about that?"

She nodded and smiled. She felt it in her blood. She belonged with him. "It's your house as much as it's mine. We built it together. And you were right when you assured me we could build a new solid foundation, better than the original."

"You think we've done that?"

She smiled. "I know we have. But you've helped me with something even more beautiful than that."

"Oh yeah?" he asked.

"You've given me love and family and shown me, even when I was too stubborn and blind to acknowledge it, a future to dream about. With you."

Epilogue

It was the hottest October on record. The temperatures had risen into the hundreds and the humidity had arrived with it, lingering in the air around them. And Sasha couldn't quit smiling. Her entire body felt fluid and loose. She was one big smile. *Continuous orgasms will do that to a girl. Mm-hm, that man certainly can kiss, woo wee.* Sasha let her aunties' words twirl through her. They were true, after all.

"Remind me again why we're baking when it's a hundred and five degrees outside?" Connor asked. He stood behind her with his arms caged around her while she attempted to roll out the dough. It was supposed to be a lesson for him, but really it was a masterclass in working through distraction for her. He kept kissing her neck and behind her ears. Not to mention, it was remarkably difficult to roll out dough with a large man wrapped around her back. A sexy, hot, large man.

To be fair, she loved this distraction game they played. It seemed to happen every time she tried to teach him how to bake. She was smart enough to know he did it on purpose, asked her to teach him, so he could hover close and pepper her skin with kisses. It had been a deliciously fun two weeks since they'd made up and he'd moved in. He nipped the sensitive skin against her pulse and caused her entire body to shiver.

"Because you can't get enough of my morning buns."

"Mm-hm." He sniffed at her. "Love this spot." He open-mouth kissed and tickled the indentation where her neck met shoulder. "All this sugar. You're right." He traced a path along her back. "I can't get enough of your buns." He gripped her dress and tugged it up to her waist.

She laughed and closed her eyes to the sensation of his hands on her legs.

"Morning buns, afternoon buns, middle of the night buns. How you hide them under these dresses and walk around teasing me. God, what these little flirty sundresses do to me. I need to touch you."

"Connor," she said on a whimper as he tugged her hips tight against his body. The rolling pin dropped from her hands, and she pushed it away with the dough.

He gently nudged against her back, bending her body over the counter. Her cheek rested against the cool marble surface, in sharp contrast to her overheated body. Powdered sugar to keep the dough from moving now tangled in her senses, on her skin. She was fully open and alive, her cells on fire for him. "You're going to get me all dirty. All this sugar." She tossed his words back at him.

"Mm."

Sara Ohlin

"Mm," she mimicked as he dragged her underwear down and helped her step out of them. His hands never left her, grazing across her skin, slipping to her ankles and back up, slowly, so slowly, she felt it achingly torturously as every cell in her body vibrated with attention, seeking him. "Connor," she panted as she pulsed her body back against his.

"What time is everyone getting here?" he asked in that deep voice of his. So steady he was. How could he even think of others at a time like this? While he teased her body through this erotic dance. His hands finally reached her bare hips, her skin buzzing for his touch.

"In a few hours...oh..." He dug his fingers into her butt, right where it met her hips, parted her and glanced his thumbs across her aching pussy.

"Right there," she begged. *Demanded*. It was all the same to her. He listened and did what she asked, pushing one thumb in along that same torturous path as before, and she could feel that touch everywhere. Right where he entered her, and along her spine, fluttering all the way to her toes. It was electric. It sent her blood quivering.

"Plenty of time to..."

She heard his shorts hit the floor, remembered again how unbelievably amazing it was, now that they'd both gotten tested and dispensed with condoms, when he fitted his cock to her entrance and slid home. *Every time feels like coming home.*

"Enjoy this amazing body of yours, this connection we have."

He banded one arm around her waist and used the other to massage her butt the way she loved teasing his fingers along her seam. She was so primed and ready when he buried himself in her and pushed against her clit. Her orgasm shot through her. She clenched and pulsed around him, feeling the way he held on so tightly to her, like he never wanted to let her go now, and he never would.

He claimed her body and thrust in, losing all control and coming as he cried her name. She relaxed against the counter in a boneless puddle, sweaty and full of joy, and gave a soft laugh. "Not so steady after all," she mumbled through her dazed and sated smile. *No, and we sure do love it when he loses control, don't we?*

"Every time," he rasped into the skin of her back. His breathing was heavy, and he still drew circles along her belly with his fingers. God, she loved that constant touch. "Every time, feels like coming home."

"Yeah," she said. It did. He was her home.

"I think I'm going to need more baking lessons, though."

She giggled against the counter.

"A lot more, buckets more. More forever with you." He pulled out and tugged his shorts up, folding himself away. Then he helped her up, tagged her underwear and led her into their bedroom. "And showers. It's so much fun getting dirty with you because then we get to the cleanup."

He had her sundress up and off before she could blink, his hands still connected to her, like he couldn't bear to be separated.

They stood under the spray, hugging. Coming down from the high.

"Connor?" she said, with her cheek against his.

"Yeah?" He stroked up and down her back, soothing her body.

"I love sex with you."

He laughed, a full-body laugh that made her smile even bigger.

"How you make me feel, how playful it is sometimes, how exciting."

"I ruined our morning buns again, got a little out of control."

Sasha wrapped her arms around him and held on, tilting her head to meet his gaze. "I love it when you lose control with me. It makes me feel so desired in a healthy way because I know you'll never hurt me."

"Never," he swore.

"I know." She put her hand to his cheek. "I know that about you, deep in my heart. Trust me?"

He searched her eyes and nodded. "I love you," he said.

She smiled and kissed him. "I know that too." He pinched her side and held her while she giggled through it.

"And?" he prompted. This had become a game to them too, or not necessarily a game, but part of their routine the last few weeks.

"And I love you too," she whispered. "So, so much. And it feels phenomenal." She leaned up and kissed him deeply, holding on to him and pouring all her emotions into the gesture, making sure he knew, without a doubt, how she felt about him.

* * * *

"I can't believe we're swimming and it's almost Halloween!" Ruby said.

"This pool is wonderful. I might live here until the temperature starts behaving." Katie bumped her innertube against Sasha's. They were in swimsuits,

298

floating in her backyard pool. "When did Corvallis get so hot?" Katie asked. "I can't be pregnant in this heat."

Natalie laughed. "I don't think you'll have to worry in a few days, you dork. It's not like you'll have nine months of these high temperatures."

Katie, Natalie, Ruby, Ford, Sasha and Ellie were all in a circle in innertubes, celebrating more than Sasha and Connor moving in together.

"I heard we might get snow next week," Ellie said.

"Hush." Katie sent a trail of water splashing over Ellie's feet. "I can't handle that extreme either. How about a few mild blue-sky fall days? How about nine months of that, so I can wear cute maternity clothes with my new boots and appear to be extremely chic?"

"I'm so happy for you," Ellie said. "How's Leo feeling?"

Katie beamed. Sasha thought her friend's smile might even be bigger than her own. "He's over the moon. I...I can hardly tell you. He cried when we found out. I can't wait to meet this baby. And the girls are going to be such good sisters."

"Jackson and I are trying again," Ellie said.

"Shut up!" Ruby said and they all laughed.

"He wants them to be close in age and I love being a mom, so I'm all for it."

"Well, goody," Ruby said. "You all go on having the babies and I'll continue being the best Auntie Ruby they've ever had."

Ruby and Lachlan didn't want kids and Sasha could understand. She glanced across the pool to the men in the shallow end. They had baby Alex in his first swimsuit and were taking turns spinning him through the water. The tiny bugger was laughing and laughing.

Thank goodness he was over his crying-all-the-time phase for now.

Cece, Rosie, Brie and Natalie's girls were on blankets in the shade, drinking lemonade and painting Brie's toenails, which were sticking out from the end of her purple cast. The dogs were also worn out in the heat and napped inside in the air conditioning.

It was Connor's turn with Alex and he blew raspberries on the baby's tummy before dipping him in and out of the water. Pure glee took over the baby's face and he kicked his little feet. She and Connor had talked about kids, and she was relieved to know he was on the same page as her, which was taking time to enjoy each other's company and build a life together, the two of them, for the time being.

Her before life had been so stressful. She'd been holding herself in a tightly wound-up ball for so long that it was remarkable to relax, to enjoy life, to be free, to be in love, to take it one day at a time, to see a future.

Connor gave Alex back to Jackson and broke away from the group of men. She dipped her body through her innertube and swam toward him, climbing on his back and wrapping her hands around him.

"Having a good time?" He brought one of her hands to his mouth for a kiss.

"The best," she said. "You?"

"Yeah, darlin'. Love this pool, love these people. Love you."

"I love you too, Connor Duggan. Thank you for sharing your family with me." She twirled her wrist. His nieces had made her her very own friendship bracelets and presented them to her today with Brie's words, *"Now that you're officially part of our family."*

"Sugar, they adored you before we got together. If anything, dating you gives me street cred in their eyes. I was a delinquent in the field of love, according to them."

Sasha giggled and kissed his neck. "Well, I love you so much. My heart is free and happy. I'm embracing a future with you. I never let myself dream of a future. I was too afraid. I'm not afraid anymore."

Connor tugged her body around to his front, so they were facing each other. "Future's looking pretty damn amazing in my eyes." He met her gaze.

"Yeah," she said. "I see it too."

Want to see more from this author?
Here's a taster for you to enjoy!

Graciella: Handling the Rancher
Sara Ohlin

Excerpt

Cruz stood at the edge of the bluff above the Pacific. The ocean brooded, inky-dark and dangerous, while the wind whipped it onto the shore. He let the cadence of wild, crashing waves and gusting wind wash over him. He loved the water in its fierce and powerful nature as much as he loved it when it was calm and patient. Wide and open, the beach stretched on, completely untouched by footprints, secluded and vulnerable all at the same time.

He took one lasting breath of the misty sea air and headed towards his farm. *His farm.* He still had moments when he couldn't believe it.

Wispy slips of fog teased and lifted around Cruz, revealing the morning dew on the grass as he made his way up towards the main house of Brockman Farms. Mornings on the farm were his favorite, the way the new light barely stroked the land, how the hues of everything were rich in those few moments of soft sun and leftover darkness. The salty air mixed with the scent of damp earth as it rose up. Home—Cruz was finally home—a place most people took for granted.

He'd been back in Graciella for five weeks after more than a decade away. His relief on hearing that his father, T.D. Brockman, was finally dead had been such that he'd nearly wept like a baby when his brother Adam had called with the news.

Thank goodness no one had seen his near breakdown. And that it hadn't lasted long. He could finally breathe clear and easy here on this land he loved, knowing the monsters were gone. He aimed to do more than breathe easy, however. It was his time to take care of the farm and all the people who depended on it—and to put his stamp on something valuable.

As much as he liked helping out at the barns, this morning dictated that he make a dent on the estate paperwork and duties. That didn't mean he had to do it without a fresh cup of coffee. Cruz entered the main house through the back to grab a mug of their housekeeper Elena's rich espresso brew in the kitchen before he got to work.

Fueled by caffeine, he sat at T.D. Brockman's old desk, going through bank statements and employee schedules. Since he'd returned, the phone hadn't quit ringing with condolences for his father's death and calls from the press. He wasn't sure which group won the award for insincerity.

Who could blame them? T.D. Brockman had taken pleasure in his ruthless way of doing business. But he'd been a wealthy bastard, owning most of the commercial properties in downtown Graciella. And the farm was spread out over two hundred and fifty thousand acres, nestled between Oregon wine country and the prized breathtaking Pacific coast. Money was involved, and where money was involved, people were curious. What would happen now that he was dead? Everyone wanted to know.

The phone rang again. "Brockman Farms," Cruz answered, the words clipped at one more interruption.

"Mr. Brockman? This is Ms. Selby from the *Oregonian.*"

Another reporter. "The family has no comment at this time."

"Please, Mr. Brockman —"

"No comment!" Cruz said through clenched teeth and slammed the receiver down. The only reason he'd left the damn thing plugged in was because there were legitimate calls from banks and people regarding T.D.'s investments that Cruz had to deal with as executor.

"You must be Cruz Brockman."

Cruz looked up at the musical voice. Normally he wouldn't have to force a smile for anyone, let alone for an elegant woman. "Hello," he said and tried to punch down his irritation. "Can I help you?"

"Do you ever wait to see who's on the other end or are you that rude to everyone on the phone?" she asked as she walked into the room. Her body language might have said *cool* and *put-together*, but the haughty tone in her voice gave away one serious, pissed-off attitude.

"Excuse me?" He pushed his chair back and stood. "This is my office and if I remember correctly, I smiled and said hello. Perhaps you'd like to start over —"

"Mr. Brockman," she snapped.

He locked his gaze with hers and came around from behind the desk. "I said, perhaps you'd like to start over." His tone was sharp, no longer concealing his frustration.

"I'm Miranda Jenks, the audit accountant. I've been trying to contact you for days to let you know when I'd be arriving, but your phone etiquette made that impossible. The times you actually picked up the phone, you hung up on me before I could say more than three words. I finally got hold of your lawyer. He should have mentioned I'd be here today."

Gorgeous and haughty, what a combination, like a goddess rising from the morning's crashing waves. The image, unbidden, teased through his temper. Cruz half-listened as he studied her. In her charcoal-gray suit and black high heels, with that tone of reprimand in her voice, she reminded him of his finance professor in college, who'd believed Cruz's choice of photojournalism a waste of time. That was where the similarities came to a screeching halt. His professor had been in her sixties, very short and very thick.

The woman in front of him certainly wasn't sixty, short or thick. In fact, she looked more like she could stand to eat a good meal or two. Contradictions surrounded her. Deep, confident and extremely sexy, her voice was like a rich port. It also vibrated with indignation. But the rest of her seemed guarded. Her long dark hair was pulled back and held in a simple ribbon at her neck. Tall and stiff, she did a good job of trying to pretend calm. Gaunt cheekbones shaped her face and dark circles rested under her eyes. Very green, very frustrated eyes. That expressive gaze and sultry voice were at odds with the rest of her controlled, veiled demeanor.

"Mr. Brockman?" Impatience sliced the woman's words.

"Accountant? Jake never mentioned you were coming today."

"Yes, I did, Cruz." Jake walked in. "Sorry I'm late, Ms. Jenks, I'm Jake Burns. We spoke on the phone."

"Nice to meet you, Mr. Burns."

Cruz watched her almost-smile at Jake and enjoyed the way her face warmed and softened a hint. *Wonder what she looks like when she really lets herself smile?*

"Cruz, good to see you." Jake smacked him on the shoulder. "Ms. Jenks, thanks for your patience. Cruz, Miranda Jenks — the accountant I told you would be auditing the books if we plan on settling this estate."

Cruz had a vague memory of the conversation. One of about five hundred he'd had about the estate since the funeral. "I apologize, Ms. Jenks," he said. "The phones have been on fire since T.D. died and I lost my patience with them days ago." He flashed her a grin in apology.

He held out his hand, and when she took it, his nerves sizzled. Every pulse point in his body awakened. He nearly tugged her closer so her entire body could touch his. She closed her eyes and quickly removed her hand, one that had trembled slightly in his and had such soft skin that he wanted to hold it again. She opened her briefcase to search through her paperwork.

"Excuse me, it seems my phone's busy today," Jake said. He took out his cell and walked into the hall.

"Ms. Jenks, thanks for coming all the way from…?" Cruz began.

"Houston."

"How was the trip?"

"The trip was fine. Shall we get to work? I'm certain none of us has any time to waste."

All business. Cruz sighed. From experience, he found accountants shallow and driven by money. But he needed one to handle the books. Cruz had lived most of his adult life traveling from one assignment to another, documenting the beauty and tragedy of the world, photographing and writing other people's stories. He had not been running a large company or settling estates, meaning he needed help to get things reconciled. Only then could he begin making lasting improvements and changes to Brockman Farms, fulfilling his dream of making this place something to be proud of.

"I'll need all the records your father kept. Bills paid, bills due, revenue, assets, expenses, wages, tax forms from the past few years, receipts, investments." She drew him out of his thoughts with her long list of demands.

Cruz looked around at the piles of paperwork covering the desk. "Most of it is here somewhere, but it's a mess at the moment, a mess I've been trying to sort through. Jake and I have some things to take care of. I know you've come a long way. How about if we begin in the morning? That will give me some time to get things more organized for you."

"Certainly."

Damn! The force of that word breathed at him like a dragon's fire. He could almost see the inner turmoil as she fought the need to roll her eyes at his incompetence. "But time isn't something you have a lot of, Mr. Brockman. I'm sure you're aware of that."

"I realize the importance of this, Ms. Jenks, but it's not exactly life or death now, is it?" He grinned at her again, trying to prod some emotion out of her. At the least he wished she'd relax. At the most he wanted to see her smile again. He liked the way it softened her face, gave her a bit of mystery, as though she was holding a special secret or two. He'd even take the fierce side of her — it showed her strength.

"That depends on how you feel about the IRS shutting you down for good."

"What the hell's that supposed to mean?" he demanded.

About the Author

Puget Sound based writer, Sara Ohlin is a mom, wannabe photographer, obsessive reader, ridiculous foodie, and the author of the contemporary romance novels, *Handling the Rancher, Salvaging Love, Seducing the Dragonfly, Igniting Love* and *Flirting with Forever*.

She has over sixteen years of creative non-fiction and memoir writing experience, and you can find her essays at Anderbo.com, Feminine Collective, Mothers Always Write, Her View from Home, and in anthologies such as Are We Feeling Better Yet? Women Speak about Healthcare in America, Take Care: Tales, Tips, & Love from Women Caregivers, and Chicken Soup for the Soul.

Sara loves creating imaginary worlds with tight-knit communities in her romance novels. She credits her mother, Mary, Nora Roberts and Rosamunde Pilcher for her love of romance.

If she's not reading or writing, you will most likely find her in the kitchen creating scrumptious meals with her kids and husband, or perhaps cooking up her next love story.

She once met a person who both "didn't read books" and wasn't "that into food" and it nearly broke her heart.

Sara loves to hear from readers. You can find her contact information, website details and author profile page at https://www.totallybound.com

Home of Erotic Romance

Sign up for our newsletter and find out about all our
romance book releases, eBook sales and promotions,
sneak peeks and FREE romance books!